DOUBLE BLIND

BOOK ONE OF THE THANATOS RISING SERIES

TIFFANY PITTS

booktrope

Booktrope Editions
Seattle, WA 2014

Cover Design by Melody Paris

Previously published as *Double Blind*,
KDP Select, 2013

PRINT ISBN 978-1-62015-203-4

EPUB ISBN 978-1-62015-299-7

Library of Congress Control Number: 2014901278

This book is dedicated to Katzuhiro.

*You were so fat. You were so loving. And sometimes
you could be a total jerk. But I loved you, Katzu.
I loved you, and I love you still.*

SEATTLE
MONDAY, JUNE 3RD, 11:00 A.M.

THE MAN APPEARED LIKE A PILLAR, eighteen feet tall and solid granite. He had muscles where most people had good intentions. Even his teeth looked buff.

It would not be a fair fight; anyone could see that. Compared to the hulking mass of muscle, Delilah Pelham looked like a doll. Her tiny frame barely reached five feet. Her short brown hair had a fairy tale quality about it. Add a bow and a couple of talking birds and she could be a princess. She even had a button nose.

The fight would be over in seconds.

Deli smiled. She liked these odds. The muscle-bound mammoth towered over her, but she knew something he did not. It wasn't about size. It was all about leverage.

He came at her, curling his fists into hams and aiming them at her head. As he pulled his arm back to take a swing, Deli threw her shoulders to the left. The man lumbered left.

Deli grinned and forced her hips in the opposite direction. The giant was unprepared for her to slip past him on the right.

She launched herself at his back, grabbing the trunk of his neck and hugging tightly. He tried swatting her off, but his arms were so massive, they couldn't reach far enough behind.

Concentrating all of her strength in the grip around his neck, Deli relaxed the rest of her body. Within seconds, Goliath had ninety-eight pounds of limp rag doll hanging on his back, pulling him down into unconsciousness. The bell over the door tinkled somewhere behind her, but it sounded to Deli like tweety-birds circling his head as she slowly knocked him out.

They teetered and fell backward—Deli first, then the senseless powerhouse. She let go of his neck as they plunged to the mat, twisted around in midair like a cat, and landed on her feet. Using the momentum of the fall, she propelled herself forward, rolling toward the rope. Then she sprang to her feet and landed on her toes at the edge of the ring, face to face with a wide-eyed Carl Sanderson.

"Carl?" she said. "What are you doing here?"

His hair had grown shaggy since the last time she'd seen him, but other than that, it was the same old dorky Carl. He wore a baggy brown suit much like a coat hanger on stilts, poked out at the shoulders and straight all the way down. Everything in between was knees, elbows, and Adam's apple. The best thing that could be said about Carl, from the standpoint of a casual observer, is that his joints always appeared to be in surprisingly good order.

"I-is that guy gonna be okay?"

Carl stared at the lump of blacked-out brawn behind Deli. She barely glanced over her shoulder before answering.

"Who, Dave? He'll be fine."

Standing up straight, Deli jogged to the corner of the ring. She didn't need to pull the ropes apart to slide between them.

She stepped lightly onto the concrete floor of the gym. "What can I do for you, Carl?"

Carl stood, still transfixed by the slumbering David. "I, uh, I called your phone but I only got your voice mail."

"Sorry, I usually don't answer unless I know who it is."

"I left a message."

"Yeah, I got it. Again, sorry. I've been a little busy with tournament training."

"I am sorry to intrude. It's just that, I thought I should probably come down and talk to you." He looked sincere, but Deli learned long ago not to trust the sincerity of Paul's friends.

"Do you have a moment? Maybe we could, um…" Carl looked down. Then he looked back up. Deli thought his ears might be redder than normal.

"Maybe we could go get a cup of c-coffee or something?"

Coffee? What could possibly be so important that her brother's roommate would come all the way across the water to ask her for an awkward cup of coffee? Shouldn't he be at work or something?

Deli couldn't think of any way to get out of coffee without lying. She didn't like to lie. She left that business to Paul.

"Okaaay," she said. He better not think this was a date. "But I need to change first."

She huffed out a short breath, blowing the hair away from her face in a clear sign of resignation, which Carl missed because his attention was focused on a point somewhere beyond her left shoulder.

"Oh, sure. Yes, of course. You're probably all sweaty and stuff." He nodded absently, still staring behind her.

Deli studied him for a moment. Paul said he was a security guard, but he certainly didn't look like a security guard. She thought security guards were supposed to be all buff and menacing. Carl looked about as menacing as a bug-eyed hamster.

What the *hell* was he still staring at? She turned to look.

On the mat, the heap of Dave had rolled over onto his side and started snoring. Deli choked back a giggle.

"Really, Carl," she said, "don't worry about him. He'll wake up in an hour or so and have a headache."

Carl blinked and brought his attention back to Deli. He was definitely pink around the edges now. Deli smiled. As far as Paul's roommates went, Carl was way better than the last guy. Sure, he was nervous and awkward and made a habit of putting his foot in his mouth—but at least he didn't collect knives. He was even kind of cute, in a Muppets meet Einstein sort of way.

Honestly, the major problem she had with him was that he lived with her brother. Deli didn't trust anyone in Paul's inner circle. She wasn't trying to be mean. It was more of a coping tactic.

And now he drives all the way here on a Sunday morning to have coffee and a chat?

Deli wasn't that stupid. Carl wouldn't be here unless Paul needed something. Either that or he was in mortal danger.

She shook her head and headed for the locker room, secretly rooting for mortal danger.

THE CAFÉ NEXT DOOR
TO DELI'S GYM

THE CAFÉ FILLED UP as the sunshine clouded over. People, drawn in by the spicy aroma of Sumatran coffee and blueberry muffins, pushed into the dining room looking for a place to sit.

Deli sat across the rickety table from Carl, or rather, the middle half of Carl. Currently, he was doubled over, scrabbling around inside a canvas messenger bag. He resurfaced seconds later with a legal-sized envelope, fumbling to place it on the table carefully. Written on the front of the envelope in serious, black ink was one word: *Delilah.*

My dearest Delilah,

I write this letter on the eve of something very big. I travel tomorrow to Hong Kong where I will meet with an investor. I cannot give you his name but I will tell you he is <u>well</u> <u>known</u>. Even you, dearest sister of mine, would recognize his name. The upshot is that he is very interested in developing a pet project of mine into a worldwide enterprise.

We will meet in a private setting. This is merely a precaution, mind you. My investor is not keen on intrusions of any kind. I am taking my tablet and phone in case of emergency but it has been requested that I keep this meeting quiet and my outside contacts to a minimum.

You may remember my roommate, Dr. Carl Sanderson (PhD)? He has generously agreed to act as a liaison. I will keep in touch with him as often as I can, but he has signed a non-disclosure agreement, so he cannot give you specifics about the project. He does not know the name of my investor, either.

All this is very complicated and you will probably not be interested, but I still must request that you do not ask.

In the event that anything should go wrong, Dr. Sanderson will be in touch with you. I specifically ask that you do not involve the authorities. My business is legal, but there are ramifications to involving the State Department and my investor has legitimate concerns.

A copy of my will can be found on file with my lawyer. (You remember Augie Terkle? I believe you once punched him in the eye.) In essence, it says that my liquid assets are to go to Mother. You may keep the contents of my safe deposit box. Carl has custody of the key.

All this planning is tiresome but necessary. I intend to return no later than the first of June. Upon my return, we will celebrate my success over dinner. You may bring Mother if you like.

Yours faithfully,

Paul S. M. Pelham, Esq.

* * *

She ran her fingers over a raised seal at the bottom of the page. Carl watched her with patient concern from across the table.

"He *notarized* it?" she asked, not sounding surprised at all.

"He felt that was best," said Carl. "So it can be taken as legally binding. Uh, if you need to, that is."

He looked away from her scowl, at the thinning stream of people marching past. Occasionally, warm, caffeinated aromas flung themselves out the door and snared a few more stragglers.

"Look, I don't mean to be rude, Carl. I mean, it was nice of you to come all the way down here, but…what exactly do you need from me?" The question should have taken him off his guard, but Carl had been a Boy Scout until the twelfth grade. He was *always* prepared.

"I just thought that, well, since he's your brother and all..." His eyebrows creased with concern. "You might want to know."

Deli's eyes went glassy and she shook her head.

"I don't think he is."

"You don't think he's what?"

"My brother," she said. "I don't think he is my brother. I think he's *adopted*."

Carl watched her eyes, trying to find a hint of irony but her stony face gave nothing away. "But, y-you guys are twins."

A thick blanket of bafflement wrapped itself around his thoughts. Deli stared at an indeterminate point over his right ear and rambled on. The serious expression never left her face.

"How do you *know*? It could be one of those things where a couple is trying really hard to have a baby but they can't, so they give up and apply for adoption. And then, as soon as the adoption is final, the stress goes away so they end up getting pregnant like, *immediately*."

The glassy look left her eyes and she focused back on Carl. "That happens all the time, you know. It happened to this lady I used to work with when I was sixteen." She ended on a high note, full of hope. Carl stared at her, not knowing what to say. He went with the obvious.

"But what about the family resemblance?"

Deli shrugged. *Was* she messing with him?

"I mean, you have to admit that you guys look a lot alike. You have the same nose and...stuff."

Of course, they weren't identical per se. They had the same individual features—bright blue eyes, delicate ears, high cheekbones—but they wore them differently. The eyes and cheekbones gave Deli a graceful, elegant appearance whereas they stretched Paul out, making him average-looking at best.

"Killjoy," she said, interrupting his analysis. "Can't you let a girl dream?"

Carl breathed easier. Clearly she was messing with him. He hoped. Either way, he tried directing the conversation back to business.

"I know you guys aren't that close, but—"

"Do you remember the party he had for his twenty-first birthday?"

Carl closed his mouth, thought for half a second, then shook his head slightly. "That was a little bit before my time, I'm afraid. We met in grad sch—"

"Well, it was *gigantic*. Fancy hotel, fancy food, fancy wine, fancy *everything*." She made wide circles with her arms to underline her point. Then she stopped gesturing and zeroed in on Carl.

"I'll give you three guesses as to which twin sister he did not invite. And the first two don't count."

"Um..."

He *hadn't* known about that. Surely, there must have been a good reason?

"Maybe it was just for his fraternity brothers?" said Carl.

"*He invited Nana and our uncle Clyde.*" Deli glared at him. After a beat, she rubbed her eyes then looked at him through her fingers.

"Please just tell me what this is all about, Carl. I don't really want to waste more time than I have to."

Carl frowned. This was harder than he'd anticipated. "I think Paul might be in some sort of trouble."

Deli put her hands down. Her right eyebrow inched up a sliver but the rest of her stayed motionless. She didn't even blink. "What's he done *this* time?"

Carl brushed the hair back from his forehead and forged ahead. "I don't think it's like that, exactly."

Deli didn't say anything. She just stared.

"I got a few emails from him since he's been gone. The first was from the airport, to tell me that he arrived in Hong Kong and was doing well. The second was from an internet café. That one was about shopping."

Deli kept staring.

"He said his suit wasn't nice enough for the meeting."

She finally reacted by rolling her eyes. Carl shrugged.

"I got his last email two days ago," he said. "It says he returned safely from the meeting and was resting in Hong Kong at some posh hotel called the Maxwell."

"Well, that's all good, then.... Isn't it?"

"No, I don't think it is."

"Why not?" She pinned him down with her stare. Carl matched it, but politely, because he wanted her to take him seriously.

"He said to expect him back on the sixth of August and that his plane gets in about 7:65 p.m." He paused to let that sink in. Deli's stare went from serious to seriously confused.

"His letter said the first of June. Maybe he changed his return date."

TIFFANY PITTS

"I thought that at first, too…but 7:65 p.m. isn't an actual time."

Deli doubled up on the confused stare.

"So I got to thinking about it. And, if you put 7:65 into military time, you get 19:65."

He looked expectantly at Deli, waiting for her to catch on. In the background, the rumble of steaming milk rose slowly to a thick shriek, and she still said nothing.

"Oh!" he said, recognizing his mistake. "Are you not a Beatles fan?"

Deli shook her head slowly.

"August 6, 1965, was the day the Beatles released the *Help!* album." Carl looked triumphant.

She finally blinked.

"You're telling me that Paul might be in danger and the most subversive thing he can think up is an old Beatles album?"

"Actually, I didn't get it at first." Carl sat up straighter. "When I did figure it out, I thought it was pretty clever."

"And let me guess, we're not supposed to contact the authorities because they're going to throw his ass in jail, *right*?"

Carl straightened up all the way now. "Actually, no. His business is legitimate."

"Don't you think we should call the cops and let *them* decide?"

Carl wished he could tell her about this mess. Then maybe she would trust him. He decided that non-disclosure agreements were a sneaky way to do business.

"They wouldn't find anything wrong if we did. It seems your brother has set everything up to look as though this was his plan all along. All the emails he sent emphasize the fact that he's not in any danger and that he'll come home when he's ready."

Deli shook her head and massaged her temples. "Dammit! Now I'm going to have that idiotic song in my head all day."

Carl's face fell. "I'm sorry," he said. His eyes softened and he bowed his head slightly. "I thought you should know what's been happening. No one expects you to…" Carl went silent. "I mean," he tried again. "You're welcome to help find him, but…don't feel obligated or anything."

Deli set her coffee cup down with controlled force.

"I don't know what I can do to help you, Carl. But I swear to *God*, if this turns out like that Augie Terkle bullshit, I will drag that bastard home so I can kill him myself."

OUTSIDE THE CAFÉ

CARL OPENED THE DOOR. Deli stepped past him into the greying afternoon. Most cities complained of heat waves by now but Seattle usually needs a running start at the summer. June is always an unreliable month.

She sauntered down the street, crossing her arms against the breeze and waiting as Carl held the door for a group of teenage girls chatting too much to thank him. After the last one stepped over the threshold, he jogged to catch up with her.

"My friends, Jake and Sacha, have been helping to track Paul down since I figured out his coded email." He paused for a moment and cleared his throat quietly before adding, "Would you like to see what we've got so far?"

Although his cheeks flushed, he managed to get the sentence out without stuttering, accidentally spitting, or doing anything else embarrassing. It wasn't weird that he was helping find Paul, because roommates would do that.

"Suuure," she said. "Let's go see what they've got."

"It won't take long. The Dungeon isn't too far from here. It's only a couple blocks that way."

He pointed toward an older section of the hill flush with money, surrounded by a regiment of horse chestnut trees. They walked in quiet contemplation until Deli got a queer look on her face and turned to Carl.

"It sounded like you just said the *Dungeon.*"

Carl's eyes widened for a brief moment, searching for an explanation that didn't make him sound juvenile.

"Yes, it's what everyone calls their apartment." He didn't add that, in this instance, *everyone* meant Carl and the two guys that lived there.

As they walked, the houses grew larger, the lawns more obsessively manicured, until finally Deli stopped in front of a boxwood hedge shaped like a teddy bear. She eyed it suspiciously.

"Why?"

Her voice remained so neutral that Carl couldn't tell if she was referring to the Dungeon or the landscaping. He went with his best guess.

"Because it's kind of dungeony? You know, all dark and cold. Not because they have any whips and chains and stuff." He snorted a short laugh. When Deli didn't laugh along, he stopped and quickly added, "At least, I never saw any when I lived there."

"You used to live there?" For a brief second, a spark of interest lit her eyes, but then she checked herself and shifted back to neutral. "That's probably more information than I need."

Carl's cheeks turned pink and he went quiet for a moment. They walked on until Deli broke the silence again.

"What do these guys *do*, exactly?"

"What do you mean, like for employment? Jake is the super for his apartment building." Carl squinched his eyes together. "I think Sacha has settlement money from a lawsuit when he was a kid." Then, as if he understood what kind of impression this might make on a girl, he hastily added, "They also have their own online company."

"Let me guess," Deli said. She was not smiling but it seemed like she wanted to. "They run a website dedicated to underground gaming."

Carl tripped over his foot in surprise. He got his balance back before he made a complete fool of himself and turned to Deli.

"How did you guess?" He started walking again, this time with a bounce in his step.

"They're computer nerds and they live in a place called *the Dungeon*." Carl didn't hear her sarcasm.

"You're totally right! They run *TerrorCity*. It's not as big as *World Domination* or *Strike Force*, but they have a dedicated following."

"Tell me again, Carl. What exactly do *you* do?"

"Me? Oh, I'm in security," he said. "Have you heard of *TerrorCity* before?"

*   *   *

The Dungeon turned out to be the basement apartment of a turn-of-the-century gothic mansion that fell into disrepair three minutes after the ink dried on the deed. It went by the proper name of Clydesdale Manor, but all the locals called it Horsey House because of Tess and Albert, the two stone horses guarding the front stoop.

Deli stood next to Carl in the living room. It looked like the bridge of the saddest, grungiest starship ever. A reticulating desk lamp drooped its head in the corner, outshone by the glow from sixteen computer terminals. They were stacked two or three tall, in a circular pattern. Inside the henge of monitors sat an impossibly cobbled structure of computer parts and cables. It lurked within the web of monitors like an overfed technological spider.

The thrum of its hardware was very difficult to tune out, and Deli struggled to hear the blond guy speak.

Jake Denny, the blond guy, had been flipping between screens for twenty minutes, trying to explain their current progress in the hunt for Deli's brother. He rumbled back and forth between the monitors, the wheels of his chair following deeply etched grooves in the clear plastic desk mats. Deli wondered if he ever stood up at all.

He droned on, pudgy arms flailing from screen to screen. After twenty minutes of acronyms and nonsense words, she was forced to assume his native language was either Fortran or Klingon, because it certainly wasn't English. Glancing over at Carl for moral support didn't help. His head bobbed in time with Jake's nerd-speak.

Traitorous know-it-all, she thought.

The other person in the room, a tall guy wearing black jeans and a penguin t-shirt, hadn't said a word. However, the nest of curly black hair sitting on top of his shoulders was making agreeable nodding movements.

She looked back at Jake and growled. "Slow down! I don't get that part."

Jake's grey eyes widened with fear. She wondered if getting yelled at by a girl was a new experience for him.

"We traced Paul's computer through different servers along his trip. We know, for instance, that he was in Hong Kong on the first of June, because his computer accessed the internet through the hotel server at ten that morning, when he checked his private email account."

"Yes, *that* part I got," she said, flipping her hand up to stop him from going on. Jake cringed.

"What I *don't* get is why you guys are convinced it's all hinky." She crossed her arms. Jake looked nervous enough to bolt.

"The server connections are pretty normal. It shows he went between several commercial providers that make sense: airport, hotel, coffee shops. That's pretty common when someone travels around. But he sent that last email from a private server in the middle of nowhere. All our data seems to indicate that it's located somewhere in the middle of the South China Sea."

Deli uncrossed her arms.

"That can't be right, can it?" she said.

"Not according to the technology we have." Jake shrugged, relaxing into the conversation. "But our data suggests that it's right...there." He pointed to a tiny spot in an ocean of pixilated blue.

"What's out there that can talk to satellites?" Deli said.

"We don't know. Sacha," he motioned to the mess of black curls in the corner, "has been searching the available satellite images for anything in the area, but so far there are no islands on or near the pinpointed coordinates."

Sacha looked up. "Nothing since you guys walked in," he said and immediately went back to scanning his images.

"If there's no natural island," she said, "then wherever that server is would have to be man-made."

Jake jerked his chin up and peered at Deli with new consideration. Carl tried to hide the astonished look on his face.

"Y-yes," said Jake. "We, uh...we were just double checking that was the case."

"And if it's man-made, you aren't going to find it on outdated satellite images unless it has been there for a year or two," Deli continued, ignoring Jake's dumbfounded expression.

"Exactly my point! Jake, listen to her." The outburst came from Sacha. His eyes popped open and he regarded Deli with a smug glare. *Go on*, it said. *Tell him.*

"Could it be coming from a ship?" she asked.

Deli felt the tension in the room increase. Sacha and Jake stared at each other from behind their respective monitors. Carl came to her rescue.

"It's possible," he said. "But that signal is staying put. If it were on a ship, they would be sailing around the area, not stationary. As near as we can tell, the signal hasn't moved so much as a meter in over thirty days."

"Well, how far can you tell? I mean, what is your margin of error?"

It was a simple, logical question, and it set the room on fire. Jake started first, followed closely by Sacha.

"That's the whole *point*, isn't it?"

"Jake's programming on the location codes is *completely* ridiculous...."

The argument fascinated Deli. The fights she usually saw had a lot more punching and a lot less color commentary on the other person's intelligence. These guys bickered back and forth like agitated hens— lots of shrill clucking and puffed up feathers but no actual blood loss, since they never left their ergonomic swivel chairs.

"Knock it off!" Carl shouted. Deli jumped slightly, then giggled in embarrassment. She had never heard Carl shout. She hadn't been aware that he *could* shout.

Jake and Sacha shut up immediately. Slumping back into their chairs, they continued to glare at each other over computer monitors until Carl spoke again. He looked both irritated and embarrassed at his friends' behavior.

"What they are *trying* to say is that they aren't sure what's going on."

Jake sat up in his seat. Sacha gasped. Both had their mouths open ready to set Carl straight, but he stopped them with an outstretched hand.

"Jake, here..." He pointed, and Jake sat back down. "Has shown the server is located in a stationary spot. His mathematical arguments are valid. The code he wrote based on the calculations is correct." Carl put his bear paw of a hand up to silence Sacha. "We all went through it four times. It's correct."

"So it's coming from a stationary target," Deli said. Carl's eyebrow raised itself in tribute to her logical reasoning.

"Yes," Carl and Jake both agreed. Sacha looked at Deli through squinted eyes, clearly doubting her intelligence.

"But Sacha here"—he turned halfway toward the sullen programmer—"has a valid concern about it coming from a stationary source. The satellite images don't show anything within seventy miles of our pinpointed location. Nothing. No island, no reef, not even a little atoll. There's nothing there but ocean."

"What about an oil rig?" Deli said.

Sacha sneered. "I thought of that, but an offshore rig takes anywhere from one to four years to build. These scans are only five months old. Even if they were hiding it from satellites, we would see wave distribution patterns indicating *something*. There's nothing there at all. No platform, no funky waves…nothing."

"So, definitely not an island then." Deli looked to Carl for an answer.

"We don't know what it is," Carl said. His shoulders slumped forward.

"Well, is Paul even *there* anymore?"

All three men looked up at her. Carl broke the silence.

"We don't know," he said.

"What *do* you know?" Deli said, trying not to sound sharp.

"We traced the credit card transactions he made in Hong Kong before he sent his final email. He stayed at the Maxwell Hotel. He also charged about fourteen dollars at a post office; thirty dollars at someplace called Hang Choy Foods; and withdrew five hundred dollars at a cash machine on Kimberley Street."

"So he mailed something, ate lunch, and went to the ATM. Then what?"

"Then somehow he travels hundreds of miles to the middle of the South China Sea and manages to send a coded message for help," Carl said.

"Okay," Deli said, digesting the information. "So, what's the next step?"

No one answered.

"Do you have any idea where to go from here?"

Jake shifted slightly in his chair, but still no one spoke. Everyone seemed to be looking somewhere else for a moment.

Deli's expression went flat. She looked at Carl. In her best *I'm not angry just tell me the truth* voice, she said, "You guys are completely stuck, aren't you?"

No one answered.

"You know, when I was a kid, if I lost something and couldn't find it, my mom always told me to put my hand where I was looking." She scanned their faces. They were blank. "It means why doesn't someone *go there and look for him*?"

"What, you mean, like, *go* to Hong Kong?" Jake said. He looked terrified. Carl looked relieved. Sacha didn't look at all; he had gone back to his maps.

"I thought about that," Carl said. "But I didn't know how to suggest it. It is kind of risky, isn't it? I mean, I'm willing to go, but I have the Euro-Stock drop this week and Jake—"

"What?" Jake interrupted. "Why would I go? He's *your* roommate!"

"...can't go," Carl spoke over the protestations. "His passport is expired."

"It is?" Jake looked surprised. "How do you know that?"

"Have you renewed it since we went to Amsterdam?"

Jake relaxed into a grin.

"I thought not," Carl said, but Jake wasn't listening. His eyes were closed and he giggled under his breath.

"Amsterdam was awesome. We should totally do that again, man." He giggled some more. "Remember those chicks we met near the Leidseplein?"

"Yeah, shut up, Jake."

"Right." Jake smiled.

"I ain't going," Sacha called from the back of the room. Everyone turned to look at him.

"No one said you had to, man," Jake said, probably more to reassure himself than anything.

Deli sighed. These guys had no idea what they were up against. She could see they were trying to help, which was sweet. But they clearly didn't know her brother well *at all*. They weren't going to track him down online. Paul was a mooch. He never spent his own money if he could help it. He could find a bored heiress in a can of tomato soup. If there was a trust fund within ten miles of Hong Kong, Paul would lock on, cozy up, and flatter the hell out of it until they were best friends. She couldn't ask them to risk their lives for her stupid brother. For one thing, he wasn't worth it. Deli only considered it her job because she knew how disappointed Nana and Uncle Clyde would be if they found out otherwise. She took a deep breath.

"I have a tournament to run in two weeks. If I'm not back here to run it, I'm going to be out of a gym."

Carl's eyebrows shot up. He grabbed the keyboard of the nearest computer terminal and plunked down in a chair.

"What if we could get you there and back before your tournament?"

"Sure, but I'm broke as hell. Paul is the one with the cash, not me." She gave Carl a look that dared him to one-up her.

"What if I said that we could get you there on the cheap?"

He typed a tornado of commands into the computer. His eyes never left the screen.

"That depends on how cheap," she said.

An official-looking screen popped up on Carl's monitor and asked for a password. He thought for a moment and typed in a string of characters. The website approved his password and linked to another, even more official looking page. A brief flash of guilty conscience passed across his face, but he looked over at Deli and it disappeared.

"Um...is free okay?"

OUTSIDE THE DUNGEON
7:00 P.M.

THE DAY SLIPPED BEHIND GATHERING CLOUDS as Carl and Deli left the Dungeon. The wind had picked up while they were inside, and the evening was cool with the promise of rain. Goosebumps rose on Deli's arms. Carl noticed her shivering slightly.

"Would you like my coat?" Despite the coolness of the evening, Carl was very warm.

"That's okay. I'm only a few blocks away. You can go if you like, I'll be fine."

"I, um…actually, would it be okay if I walked you home?" He wanted to talk with her about her trip. He wanted to suggest that she not go by herself, but he was having a difficult time finding a way to broach the subject.

Deli gave him a dubious look but didn't say *no*, so Carl kept walking.

"I *can* defend myself, Carl. I'm not helpless, you know."

"Yes, Paul told me about your black belt in karate," he said. His forehead wrinkled. "Are you sure that guy is going to be okay?"

She stared blankly at him until her eyes lit up and she laughed. Carl smiled and glanced quickly down to the sidewalk. Grass growing through the cracks started to sway in the wind and he noted the storm was coming in from the west.

"Seriously, Carl, he's fine. He's actually a pretty good student. He just keeps forgetting about core leverage. And it's *bodu kura*, not karate."

She hopped lightly over the broken concrete and stopped. They had come to the end of the street. Carl caught up to her and tried to look unsure of which way to turn. She looked at him with skeptical eyes. Carl didn't panic, but it was a close thing.

"What else did Paul say?" she asked.

He didn't expect that reaction. It made him grin. Carl knew Paul and Deli didn't get along well, but he could never figure out why.

"He said you have issues and that I should watch my ass because you could kick it from here to Hanoi."

She shivered. Carl shrugged the coat from his shoulders and handed it to her. Deli shimmied into it without hesitation, then turned left, into the wind. Carl followed.

"He's always been a sore loser."

She said something else but the wind was getting enthusiastic about the upcoming storm and Carl had a hard time hearing over it. He opened his mouth to ask what she'd said but Deli shook her head and pointed to her ear. After a while, she turned up a set of concrete stairs. Carl followed.

The alcove at the top of the stairs was a mixture of Art Deco styling, modern security, and street tags. Deli punched in the security code by rote. Carl watched and filed the numbers away for later as the door buzzed its approval. He wasn't trying to be sneaky. Carl filed everything away for later.

Out of the rushing wind, Deli hunched over, searching her purse for something.

"What's that?" Carl said, watching her search.

"My mailbox key." She jingled her keys in his face.

"Um, no. The Bora Bora thing."

He smiled cautiously. As short as she was, she was still a little scary to talk to.

"Oh, sorry, bodu kura. It's a discipline of mixed martial arts, but I'm not a black belt."

"Why not?"

Deli ran her fingers along the wall of aluminum mailboxes, stopping at the one marked *Pelham*.

"Because there are no black belts in bodu kura. You either win a match or you don't."

"What happens if you don't?"

"Usually, you go home. Sometimes, you go to the hospital."

"Oh," he said and turned away to hide his shock.

Directly across from the mailboxes sat a mahogany staircase, six feet wide and topped with an ornately carved bannister. Though the sides were gleaming with polish, the stairs were worn and dull in the middle from years of use. He was inspecting the carved wood pineapple sitting on top of the bannister when Deli clicked the mailbox door shut.

She rounded on Carl.

"Look, Carl, *this*"—Deli pointed at him, then to herself, then back to him three times in rapid succession—"isn't going to happen. You understand? You're cute and all, but *no*. You're Paul's roommate, and I have rules. Well, just the one, really. But it boils down to this: I'm not having sex with you."

Carl's blush started somewhere near his stomach. It took a few minutes to reach his neck. It had a long way to go.

"I-I don't. I'm not...um...I..."

Deli seemed satisfied with his reaction.

"Good. Just so we're clear." She kept smiling.

"I, um, I didn't mean to..."

The roots of his sandy blond hair prickled as the flush crept to the top of his head. He hadn't intended to offend her. He only wanted to talk to her about the trip without Jake and Sacha making stupid comments in the background. It's true that she was the most interesting person he'd talked to in months, but compared to the people he talked to on a regular basis, Delilah Pelham was almost foreign. He wasn't trying to, well, get in her *pants* or anything like that. Frankly, he was a little intimidated by her pants. He wouldn't even know where to start.

Carl fiddled with these uncomfortable thoughts until Deli broke his trance.

"Now, do you *still* want to walk me to my door?"

He didn't know if that was an honest question or a threat. "I-I just wanted to make sure you got home safe."

He ran a hand through the thick mop of hair on his head, trying to will the blush in his cheeks to subside. Realizing how pathetic he must look, he made up his mind to leave. Deli would be fine on her own. But even as he thought this, she punched him in the arm.

"Okay, then, come on," she said and started up the stairs.

Paul was right. His sister was scary.

* * *

He followed Delilah up the first flight of stairs. The view in front of him was distracting, so he concentrated on the banister instead. He knew he was being stupid. Clearly, she was able to take care of herself. But walking away now would give her the impression that he really *was* only interested in her pants and that—well, that simply wasn't true. No matter how interesting a woman's pants may be, Carl was no cad.

They reached the second-floor landing and continued up another flight. As they ascended, the railing grew less ornate, the stairs more scuffed and worn. The last stair was much shorter than the rest, almost like someone had made an extra stair and stuck it on as an afterthought. Carl looked at it more closely and saw that it was made from plywood and painted brown.

"Watch out for that one. It's an omen step. I usually jump over it."

"What's an omen step?" he asked, stepping over it into the hallway.

"It's an added stair so there aren't thirteen in a row. A lot of old buildings have them, just like a lot of skyscrapers have no thirteenth floor. "

He studied the rest of the stairs. Sure enough, there were thirteen original risers.

"Why didn't they just build fourteen stairs, then?"

"Thirteen wasn't always considered unlucky," Deli called to him as she walked halfway down the hall. She stopped at her front door and whispered, "What the hell?"

Carl heard her whisper and immediately went quiet. Walking softly down the hall, he joined her in front of apartment 3B.

The heavy wooden door looked like it had once been the entryway to a small cottage. It was solid oak with a tarnished brass spy hole set so high that Deli probably had to stand on a step stool to use it. The problem they encountered now was that the door, as imposing as it looked against the chipped plaster walls of the hallway, was ajar.

"Are you expecting someone?" Carl whispered as quietly as he could.

Deli shook her head.

"Should we call the cops?" he whispered, even lower this time.

Deli shook her head sharply while pressing a finger to her lips—the universal sign for *shut the hell up*. Carl shut the hell up.

Deli did something jujitsu-like with her hands, which Carl did not understand until he realized she was only untangling her purse from her shoulder. She handed it to him, and he took it without question. Then she reached out gently with her foot and pushed the door open from the bottom. It opened silently.

A soft glow came from farther inside the apartment. Deli crept toward it. Carl tried to slink as she had, but his feet were too large to properly tiptoe, so he heel-toed as softly as he could.

Light from the outer hall illuminated the entryway. Carl could make out a few of the pictures lining the walls. Most were of Deli and friends, though he recognized Paul in one of them. They *did* have the same nose.

He crept past a closed door on the left, and the sweet smell of honey and almonds drifted toward him. It was a nice smell—probably some sort of shampoo or something. He shook his head and tried not to think about it.

Three more steps took them to the end of the hall. A dim light shone through from the kitchen. Deli held up a tiny hand to signal stop. Carl stopped.

There was a muffled clink followed by the *schwoop-hiss* of a refrigerator door closing. In the next room, the dim light went out.

Deli turned to Carl and patted the air toward him in the universal sign for *stay put*. Carl didn't want to stay put, but he did as she asked. He was still holding her purse.

He watched as she snuck around the corner, ducking low. The light from the outside hallway made the rest of the room dim with shadows. He could see big things like a couch and maybe a table, but everything else was a confusing jumble of dark patches. Carl thought about calling the police, but his cell phone was tucked away in the secret pocket of the jacket he'd given to Deli.

Scuffling footsteps filled the kitchen, followed by a sharp thud. The lights flicked on. Carl stood up and walked into the room, blinking but determined to help if Deli needed it. She did not need it.

"Jesus H. Christ on a bike! Ramón what the hell are you doing here?"

The man named Ramón balanced a bottle of beer while tottering to his feet. He wore blue nylon sweatpants, the kind that unzip from the ankles up. They were unzipped, showing off coffee-colored muscles built from speed and practice. His curly black hair swished back and forth as he rubbed the back of his head. After a second or two, he gave up rubbing and used his beer as an ice pack.

"Keeping my skills sharp. Dammit, Del, why'd you hafta hit me so hard?"

"Because you broke into my goddamn apartment again! I told you *last* time that I was going to kick your ass if there was a *next* time. You're lucky I've got company or I would tear you apart."

"You're lucky I wanted this beer so badly or I would have brained you with it, as I so easily could have" he said, before noticing Carl. "Who are you?"

Carl opened his mouth to answer, but Deli did it for him.

"That is Carl. Carl, meet Ramón, my sparring partner. He's also a jackass. Please, don't mind him."

"Oh," Ramón purred, eyeing Carl and waggling his eyebrows up and down. "I get it. She's right, I am an asshole. You don't have to worry about little Ramón, sweetheart...unless you're interested in that sort of thing."

Carl looked at him quizzically for half a second before blushing again.

"Shut up, Ramón." Deli growled. "He's Paul's roommate." Ramón's head snapped back to Deli.

"The one that went to jail?"

"What? No! That guy's been in prison for like, two years. Don't change the subject!"

Ramón took a long drag from his ice pack/beer. Then he shook his head and started poking around the kitchen for a plastic bag.

"Ugh, are we really still talking about this?"

"Yes we *are*! You left the door open, you jerk! Did Toesy get out? Because if he gets into the neighbor's apartment again, I'm holding you responsible. Those people made me pay for their dog's therapy last time."

Carl drifted out of the argument to look around. He was standing in her living room, crowded with secondhand furniture. A misshapen orange couch and an equally monstrous ottoman stared at each other from across the room. Between them sat a worn-out coffee table, strafed with rings of red wine. A bookshelf cowered in the corner, crammed so full of books that they spilled out onto the floor, three layers deep. The room was carpeted in white shag, but for some reason, Deli had plastered over it with a tessellated layer of throw rugs, probably to keep the blood off the carpet—or maybe something less violent, he hoped.

"I don't give a rat's ass what you needed to *try out*—you pick that lock one more time, and I'm going to knock your ass from here to Canada. *Do you hear me?*"

"Really, Del, you need to get a better lock. I keep telling you."

"I *got* a better lock, you jerk. I got *four* better locks. You keep picking them! It's not a candy store, Ramón, it's my goddamn house."

It was time for Carl to leave. Obviously, Delilah was fine here with Ramón. If he were being honest, he was beginning to think that Ramón wouldn't stand a chance against her. He needed a way to extract himself, so he walked over to the bookshelf and started reading titles.

He skimmed the titles of three full shelves before finding a book he hadn't read. He prised it from the shelf, trying not to take any of the others with it, and cleared his throat.

"Um..."

Both Deli and Ramón looked at him; they had been fighting for a solid five minutes and forgotten he was in the room.

"I'm sorry, Carl," said Deli without the faintest trace of embarrassment. She shrugged out of his coat and handed it back to him. "Thanks for walking me home."

"Oh, no problem." He was relieved the argument had stopped for a minute. "Do you think maybe I could borrow this book?" He held it up so she could see it. She gave him a puzzled look.

"Sure, if you like."

"Thanks. And, uh..." He didn't know how to phrase the next part. "Do you need me to call before I show up tomorrow?"

"What? Why?"

Carl saw Ramón's eyebrows raise an inch.

"Don't you need a...ah...ride to the airport?" Before she got the wrong idea, he added, "I just thought that since your flight left so early, you wouldn't want to take the shuttle."

Deli stared at him for a beat and then smiled. "Sure, Carl. That would be great. I'll talk to you tomorrow then."

Certain that Ramón was now laughing his ass off, Carl left before he could embarrass himself any more. On his way out, Ramón called after him.

"Bye-bye, lover boy! Don't forget my offer!"

He was trying to think up a witty retort when he heard the kind *oof* someone makes when they get punched in the stomach really hard. Or at least he hoped that's what it was. Either way, Carl smiled and remembered to skip over the omen step.

On his way down, he passed a man wearing a black track suit with white stripes up the legs. The man carried a handful of mail in his left hand and jingled a key ring in his right. As they passed on the landing, Carl noticed the man had a scar around his right eye. It made him look rugged and a little bit scary. He smiled as they passed. The man only nodded in acknowledgment.

As he stepped into the gusty night, Carl heard the hollow thump of someone tripping over the omen step.

SEATTLE-TACOMA INTERNATIONAL AIRPORT TUESDAY, JUNE 4TH, 5:30 A.M.

DELI CRINGED AS SHE SIPPED the latte. It tasted like moldy pickle-water. She shivered and thought how deeply she hated bad coffee. Then she looked up from the cup of hot swill and realized that it wasn't even six in the morning.

She hated everything at not-even-six in the morning. No sensitive person should ever have to deal with horrible coffee, let alone four thousand people wielding suitcases and sticky toddlers, at not-even-six in the morning.

To prove how much she hated this morning, she found the nearest feral beast, a girl of roughly five years old, dressed in a red tutu and clutching a doll for comfort. Deli smiled to get the girl's attention, then pulled a monstrous face. The girl's eyes grew wild for a second but soon relaxed as she volleyed a rude gesture back. Deli approved of her blue sparkly nail polish.

That has to be the cutest bird anyone has ever flipped me, she thought before turning to glare at Carl.

He sat next to her on the vinyl bench, which was designed to be as uncomfortable as possible. His lips moved as he recited to himself all the pertinent information about their plan. Deli still couldn't figure out why he cared. It was nice that Carl wanted to help, but she had a difficult time believing people were that nice for no reason, *especially* to Paul.

Well, she thought. *At least someone knows where I'm going this time.*

She'd tried to call her mom last night to tell her the flight plans, but, as usual, the recorder announced that she was off photographing the magical Piddle-Widdle bird of the High Sonoran Desert or some such nonsense. Deli was not surprised.

Samina Pelham was not just a bird watcher; she was Queen Loony Bird herself. She took in abandoned fledglings as though they were her own children. Indeed, she seemed to understand those ugly little birds in a way that she'd never understood either Deli *or* Paul. Deli didn't take it personally. She enjoyed seeing her mother at peace, even if that peace was a shrieking mess of feathers and talons.

It *did* make visits somewhat of a hassle, though, since it was always a crap shoot (sometimes literally) as to what she was fostering at the moment. Usually it was something sweet like barn swallows or starlings but she had been known to take in the occasional falcon or osprey. Deli remembered the screech owl and scowled. She'd *warned* Paul not to taunt it like that, but would he listen?

And after he was discharged from the emergency room, he swore he'd never visit Samina's house again. Now they had to spend Christmas at Nana's nursing home, listening to their mother explain the difference between lesser and greater barn nibbits *without* the added benefit of juvenile nibbits comically attacking Paul during dinner.

Deli mostly hated Christmas now.

She wasn't too fond of Paul at the moment, either.

Why was she doing this? She should go home, back to bed. She didn't *have* to do this, did she?

She grimaced. Yes, she did. Nana would never forgive her if Paul disappeared.

Ugh, now she hated Paul even more.

She looked at Carl, spinning through his mental notes. It was sweet of him to drive her to the airport, but she wished he wasn't so prepared. Deli didn't know anyone who took the three-hours-in-advance rule seriously when traveling internationally.

Someday, she thought, *he's going to make someone a great wife.* He must have felt her gaze on him because as soon as she thought it, he looked up.

"Do you have your passport?"

Since it was the seventh time he'd asked, Deli gasped in mock anxiety and jumped to her feet. "Oh no! I think I left it on the counter next to the Oscillation Overthruster!"

Carl stood up, momentarily flustered. Deli snickered and he sat back down with a *whump*.

"I'm just making sure you get there, okay?" She knew he was worried but smiled anyway.

"Lighten up, Carl. You've already gone through your checklist twelve times. I've got the phone your boys rigged up for me."

"And the computer?"

"Yes, Q, and the tiny little computer. And the fountain pen with acid and the cyanide button for my shirt."

Either it was too early or Carl had never seen a James Bond movie in his life because he stared back blankly. She sighed as dramatically as she could at not-quite-six in the morning.

"Never mind. I have all the gadgets. I'll phone you once I get to Hong Kong."

"Jake has a tap on this phone in case you have it stolen."

"You told me that already, Carl."

"And Sacha boosted the satellite reception. It should work anywhere, providing, of course, you aren't under three hundred feet of concrete or something."

"Yep, told me that, too."

"And the same with the computer."

"Yes, Carl. We've gone over all of this." But he wasn't listening. He was running his list again. Deli sat quietly and waited for him to finish.

"And you've got reservations home on the tenth, at the same airport."

"Thank you, Carl. I appreciate all you've done for me. Everything will be just fine. I'll go out there, find Paul, and drag him home screaming if I have to. With any luck, you and he can still go to Trivia Night on Wednesday."

"Oh." Carl sounded surprised. "We don't really do that anymore."

"Whatever," she said, and stood up to stretch her legs. She walked over to the garbage can and threw in the half-empty coffee cup. *Good riddance to bad coffee.*

"Look, it's getting to be an almost decent hour, and I need to get through that security line before too long, or I won't be able to do any duty-free shopping. Do you want me to bring you back anything? Case of cigarettes? Perfume? Kinder Egg?"

"No…thank you," said Carl. "I don't smoke, and Kinder Eggs are illegal, aren't they?"

Deli nodded.

"A national tragedy, if you ask me," she said, walking back toward Carl.

"Thank you for the…help, Carl. I'll find Paul. I usually do. Then I'll bring him back, and you can have him if you still want him."

"I live in his house, Delilah. I'm holding his assets in escrow."

Deli found not a trace of irony in his stare. "That's exactly what I mean. You sure you want him back?"

"He's your *brother*, Deli."

She rolled her eyes. "He's a *jerk*, Carl. I'm only doing this because my Nana will be pissed if he isn't home for Thanksgiving."

Carl's eyes went wide and his eyebrows shot up. "What about your cat?" he asked. "Do you have someone to feed him?"

"It's funny that you ask that, because yesterday, I wasn't sure if you were coming with me or not, so I called Ramón and asked him to watch Toesy for the next few days."

For half a beat, Carl didn't say anything. He looked at the security line.

"Oh," he said at last.

"I only mention it because I'll be staying at the Dungeon for the week and your apartment isn't very far. You know." He paused. "If you need…"

"Really? Because if it's not a huge bother, that would be awesome."

Carl frowned and shook his head to show her it how trivial the inconvenience would be, but Deli was bent double, scrabbling for something in her bag and missed it.

"Except for the serial breaking and entering, Ramón is a great guy. It's just that I'm not sure he understands how cats work. The last time I asked him to look after Toesy, he filled the bathtub to the overflow valve and emptied an entire bag of kibble onto a cookie sheet. When I got home, the kibble was gone and Toesy was so bloated he couldn't move."

She looked up at Carl, made a disgusted face, and stuck out her tongue. "He farted for *days*."

Carl's face froze into a careful grin and he shrugged his shoulders in a way that suggested unimpeachable cat-food-measuring skills.

"Shit." Deli gave up searching through her bag and stood up.

"I can't find my keys, and I left my spare at the gym. My super will let you in, though. Just tell him you're there to feed Toesy. He's usually too stoned to go anywhere, so I don't think it will matter if you call ahead or not. I'll text Ramón from the plane."

"No problem," Carl said. There may have been a hint of regret in his voice. It was hard to tell.

"The line is getting longer. You should probably go. I'll take care of Toesy." He leaned over, picked up Deli's duffle bag, and untangled the strap before handing it to her.

"Thanks, Carl. I appreciate that." She hoisted her duffle over her shoulder easily.

"Ramón will be happy to know he's off the hook. For some reason, Toesy makes him nervous."

Together, they walked down the gauntlet of grumpy travelers waiting to get through security.

"You should get going, too, or you'll be stuck in morning rush hour." They reached the end of the line. Deli set her bag on the flecked white linoleum and kicked it a few inches in front of her.

"Thanks for the ride," she said, but it didn't seem like enough, so she added, "Thanks for everything."

There followed an awkward moment when neither of them knew what to do. In the end, Deli broke the stalemate by giving Carl a one-armed hug. He looked genuinely pleased.

"Remember to turn the phone on when you can so we'll know where you are. I installed a pinger app on it so you won't waste power."

"Carl!" Deli interrupted his mental listing. "You have to leave now, or I'm going to get out of this line and strangle you."

"Right," he said, listening to her this time. "Good luck and I'll see you on the tenth."

"Thanks, Carl."

"You're welcome." He gave an insecure wave then turned and walked away. Deli watched him go, certain that he wouldn't leave until she was through security.

Thirty boring minutes later, Deli was at the counter, taking her shoes off and unpacking the tiny computer that Jake and Sacha had put together for her on the fly. She looked toward the entrance of the security area and saw a tall, sandy-haired mop of cowlicks duck into a shadow and out of view. She yawned to keep herself from smiling.

Carl watched as Deli unlaced her red high-tops and put them in the grey plastic tub. When she turned and looked in his direction, he melted back into an alcove, embarrassed that she might catch him still here when he should have left half an hour ago. He told himself it was to make sure she got through security without any problems.

Honestly, he couldn't be sure if some of the stuff the guys had cobbled together for her was even legal. It would be entirely his fault if she were stopped at customs trying to take a satellite descrambler out of the country without a permit. He didn't think you needed a permit for a satellite descrambler, but he couldn't leave her to figure it out on her own, could he?

He risked another peek around the corner. She was dumping change from her pocket into a small dish near the metal detector. Carl thought again about the conversation he had with Paul months ago.

She's weird, Carl. I mean, I know she looks all hot and stuff, but trust me, man, don't get involved. She's got a serious Edible complex. Plus, I think she might be a lesbian.

Carl didn't ask Paul any more questions after that.

Now, seeing her twirl through the metal detector on her way to a city she'd never been to, without a guide and no ability to speak the language, Carl didn't find her weird. He thought she was strong and brave and slightly crazy, but not weird.

He watched her lace up her shoes, transfixed by the grace of her movements. When she finished, she spun around on her left foot and shouldered her bag in the same motion, then came to a stop, facing him. He wanted to duck away again, but it was too late. She blew him an exaggerated kiss and skipped off to her gate.

Carl's cheeks burned. She knew he was there the whole time! What an idiot thing to do. He scanned the crowd beyond the security gate without any real hope of seeing Deli again.

He made up his mind to leave when he noticed a lanky man sitting on the bench beyond security, lacing up a pair of track shoes. Something about him reminded Carl of white stripes.

He focused on the man and slipped forward through the crowd. The man straightened up and took his carry-on luggage from the security tub. The X-ray technician spoke a few words to him and Carl watched as he turned to reply. In the fluorescent lighting of the security area, the half-moon scar around the man's eye looked pink and new.

Carl stood motionless, thinking of any number of plausible explanations for the scarred man to be at the airport. The man had a conference to go to. He was going on vacation. He was moving to the Baltics.

He was trying to convince himself that the man did not follow Deli down the concourse when his phone interrupted his thoughts with a polite chirp. It was an incoming text.

Please tell the boys thank you for the upgrade. I'll drink to them in first class! Call you from HK. Cheers!

Carl had Jake on the line in less than three seconds.

"Did you upgrade Deli to first class?"

"No. I couldn't, remember? It was only available if she went through San Fran."

Carl didn't say anything.

"Why are you asking?" Jake said.

"Something's wrong."

LONG-TERM PARKING LOT

"CALM DOWN, WE'LL GET YOU BOOKED." Jake tried to sound assuring but ruined the effect by immediately sucking air through his teeth.

"What? *What is it?*" Carl wasn't shouting. He was speaking very loudly, but that was different from shouting.

"Well, we can't do the reservations stunt so close to takeoff, man. You sure you want to do this? It ain't gonna be cheap."

"I don't care about the money, Jake. Just get me on a plane." He tore through the glove box, trying to find his charging cable. He fished it out and shoved it into his messenger bag.

After he'd gotten home from Deli's apartment last night, he'd packed a lot of things in his car—never intending to use them, of course. He only wanted to be prepared in case Deli needed something.

His suit was there because he'd picked it up from the cleaners on Saturday. In all the excitement, he must have forgotten it in his car. That was not unusual. People forget stuff like that all the time. He didn't really have an excuse for the shoes, though.

"I'm in." Sacha cut through his packing trance. "Northeast okay?"

"Fine. Anything is fine," Carl said, excavating an old laptop from the trunk.

"He doesn't want to fly Northeast, Sash. They charge you for an in-flight meal. Look, Carl, I'm in at Alzona Air. They don't have the best snacks, but I think I can get you a comped first-class upgrade."

"Whatever." Carl didn't care what plane he got on, as long as it left before nine.

Several minutes went by in which more frenzied tapping could be heard over Carl's panting, as he ran back to the airport from the long-term lot.

"Okay, I got you on the eight-fifteen flight to Vancouver. From there you're on the ten a.m. nonstop to Hong Kong, but you'll have to run to make the connection. You should arrive two hours after Deli's plane lands."

"Thanks, Jake."

"Hey!" Sacha shouted.

"You too, Sash."

"Yeah, man, no problem. Go get your girl."

"She's not my girl, Sash."

"Then bring her back for me," Sacha said. "She's pretty tasty. Why was she hanging out with you, anyway? I think she was into me. Did you guys see the way she was looking at me?"

"She was trying to figure out if you were alive, you moron," Jake said.

Carl didn't want to get in an argument about Deli right now. He wanted to get on the plane. He could kick himself for letting her go alone. He changed the subject.

"I have a huge favor to ask you guys," he said.

"Holy crap, what now?" Sacha said this with a sarcastic whine, but Sacha always spoke with a sarcastic whine. Carl knew better.

"I need one of you guys to take care of Deli's cat." He heard the intake of breath as both Jake and Sacha tried not to laugh.

"You serious, man?" Jake asked.

"Look, I told her I would do it, but obviously I can't now. Please, can one of you get over there for me?"

Jake snickered, but Carl didn't hear him. He was jogging toward the Alzona Air counter, messenger bag smacking against his leg in heavy thumps.

"Whatever, dude. I'll take care of her cat for you. But you gotta promise me this ain't gonna go the way it did with Heather," Jake said.

"Heather hated pets," said Carl. He approached the counter, phone balanced between his ear and shoulder, patting his pockets down. He found a passport-shaped lump and fished it out.

"Heather hated everything, man," Jake said.

"Not everything." Carl handed his passport to the blonde woman behind the counter.

"Whatever you say," Jake said, not sounding convinced at all.

"Dr. Sanderson?" The woman glared at Carl.

"Look, I gotta go. I'm checking in," he said into the phone. Then he held the receiver away from his ear and whispered, "I apologize. They're having a meltdown at work."

"Where are you headed, Dr. Sanderson?"

"Ooh, she sounds hot!" Sacha's tinny voice squeaked from the phone. The blonde woman ignored it by glaring harder at Carl. He snapped the phone back to his ear and growled.

"Shut up," he said into the phone. "I'm hanging up on you now." Carl made a dramatic gesture of hanging up his phone and stuffing it into his pocket. "I am sorry about that," he said. "I'm going to Hong Kong through Vancouver."

"You're rather late to be checking in, Dr. Sanderson." The polite smile plastered to her face stopped short of her eyes. Her voice had icicles in it.

"Yes. I apologize for that. I have been trying to put out fires for the last three hours and it's not easy…" He rolled his eyes toward the pocket he stuck his cell phone into.

"…when you work with animals."

The blonde woman's eyes warmed up after that.

THE DUNGEON

JAKE HATED LEAVING SACHA ALONE for the evening. He *knew* that asshole was going to eat the rest of the pizza as soon as he left. They'd been working together for three days straight, though, and he desperately needed a break. Plus, he wanted to look at Deli's system setup.

He wasn't planning to be gone for more than a few hours, so he only packed a laptop, the smaller portable hard drive, and a few other gadgets he thought might be useful. Jake wasn't sure what kind of system Deli had. Maybe he could make a few improvements on it while she was gone.

"See you later," he called over his shoulder on the way out the door. "Don't eat all the pizza, you mooch."

"Kiss my skinny ass, Jake. That pizza's as good as gone."

He gave Sacha a one-fingered salute and slammed the front door behind him. Outside, the air was warm and sunshine sparkled through the trees. It was a nice change from the storm yesterday.

Jake loved summer. The chance of seeing girls was exponentially higher than any other season in the Pacific Northwest. You could go for weeks without seeing one during the winter, but when the rain dried up, they emerged from their secret lairs in a haze of gauzy-skirted, strappy-sandaled glory. Truly, it was a magical time of year.

He walked across the lawn with a bounce in his step and pulled out his phone to text Sacha.

I hawked on one of those slices.

<3 J

Then he smiled broadly, slung his bag his shoulder and walked off down the street. From back near the house, he thought he heard faint sounds of shouted obscenities, but he could have totally been imagining that part.

Delilah Pelham lived closer than he realized. Within ten minutes, Jake was tromping up the steps to her apartment building. He looked around for the elevator and swore loudly when there wasn't one.

What kind of asshole lives on the—he read the mailboxes to see which was her apartment—*third floor of a building with no elevators? Carl owes me for this shit.*

It took an additional two minutes for Jake to tackle the stairs. As he crested the top, something reached out and grabbed his shoe so that he toppled forward and fell flat on his face. After dusting himself off, Jake looked down to inspect the stairs. An omen step? You didn't see many of those in Seattle.

Whoever designed this damn building is a total douchebag, he thought, and stomped down the hall to find Deli's apartment. Thankfully, he didn't have to go far.

Jake was a natural-born superintendent. He had managed Horsey House for over a decade now and you didn't get that far in the superintending business without learning a thing or two about entering locked apartments sans key. He inspected the door and determined it to be the simple pop-on-the-corner-and-jiggle-the-handle-while-jimmying-the-lock-with-a-pick-type lock. He popped. He jiggled. He jimmied. He opened the door.

Even though he knew no one was home, Jake still called out as he entered. He'd learned *that* lesson the hard way.

"Hello? Hello? I'm just here for, uh…the cat." His voice wobbled as he searched for the cat's name. He couldn't remember it.

When no one answered him after two minutes, Jake pushed his bulk through the door and closed it with a *snick*. The silence of Deli's apartment crowded around him, making him feel out of place.

He tiptoed to the living room and stopped, fully aware that he was staring at a couch Delilah Pelham slept on at least *occasionally*. Because Carl was his best friend, he tried not to think about what she might be wearing when she slept on it.

He removed his shoes as a sign of respect (and *not* because his feet had gotten all hot and sticky on the walk over) and left them near the couch. Then he headed to the kitchen and rooted around the refrigerator until he found something he thought might be a soda. It turned out to be rhubarb-flavored soda water; more proof toward his long-held belief that girls were alien creatures who did weird shit.

"C'mere, uh, Puss-Puss..." Jake made a clicking noise in the back of his throat to call for the cat again. The cat did not appear. "I'm supposed to feed you, cat. Where the hell are you?"

The cat continued not making an entrance, so Jake did what he could. He found a stubby can of cat food and dug around in the drawers until he unearthed a can opener. As the opener bit into the can, the pungent odor of wet cat food whooshed into the room. He had the can halfway open when a piercing wail caused Jake to nearly jump out of his shorts in fright.

Lazing behind him was the most massive house cat Jake had ever seen. He estimated it weighed thirty pounds, *easily*. It was striped grey with sharp fangs that poked out even after it closed its mouth. It looked like a fuzzy, overweight vampire.

It yawned wide then licked at a paw containing several more claws than normal. Jake finally remembered the cat's name.

"Hey, Toesy! You hungry, man?"

MeEEEROOooow, said the cat.

Its sleepy, golden eyes never left Jake as he put the entire can on the floor. He backed away, leaving the cat to his symphony of feral chomping and soggy purrs.

Operation Feed the Cat accomplished, Jake looked around for Deli's laptop. She probably hid it somewhere. He searched the dishwasher and through all the cupboards but found nothing, so he went back to the living room.

One of the cushions of the couch sat higher than the other two, and Jake laughed at her idea of security. He extracted the computer and plunked down on the couch. Then he pawed through his bag and pulled out his own laptop.

Before all of the excitement about Paul, they had planned to run the off-site pen test on the new security patches. Just because Carl was now running around Asia with a super-hot chick didn't mean that the pen test could wait. Jake figured he could use Deli's computer setup as a foreign competitor and see how far into the home system he could hack. Particularly the encryption code Sacha wrote. He loved finding bugs in Sacha's work.

It was shaping up to be a good afternoon.

FLIGHT TO HONG KONG

"DR. SANDERSON, YOU SHOULD BE in your seat right now."

Jenny the flight attendant stood in the galley behind the bathrooms, bracing herself against the wall. She had been looking for a reason to talk to Dr. Sanderson for most of the flight. So far, all she'd gotten was the introduction on takeoff and his decision on breakfast. She smiled but in a conspiratorial way, as though the two of them were sharing a joke.

"There's some turbulence up ahead, and we wouldn't want for you to get hurt."

"I'll go straight back to my seat, of course, but do you mind if I use the restroom first?" Carl looked deep into Jenny's eyes and said it as sincerely as he could.

Jenny didn't notice the smile; all she saw was a lost little puppy dog with the most beautiful blue eyes. She wanted to scratch him behind the ears and tell him he was a good boy. Then she wanted to find out if there was a *Mrs.* Dr. Sanderson.

"If you promise to get back to your seat just as quickly as you can, I'll forget I saw you." When Carl smiled again, she blushed.

"Thank you." He ducked into the bathroom and locked it behind him.

Jenny swooned. She didn't often do that anymore. He was cute, in a Silicon Valley way, which is to say that he was awkward and goofy but had a lot of potential. He also looked like he might be rolling in dough.

She heard the bathroom door lock and hurried over to his seat, intent on getting a peek at his stuff. If he caught her here, she would use the pretense of finding an extra magazine or a pillow. Or maybe she'd just tell him flat out that she found him attractive and ask if he was busy this evening.

The man in the window seat snored lightly but didn't wake as Jenny searched Dr. Sanderson's area. In the seat pocket, she found a street map of Hong Kong and several pages of notes. She tried to decipher his scribbles, but either he had terrible handwriting or it was in a foreign language.

The muffled sound of a toilet flushing caught her attention and Jenny stood up. She opened the overhead bin and dove for a blanket but the damn thing had settled so far back into the bin that she had to step forward to reach it. As she did so, the heel of her shoe crunched on something hard, like plastic.

Jenny bent over to pick it up, abandoning the blanket ruse. It was a strange sort of identity card. Although it was the same size as the ID badge she carried for airport security, this card was much heavier. It had the outstretched eagle seal of the United States Department of Defense and a quirky picture of Dr. Sanderson—less than flattering, but still kind of cute. Below the photo, his name: Carlton Leif Sanderson, ICSD. The rest of the card was blank.

He must work for the government.

Jenny heard the *snick* of the bathroom door unlocking and straightened up. She closed the overhead bin and hurried back to the galley, ID card in hand.

"I think you must have dropped this, Dr. Sanderson." She took his hand, still wet from the sink, and put the card into it. She didn't let go of his hand immediately.

"Oh! Thank you very much, Jenny. I would hate to lose that." As he pocketed his ID card, Jenny swooned again. He remembered her name.

"Is there anything else I can get you before you sit down, Dr. Sanderson?"

"Thank you, but I'm all set," he said. Then his eyes brightened. "Actually, there *is* something I could use a little help on. You wouldn't be willing to help me in an official matter, would you? I don't want to get you in trouble or anything."

He bowed his head sheepishly, like a kid asking for a second cookie. Jenny smiled. This was the opening she'd been looking for.

"Certainly, Dr. Sanderson. How may I be of service?"

"I'm unfamiliar with the layout of the Hong Kong airport."

"I have a map if you'd like." She smiled to the corners of her eyes.

"Oh, I have an accurate map; I just need a few extra details. Could I pick your brain for a moment?"

The plane bucked again, causing the deliciously tall Dr. Sanderson to stumble forward. He caught himself with an outstretched hand before he squished Jenny against the bathroom door. Trapped between Mr. Sanderson and the door, Jenny tried not to lick her lips.

"Uh, after the captain has turned off the seatbelt light, of course," he said and straightened up awkwardly.

"I'd be happy to," she said. "Is there anything *else* I can do for you?" She emphasized her meaning with a raised eyebrow.

"Well, there *is* one other thing I need, but I wouldn't want to inconvenience you in any way."

"Tell me what you need, and I'll see what I can do," Jenny said with a grin. "I think you'll find that I can be *very* accommodating."

Dr. Sanderson started to blush.

DELI'S LIVING ROOM
LATER THAT EVENING

BECAUSE OF HIS SIZE, most people assumed that Toesy was more dog-like. To some extent, that was true. He liked to go for walks. He liked chasing cats. He even played a very specialized game of fetch, which could be very rewarding—provided, of course, you were in need of a dead bird or half a rat.

But in some important ways, Toesy was very feline indeed. For instance, the second Jake's breathing slowed from the syncopated wheeze of someone doing too many things at once to the drawn-out rhythm of sleep, he pounced.

No, *pounced* is too harsh a word. He *crept*, as well as any thirty-two pound cat can creep, from the far side of the couch to the man's lap. It wasn't easy. The man had minimal lap to start with and it currently held many electronic whatsits. However, Toesy's ability to squish all thirty-two pounds of himself into tight spaces was quite remarkable, and soon he was cozied up between the man, his gadgetry, and the back of the couch.

After a while, the man woke up enough to move the whatsits from his lap to the coffee table. He discovered Toesy tucked in by his side and took the opportunity to reclaim the other half of the couch by propping his feet up on it. Toesy allowed the man to get comfortable before stretching out again. Delighted at this turn of events, he began to purr.

"You're not such a huge monster, are you?" The man mumbled more contented laziness at him and scratched behind his left ear. A small drop of saliva gathered on Toesy's lips.

The man must have been very tired because he soon returned to snoring. Toesy took advantage of the situation by climbing up to sleep on his chest.

Toesy considered his mistress a near-perfect human. She was easy to live with, generous with the catnip, and willing to stay in bed until noon on Sunday mornings if it was raining outside. Yet for all her fine qualities, Delilah Pelham had one major flaw. She was too small for him to sleep on.

Usually, as soon as he achieved the prime comfort position, she complained that he was too fat or that she could not breathe. Sometimes her arms fell asleep. Toesy loved Deli endlessly, but occasionally he suspected that she might be a bit of a wimp.

This man, who knew to feed him the Seafood Flavor without any prompting, would not complain about Toesy's extra girth, for he had extra girth himself. Toesy suspected he might be a holy man. Certainly, no regular human he ever met had been so awe-inspiring.

He kneaded the lumps of stuff in the man's shirt pocket into an arrangement conducive to long-term napping. Perfection attained, he tucked his nose into his furry belly and purred himself into a trance.

Or at least that's what he intended to do.

A few moments into his joyous nap, Toesy heard a faint *tick-tick* sound and opened his left eye halfway. Normally, he didn't allow *tick-tick* noises, on the principle that they always precluded some sort of funny business, like a bird or a squirrel. Then he would have to go kill something, eat it, and spend the rest of the day fighting off vermin-induced heartburn. But thanks to this great man, he wasn't hungry just now. He refused to allow one *tick-tick* to ruin his repose. He closed his tawny eye.

Another *tick-tick* ticked. Both of Toesy's eyes shot open.

One *tick-tick* was understandable, but *two* tick-ticks? He would not stand for it. Toesy was a sweet creature as far as sharp-fanged, mildly feral cats go, but there was a streak of murder in him that would not stand for a good nap to be ruined by ticking jackassery.

He lifted his head to look at the nearest window. If that crow was back again, he intended to kill it *completely* this time. But the kitchen window was empty.

More ticking ticked, this time followed by faint *scritchy-scratchy* noises, which confused his senses. Toesy closed his eyes and focused his ears on the unusual sound. It came not from the window, but somewhere close.

He flicked his ears twice, once in recognition and once in disbelief. The ticks were coming from the man's trouser pocket!

Toesy searched until he found the fold of the man's pocket and cautiously stuck his nose inside. The smell of cheese overpowered him for a moment, so he lay still and waited for his brain to adjust. After a moment, he was able to pick out more subtle scents. The tangy brine of coins, oily keys, and the cold, blank smell of glass—all surrounded by a diffuse aroma that Toesy could not place. It smelled *awake*.

TICK-TICK.

The glass jumped toward him, hitting him in the nose. Toesy backed away, affronted.

Surely this man does not want all this tick-ticking in his pocket, he thought. *I must put a stop to this nonsense.*

He reached in through the folds of cloth with a giant furry paw. The glass surface was round like a tube, with a little fluff stuck in one end. As Toesy rummaged, the tube slid free from the man's pocket and started to roll away toward the floor. He flashed a claw and caught it by the fluff.

Inside the tube, small bugs hopped and popped. Normally, Toesy wouldn't bother with bugs of this size, as he preferred something juicier. However, these particular bugs had just punched him in the nose and obviously needed a short, sharp lesson in consequences.

The wad of fluff at the end of the tube squeaked along his claws as Toesy dug deeper. He got a good grip and shook hard, loosening the cotton until suddenly it jerked free. This caused the glass tube to shoot across the room, where it hit the television with a *tink* and dropped to the floor.

Toesy did not want the bugs to escape before he could inspect (and possibly eat) them, so he power-jumped across the room.

When using all the muscles in its hind legs, the average house cat can jump six to seven feet from a resting position. Toesy, however, was *not* an average house cat. He was more like two or three average house cats shoved into the body of one. The force exerted by all thirty-two pounds of Toesy, power-jumping off the man's sleeping abdomen, was approximately equal to being sucker punched by a gorilla.

That's why the man woke up gasping for air and clutching his gut. He tried to roar, but without any breath, it came out a thin squeak.

"What the..." *Wheeze.* "...hell..." *Gasp.* "...are you *doing*?" *Cough, cough.*

Toesy had no attention to spare. He landed within inches of the glass tube, all thoughts laser-focused on the floor.

Now that he was better able to see them, the bugs didn't look like bugs at all. They looked like shiny, hopping beans. He sniffed them. They smelled like shiny, hopping, *metal* beans. He reached out with a tentative paw and batted at them. One of the beans popped up, half an inch into the air. Toesy quickly clamped his paw down on it.

"What have you got there, Toesy?" the man asked after he went back to breathing right.

Toesy flicked his tail in deference to the man but did not turn around. He was trying to figure out how to let go of the shiny bean and eat it at the same time.

"Let me see, boy."

The man was on his knees now, shuffling around on the floor next to Toesy.

"What's this?" he said, holding up the cracked glass tube. "That's not... No, it can't be. What have you got?" His voice grew alarming and insistent.

"*No! No, no, no, no, no! What have you done?*"

Toesy admired his volume as the man yelled and scooped two of the beans back into the cracked tube.

"What are you doing with the Elevators? You can't have those! They don't even work! Carl is gonna *kill* me!"

Another bean popped into the air. Toesy clamped a free paw down on it while his eyes dilated all the way up to crazy. He loved everything about this day.

"What the—?"

The man sat back on his haunches and examined the two beans he captured earlier. They sat at the bottom of the tube, vibrating back and forth gently.

"That...has *not* happened before," he said. Then he looked at Toesy and added, "Do you see this?"

Toesy, still splay-legged with trapped beans, rejoiced at this turn of events. The man was getting in on the game, too! They would eat the beans together! He broke into spontaneous purring. The beans under his feet began to wiggle around, and he dug his claws into the carpet wildly.

The beans in the man's hand vibrated faster. He peered at them, then he peered at Toesy. He brought the beans closer to Toesy. They began to pop inside their tube. He drew the beans away from Toesy. They quieted down.

"Holy shit," the man said. "Cat, do you realize what this means? I could kiss you!"

But he did not kiss him. Instead, the man leaned over, lifted Toesy's right paw and extracted the bean from underneath. Then he tousled Toesy's shredded ears. Toesy dug the claws of his other paw deeper into the carpet. He did not want the man to take away his last bean.

"You," he said, pointing to Toesy and smiling huge. "Are the most awesome cat in the universe! I gotta tell Carl."

He stood up, grabbed something from the table, and walked to the kitchen. He was making little *boop-boop* noises on the electronic whatsit when he stopped suddenly.

"Shit, he's still on a damn plane." He turned to Toesy and continued talking. "I'll have to email him about how awesome you are, Toesy."

At the mention of his name, Toesy purred louder. The bean struggled beneath his paw.

"Now, where does Deli keep your cat treats?"

The Great Man continued to talk at him as he combed through the kitchen, but Toesy had stopped listening after *cat treats*.

There was no doubt in his mind now that this was indeed a holy man. Toesy loved him, whisker and claw. Deli was gone for now, but she would return. When she did, could he convince her to let this man stay? The thought of him sleeping on the couch forever made Toesy purr even louder.

The bean beneath his paw struggled again. Cautiously, in case it escaped, Toesy lifted his foot. The bean popped up but fell back down in the same spot, seemingly resigned to its fate. Toesy sniffed it twice, then ate it.

It tasted of metal and victory.

HONG KONG INTERNATIONAL AIRPORT
WEDNESDAY, JUNE 5TH
4:55 P.M. (LOCAL TIME)

THE CUSTOMS AGENT STARED AT DELI for a second before diving into her unmentionables. Deli couldn't tell if he was bored or suspicious—probably both. He even opened her toothpaste. She did not protest.

He pulled out her computer and in an accent so thick she barely understood, requested that she turn it on. She did so. He repeated the same process with her phone. After three tense moments, he waved her through. Deli grabbed her stuff and walked as fast as she could toward the exit.

She didn't get very far before a slender man tapped her on the shoulder. He was wearing shiny black glasses that accented his shiny black hair.

"Excuse me, Miss. My name is Detective Zhi-ying." He flashed an official-looking ID badge at her and pocketed it quickly. "If you will please come with me for one moment?"

Deli turned to face him. He was taller than she was, but not by much. She could easily take him in a fight.

"What's the matter, Detective?"

"I only require seconds of your time. Please, come." He grinned. Something in his expression made the hair on the back of her neck stand up.

She shifted her duffle bag from her right shoulder to her left, using the move as an excuse to free her dominant hand. If it came to fighting, she wanted to be ready.

Another dark-suited man stood watching them from a few feet away. He had the hard, corrosive look of a henchman. She looked pointedly at him, then back to the detective. The detective read her movements.

"Oh, that is Johnny. Do not worry about Johnny. He is here to take care of you. Please…" He swept his hand forward in an after-you gesture. "Come with me."

If she ran right *now*, she might be able to make the main entrance before Johnny reached her. He didn't look particularly nimble, but judging by the bulge under his suit jacket, he didn't have to be. She tried convincing herself that Johnny looked like the shoot-'em-in-the-leg type of guy. It wasn't working.

She bent down to adjust her shoe and subtly check out the closest exits. Of the two she could see, one was too far to reach and the other was behind Johnny. She took a deep breath and calmed her mind, trying to visualize a route around Johnny while silently cinching the duffle bag's strap close to her chest.

"Miss Pell-ham," said a voice, lilting and slightly feminine.

She looked up to find Johnny standing directly in front of her. Being nearly as tall as he was wide, he had surprising stealth. She never even heard the squeak of his knock-off Italian loafers. She straightened up.

"Today I wish fortune upon you, Miss Pell-ham," he said. "To make good decisions. *Wise* decisions." He menaced her with a smile full of yellow teeth and staggering halitosis. Deli smiled back.

"I guess it's my lucky day, then," she said. Her hand fell away from the duffle strap.

"If you please?"

"Certainly," she said and allowed herself to be herded from the room.

TWO HOURS LATER

DELI PUSHED THE AIR OUT OF HER LUNGS and tried not to inhale too deeply. She couldn't get the stench out of her nose. It smelled like someone had stuffed a barn full of chickens into the ventilation system, then sat down to enjoy a lunch of fried garlic with a side of burnt rubber. It made her eyes water.

The only other people in the room were the detective and Johnny. Neither of them appeared to notice the smell at all. She sat behind a bare wooden table at the far side of the room and breathed through her mouth.

Johnny sat to the right of the door, Deli's duffle bag stashed at his feet. He hadn't officially confiscated it, but Deli didn't think she was getting it back any time soon.

Detective Zhi-ying stood across the table from her wearing a smug I've-got-you grin that made her want to take up full-contact dentistry.

"Miss Pell-ham, you still say you know *nothing* of this?"

"For the last time, *no*. I don't have a clue what you're talking about," she said, then slumped over in her chair again. The detective bristled.

"I think you do, Miss Pell-ham. And this will go very badly for you if you do not cooperate." He slammed his hand down on the table for emphasis. From the corner of her eye, Deli noticed Johnny turn his head slightly in their direction.

"We have your fingerprints at the scene of the crime, Miss Pell-ham. We know what you have done!" The detective grew three sizes with his bravado. He towered over her now, seething with anger.

Deli hated it when people shouted at her. It brought out her natural reaction to shout back.

"*Now, just a minute you bantam-weight jack-off.* Are you accusing me of a crime? Because if you are, you need to make up your mind and do it. Put the handcuffs on and haul me off to jail. Be warned, though, whatever you do, you had better be well and truly lawyered up because I haven't done a *damn* thing, and I'm an *American.* Do you know what that means? It means I was born with a football team full of lawyers just *waiting* to put you in a grave. They will be on you so fast you won't know if you found a rope or lost your horse. I've never been to Hong Kong before today, and I'm not going to sit here and listen to this insane bullshit. If you can't do any better than 'We know what you did,' then you better step off, jackass, because I am *out* of here."

With that, she shoved her chair backward from the table and stood up to leave. The table was wide, and she had to kick it to the left an inch or two in order to step around it. Johnny watched her intently from his chair in the corner, but he did not stand up.

"Sit down, Miss Pell-ham. You are not going anywhere."

Zhi-ying cracked his knuckles. If he threw so much as an overzealous hand gesture her way, she was going to break his right elbow, then his left shinbone before dislocating his left shoulder. She hadn't planned much more than that. She believed in letting these things happen organically.

But Zhi-ying did not hit her. Two seconds after his knuckle display, the door opened a few inches and a head of glossy black hair popped through the crack. The hair barked out an order or maybe a phone message. Deli didn't understand a word, but judging by the way Johnny's eyebrows went up, it wasn't good news.

The detective turned and stiff-legged it up the steps. He stopped in the hallway to argue with the messenger before slamming the door shut behind him. As soon as he left, Johnny went back to being an overfed doorstop.

The detective was not gone half a minute before the doorknob rattled. It opened an inch and stayed there. Someone on the other side was holding it steady. Through the crack, Deli heard a volley of irritated mumbles growing quickly in volume as the mumbler ran down the hallway.

"I understand your position, Detective, but I fear you misunderstand mine."

The voice was just on the other side of the door. It was a serious voice full of responsibility and fortitude. Deli was amazed at how much it sounded like Carl. But Carl was sixteen hours away in Seattle. No way could he get here fast enough.

"I am not asking you, Detective, I am *telling* you. I'm here to take her into custody. I don't know how you got the jump on my investigation, but believe me, *sir*; you do not want to be the one holding this fugitive back from facing justice on American soil."

The door opened. Deli had to bite down hard on her tongue to keep her mouth shut. It *was* Carl, but not the one she knew. His sandy hair had been combed into something resembling a style. He wore a charcoal grey suit tailored to make him look less like a scarecrow and more like Atticus Finch. His jaw was a hard line of authority.

"Miss Pelham," he said, looking her in the eye. "Also known under the internet moniker as *Bunny the Spider*?"

She had no idea what he was playing at, but she didn't care. At that moment, Deli would cop to anything Carl said as long as it ended with them getting the hell out of there. She pushed out her chin in defiance of the silly name and glared pretend daggers at him. His expression did not change, although Deli thought she saw a mischievous light come on behind his eyes.

"My name is Agent Carl Sanderson. I represent the United States government." He stood in the doorway, holding up a badge. Justice glinted off the official seal in the fluorescent light.

Deli looked at Carl and tried looking angry or put upon or *anything* other than impressed. Where did he get the suit? She shook her head slightly.

"Do not get comfortable here, Miss Pelham, you are not staying. You will be brought back to the United States to face charges leveled against you by the States of Washington, New York, and Alabama. Please," Carl said, nodding slightly toward the immobile Johnny. "Do not make this any more difficult than it needs to be."

Deli kept her expression as put-upon as she could and braced herself. Carl took two steps toward her, glancing up to the ceiling and back down again as he did so.

"This is *bullshit*," said Deli, slamming her hands into the table and jumping to her feet, hoping that's what he meant by the eye thing.

"Bullshit it may be, but you will not hide from the American people, Miss Pelham."

He walked past Johnny, pushing the table out of the way with his foot in order to reach Deli. From his suit pocket, Carl produced a pair of shiny steel handcuffs. He fumbled them slightly; Deli saw his hands shaking and stepped forward in time to make it look like her fault.

They were face to face for the first time since the airport back home.

"Miss Pelham, has anyone officially arrested you here, on Chinese soil?" He looked hard into her eyes.

"No. I have no idea what these idiots are talking about. I don't know what you're talking about either, *asshole*."

She added the last bit for character. Most of Carl's face remained impassive but his right eyebrow could not contain itself. It crept up his forehead in spirited approval.

"In that case…"

He grabbed her wrist and zipped a handcuff on it. Deli resisted the urge to smile. Instead, she twisted away from him slightly so that Carl had to reach across her body to grab her other hand. He held her wrist steady and clicked the second cuff in place with more force than necessary. Deli felt a spike of adrenaline through her stomach.

"Miss Delilah Pelham, I am arresting you for suspicion to traffic in illegal firearms, funding a major terrorist network through fraudulent means, and the kidnap, subjugation, and trafficking of no less than thirty-five human souls. You are also being arrested for suspicion…"

"You cannot do this! *Who are you to do this?*"

Compared to Cool-Guy Carl, the detective was pint-sized. He couldn't walk into the room without immediately becoming the shortest rooster in it, so he stayed at the top of the stairs and crowed.

Carl brought his temper up to simmer. He faced the man squarely from across the room, and even though he was well out of reach, Zhi-ying flinched.

"I have told you, *sir*." Carl's voice was solid with authority. "My name is Carl Sanderson. I am from the US Department of Homeland Security, ICS Division." He held up his fancy ID card with its super-justice seal. "And I am taking custody of this woman on charges

leveled against her by the United States government." He ended by
turning back to Deli and grabbing onto the short chain between the
handcuffs on her wrists. This made her jerk forward half a step.
Wow, Carl, you are on fire, she thought.

"You cannot take her anywhere!" the detective shouted. "I am in
charge here!"

"Detective Zhi-ying, are you aware of the anarchist network known
as *Spies Like Us?*"

The detective didn't speak. The crease in his forehead answered
for him. He was *not* aware. He substituted this lack of knowledge
with an overabundance of posturing, but Carl did not pay attention
to his upturned chin or downturned mouth.

"It's a small group of individuals dedicated to the art of misdirection.
They're hackers, Detective. And they are paving the way for other groups
to commit cyber-based crime. To date, the Spies Like Us network has
carved enough money from the international economy to fund a small
country. They don't care where their money comes from. They will,
and have, sold their abilities to the highest bidder." Carl paused to let
that sink it, meeting the detective's glare with one of his own. "Guns
and sex are hot commodities, Detective. But the real money-baby is
terror." He paused again, this time for dramatic effect. It worked. The
detective lowered his chin by half an inch. "I understand if you haven't
heard of them—they may have dealings in China under different names."

"Of course I know of this!" Zhi-Ying shouted in a shower of self-
righteous saliva. Carl's hint of condescension riled the detective, and
he stepped down into the room. Even Johnny tensed. "You think I
do not know this? But this Bunny Spider is detained by *Chinese*
customs. She will be brought to *Chinese* justice."

"Detective Zhi-ying, I respect your position, but I must warn you
that if you insist on prosecuting this suspect here instead of allowing me
to take her back to the United States, you put three years of investigation
at risk. This woman whom you have detained is a hacker known to have
direct links to a man responsible for funding several major terrorist
organizations." Carl still held the handcuff chain in his hand, and as
he spoke, he took a short step toward the detective. "Officially, we
have no extradition treaty with China. If you would like to open talks in
that direction, I can personally bend the ear of the President for you."

Carl took another step toward him, dragging Deli along, and let his implied threat hang in the air for a moment. Then he changed his tack. "She doesn't look dangerous, does she? And by herself, she's really not. She's only a laundress." He stepped in front of Deli so the detective did not see her roll her eyes. Johnny saw it, though. And because he watched Deli's face, he completely missed the fact that they now stood closer to the door.

"But if you need something covered up, this is the person who can do it. Now, if you will please excuse me, I have arrested my suspect, and I'm leaving."

"You cannot do that! You cannot arrest this woman!"

"With all due respect, Detective, I am arresting her at this very moment." Carl took another step, larger this time, more intent on leaving than getting a point across.

"Johnny..." Zhi-ying started to give an order, but Carl's shout cut him off.

"*Are you aware that the United States government will want to know why a known international criminal of such caliber was allowed into China without contacting the foreign countries involved in prosecution of said individual?*"

That last part sounded like bullshit to Deli, but it was sexy, legalese bullshit, and Carl's suit was sharp enough to pull it off. She kept her eyes on the floor, not wanting to give Johnny anything interesting to look at. Carl steamed ahead with jerky little steps, dragging her by the handcuffs on the downbeat.

"The United States and China do not always see eye to eye, *sir*. But there are *accords*, you understand? Not promises, per se, but *accords*. By now, my superior back at ICSD knows who you are, *Detective*, and she knows your position in this operation."

Carl softened his voice, almost to a croon. "Detective, you can be the weight that tips the scales of justice for a three-year investigation into the manipulation of funds to three of the world's largest terror organizations. Or, you can be the reason that global terror is still a thriving business market. Believe me, Detective, if this woman slips away, the governments of many economically viable nations will be looking for a reason why. Do you really want to bring that headache down on yourself?"

Zhi-ying closed his eyes for a second. A small bead of sweat shone on his forehead. His shoulders sank slightly under the weight of Carl's argument. No longer pretending to be asleep, Johnny watched the detective through half-lidded eyes. He reminded Deli of a snake, tasting the air with his tongue.

"Detective." Carl's tone suggested commiseration. "This woman was able to get through your customs department with an unlicensed satellite descrambler. The implications of that *alone* would decide it for me." He shuffled his feet, somehow ending up closer to the doorway in the process.

That *had* to be bullshit. Deli was almost certain of it. But she kept her head down and stayed silent. Carl and his imagination had everything under control. She inched along behind him, ready to run.

"*If* I were in your shoes, of course. I mean, nobody likes a slipup at customs. Least of all the American people, sir."

Shuffle.

The detective looked dejected for another beat. Then he stood straight and resolute. "You must take this prisoner out of here now! We do not want your filthy American scum here on wholesome Chinese soil. Take care of your criminal problems, Agent Sanderson."

He turned to Johnny and shouted, "Johnny! Make sure she leaves and does not come back here." Then he marched up the stairs and down the hall.

The doorway cleared for a moment but filled quickly with the voluminous silhouette of Johnny. He glared at Carl. "I do not believe you," he said.

"You don't have to. Your detective just gave an order. I intend to heed it." Carl leaned down and grabbed Deli's bag from the floor.

"I will accompany you to your return flight," Johnny said. His eyes flashed with indignation.

"That won't be necessary. We have an appointment with my superior in an hour. I am well trained in prisoner transport, especially one this tiny."

Carl jerked Deli's handcuffs with more force than she expected, causing her to stumble forward and nearly fall. She caught herself with her left foot and swallowed hard. Not until that moment had she thought about Carl as an adversary. His height gave him a huge advantage. He probably had more muscle power in his legs than she did in her entire body.

"What did you say your title was, *Mr.* Sanderson?"

"Special Agent Sanderson, acting under orders from the Department of Homeland Security. And if you don't like that *Mr.* Johnny, you are welcome to lodge a complaint after we leave. Would you like the phone number for the help desk?"

"I would like a great many things, Mr. Special Agent. One thing I would like is for you to tell me who you really are."

"My name is Carl Sanderson. I was born in Edmonds, Washington. The last car I bought was a black Volkswagen Jetta, and I have no known food allergies. There, now you know everything about me. Kindly step aside."

Johnny's face went from red to purple. His right hand began to flex open and closed. When he spoke next, the little bubble of spit at the corner of his mouth glistened in the overhead light.

"Leave while you can, Carl Sanderson—you will not have a chance later. I will check your story, and when I find out that everything you said is false"—he gave Deli a look full of venom—"I will find you."

Deli made sure to accidentally shoulder-check Johnny as Carl pulled her out the door.

DELI'S COUCH, SEATTLE

DELI'S COMPUTER WAS LAUGHABLE. Jake couldn't even log in to the home server until he cleaned her hard drive and upgraded her security software. It put the pen-test off until the morning, but he didn't care. He was so delighted with her complete lack of computer knowledge that he would have built her a brand-new computer if she needed one. Hell, the girl didn't even have a firewall in place.

He smiled with relief. She may be smokin' hot, but a computer genius she was *not*.

He spent an hour strolling through her email and other stuff—not snooping, mind you. He was doing research. She seemed legit, but Jake knew her brother, and if she turned out to be half the twit he was, there would be problems. He wasn't about to let Carl waste two more years on another devil woman.

Her email history didn't tell him much that wasn't about birds, library books, or something called bodu kura, whatever that was. Some guy named David certainly wanted to know a lot about it.

Jake assumed David was her boyfriend until an email exchange with someone named Stacy blew that theory out of the water. If exclamation points and emoticons were any indication, Stacy was knee-deep in teenaged infatuation with David. Deli supported her decision kindly until the emails devolved into long strings of exclamation points with very few actual words in between them. Deli's final reply was short, sweet, and to the point:

> *Please, will you just sleep with him so he can get his head back on training?*

He decided he liked Deli quite a bit after that.

Additional research led him to a file of pictures labeled *Vegas*, which he clicked on immediately. There he discovered something *very* relevant to his interests: Deli was friends with the delivery girl from Pizza Joe's.

He spent the better part of an hour making sure there were no scandalous or blackmailable images in the Vegas file. Unfortunately, there weren't. But he *did* learn that Deli knew a lot of girls who wore black bikinis, and the delivery girl from Pizza Joe's had a tattoo on her right thigh. He thought it might be a dolphin, but to be on the safe side he saved the picture on his portable drive for further study. It *could* be a gang sign. You never knew about these things.

The upgrade on the computer system finished. Jake logged into the home server and navigated his way through to Sector Nine.

The bulk of Sector Nine was old game programming they didn't use anymore but didn't want to get rid of because it came in handy once in a while. However, hidden beneath the outdated files sat a digital porthole of Carl's design—a masterpiece of hidden data storage, almost impossible to find and even more impossible to hack into.

Well, *one* person had been able to find it. But Jake didn't like thinking about her, so he forgot her every chance he got. He wound his way through files and opened up the security login.

Please enter password for access to Sector Nine.

Jake typed in the password and hit Enter.

Password Incorrect. Please try again.

Jake tried again.

Password Incorrect. Please try again.

Carl wouldn't change the password without telling him, would he?

Jake studied the clock, counting off hours in his head. It was late in Hong Kong, but Carl would probably still answer. Then he thought of Deli in her black bikini and decided it might be better to check with Sacha first. He picked up his phone and dialed.

"Sash," Jake said into the receiver. "Did Carl change the password for Sector Nine?"

"Jake! Where are you, man? You been gone for like, *hours*. What are you doing?" Sacha sounded forlorn over the phone.

"I'm still at Deli's." Jake turned to look at Toesy, curled up and purring his way through a catnip haze at the other end of the couch.

"I'm hanging with her cat. The thing is huge. It's like the size of a coug—"

"MAL-FUNC-TION. ER-ROR. ER-ROR." Sacha's voice went all roboty. "TOO. MANY. PUSSY. JOKES. CAN. NOT. DECIDE."

"Shut *up*, Sash," Jake said, irritated that he hadn't thought of the pussy line himself. "Do you know if Carl changed the password to Sector Nine or not?"

Sacha sniggered, "Nope. Not that I know of. Did you try calling him?"

"Not yet. I didn't want to *bother* him, if you know what I mean."

"Ooh, good point. He might be making out with his lady friend. How about Seraphim22? Will that work?" Sasha was typing before Jake could stop him.

"No! Don't do that! It will—"

"Shit," Sasha said. "It locked me out."

"Damn it, Sacha! Now I can't get back in for four hours."

"Sorry about that, man," Sacha said. "I forgot about the remote lockout."

"Ah, screw it," said Jake. He yawned. "It doesn't matter. I think I'm gonna get some sleep."

"You gonna stay there?" Sacha sounded giddy. He was probably high on leftover pizza.

"Yeah, I'd come back, but honestly, her couch is way more comfortable than ours. Plus, the bathroom doesn't smell."

"Hey! I cleaned it last week."

Jake rolled his eyes at the receiver. Sacha was the world's premier time-travelling housekeeper. He always cleaned things *last week*.

"Whatever. I probably won't be back until tomorrow afternoon. I've got some more stuff I want to do, and the cat seems pretty lonely."

"Niiice." Sacha said. "I won't tell Carl you're sleeping with his girly-friend's pussy."

"Asshole."

"Aw, you *do* miss me, Jake." Sacha made loud kissing noises into the phone as he disconnected the call.

Jake yawned. He was exhausted from the past few days spent trying to find that bastard, Paul. Carl should have never hooked up with that guy. He was smarmy and slick and didn't have a damn clue what he was talking about when it came to robotics. Oh, he knew enough to pass for a geek in most circles, but when it came right down to it, the guy's knowledge of simple physics was nothing more than an arsenal of dirty jokes involving the right-hand rule.

But Paul got them cash and Jake needed some pretty fancy stuff to build these expensive little pieces of crap, which, until now, had done nothing more than sit at the bottom of a vial and cost money. Who knew that all they'd needed was a monster cat to purr at them?

He shuffled all the computers to the coffee table and stretched out on the couch. Toesy, nearly cross-eyed with serenity, chirruped at him from the ottoman.

"You're right, Toes-man. It's definitely bedtime. Come on, dude."

Toesy yawned and sat up. He waited until Jake was comfortable and then moved in, spreading himself out enthusiastically over the bulk of Jake's belly. Within minutes, both man and cat were fast asleep.

*   *   *

The little metal bean that Jake forgot struggled in Toesy's digestive system for a long time before it was able to gain purchase. Finally, it lodged itself within a fold of tissue. If Toesy felt the bean wrap itself up in the lining of his stomach, he did not heed it in any way. In fact, he continued to sleep as though nothing was wrong. Technically, nothing *was* wrong.

Technically, everything was going *right*.

The bean did not know the difference between stomach lining and subdermal adipose tissue, but the environmental humidity and temperature requirements had been fulfilled, so that distinction became unnecessary. It noted the pH of the surrounding fluid was far lower than optimal and compensated by increasing hydrogen carbonate synthesis. Toesy farted quietly, but otherwise there were no discernible effects.

The bean woke up each part of its directive. Some of the coding was off by a few positive/negative couplings, but its fallback programming took over, compelling the bean to make changes where necessary with minimal damage to tertiary structure and cataloguing the splice variants so that it could learn from previous mistakes.

BAGGAGE CLAIM, HONG KONG INT'L AIRPORT 6:30 P.M.

THE BAGGAGE CLAIM AREA LOOKED exactly like all other baggage claim areas: crowded and dirty. Except this one was in Hong Kong, so it was crowded and spotless. The floor shone with the pride of Chinese floor polishers. Windows glinted with the legendary work of Chinese window washers. Digital displays announced the next round of lucky passengers, ready to claim their pampered luggage.

Deli had only enough time to notice that the hall was cavernous before Carl tripped into her. They ended up smashed into a phoneless phone booth near the elevators.

"What the hell, Carl?" He was scrabbling for her wrist, and she realized he was trying to uncuff her hands.

"Don't do that yet! They are *totally* still watching us, you idiot!"

"Actually, I don't think it matters. There's an eighty-seven percent chance that we're going to have to run for it in less than..." Carl looked at his watch for reassurance and nodded. "Two minutes."

"Wow. Okay, quick."

She shoved her hands out to Carl. He fumbled the key, almost dropping it in the process. Deli snatched it away and unlocked the cuffs herself. She slipped them into her pocket and made to step out of the booth. Carl grabbed the back of her jacket and gently reeled her back in. Deli bristled.

"Not yet," he said in a low whisper.

She turned to him, bouncing on her heels.

"Carl, I'm glad to see you and everything but, *do you have a plan here?* We can't hang around until our buddies back there figure out the story you gave them was bullshit. They'll throw both of our asses in jail. And I don't want to go to Chinese prison, Carl." She gave him a look somewhere between worn-out patience and bad-dog. "I *really* don't."

Carl, focused on a point across the baggage claim area, shook his head slowly from side to side.

"They can't take you to jail, Deli. They weren't police."

"*What?* How come they had me in custody?"

"That wasn't custody. That was an empty quarantine room for animals passing through customs." Deli looked shocked, then a light came on behind her eyes.

"Actually, that explains a lot. But how did you find me then?"

"That"—he pointed to the watch on her wrist, the one that Jake had insisted she wear—"has a tracking signal on it."

Deli looked from the watch to Carl. "Yeah, that's not creepy at all."

Carl didn't respond. He stared across the room.

"But what about everything you told them? That was all bullshit, right?"

"So far as they're concerned, no. I'm not one hundred percent legit, but I'm legal enough to scare one phony detective."

"If he isn't a detective, what the hell was he?"

She said it loud enough, but Carl didn't respond, so she poked him in the shoulder. He'd gone rigid.

"Please give me a moment. I'm watching the door."

She followed his gaze to the bank of glass doors on the far wall. Outside, cars lined the sidewalk, three deep in some spots.

There were people everywhere. Students, businessmen, grandmas—they all wove between backpacks and suitcases, tracing complicated patterns of movement. Deli watched Carl's eyes follow the movement, look down at his watch, and then back to the movement. He repeated this process a few times.

People.

Watch.

People.

"Okay," he said, looking at his watch again.

"We need to go"—his head beat a three-second rhythm—"now."

He took Deli by the arm and plunged into the crowd. They slipped between a family of four and their overloaded luggage cart. No sooner had they passed than a tour guide with a sign in Dutch directed a gaggle of blond skyscrapers toward the carousel behind them. People rushed near, around, and beside them, but they always moved at the right time.

Deli felt like she was travelling through a very dangerous tunnel that only Carl could see. Part of her wanted a nun, an old granny, and a lady with a baby carriage to weave in front of them, just to see what he would do.

They made their way to the street in less than a minute. The humidity outside neared the saturation point, and Deli drank the air in great gulps as they ran. Carl aimed them toward the outside lane of traffic where a taxi driver was deep in negotiations with a shrewd-looking elderly woman and her husband.

He approached the couple from behind, but they paid him no heed. He waited for a few seconds before coughing politely. The woman's hands flew up over her head and she ducked.

"Sorry to bother you, but do you happen to know how I can get to the Four Seasons from here?"

Carl spoke brightly with his apple pie cheeks and an All-American smile. The cab driver leered. There were dollar signs in his eyes.

He spat a few phrases at the elderly couple, punctuating his remarks with a dismissive hand gesture. The woman turned to glare at Carl. She said something in Chinese, then smacked her husband on the shoulder and marched off in a four-lettered huff. When Carl called out with an apology, her hand shot into the air signaling that he was the *number one* most unforgiven person in all of Hong Kong. Her husband shuffled along behind, carefully concealing a grin.

Without negotiations of any kind, Carl opened the back door of the cab and threw Deli's duffle bag across the seat. Then he held the door and she threw herself across the seat. The cab driver, ecstatic at this turn of events, scrambled to get behind the wheel.

Through the rear window, Deli saw a man in a dark suit run out the doors and into the slow-moving traffic. He tore through the cars, investigating each as he passed.

Another knot of blond skyscrapers stood in the road, surrounded by suitcases and arguing over a car many times too small. Deli looked back at the man in the suit. He was three cars behind and headed straight for them. She grabbed the back of Carl's neck and folded him neatly in half before folding herself in half as well. The cabbie, fed up with Scandinavian antics, jerked his steering wheel to the left and gunned the motor. He missed the lead skyscraper by mere inches.

Carl and Deli stayed as hunkered down as it was possible to hunker and still look nonchalant—sort of a casual-hunker. Not until they felt the motor pick up speed did they hazard a look out the window. They were on a freeway heading toward the city.

"That was amazing," Deli said, immediately wishing she hadn't. In order to speak, she used the rest of the air from her lungs and took a deep breath to replenish it. Her lungs were now fighting against an aromatic assault of blueberries, coconut, and something that could only be described as *mentholated grandma*. Did all of Hong Kong smell so violently? She inhaled as shallowly as possible and talked out of the side of her mouth.

"How much of that was true back there?"

"Most of it."

Carl whispered loud enough for her to hear but not loud enough for the cabbie to listen in. He was still bent over, fidgeting with her duffle bag. Deli noticed that the back of his neck had turned bright red—probably from all the running. When he finally sat up, she saw that his whole face had lit up like a stoplight.

"Oh, come on," she said. "All that hooey about the Spies Like Us network and the terrorist organizations? That was pretty film noir."

She leaned into Carl as she spoke. Partly to hide what she was saying from the cabbie but mostly because the smell of Carl was a lot easier to take than fruity, mentholated grandma. He only smelled of airplane food and soap. If he noticed Deli's surreptitious breathing, he didn't comment on it.

When he didn't answer, she sat back enough to look at him.

"Tell me, Carl, what kind of security did you say you do?" She always assumed he was a security guard.

"Computer security."

To Deli, *computer security* meant geeky guys with bad haircuts, talking in acronyms. Carl certainly fit that description better than night watchman.

"I thought you worked at Paul's law firm."

"I do. I'm the security officer."

"Then how do you know all that other stuff?"

"Because sometimes I work for other people." Carl gave her a half smile then stared straight ahead.

"That doesn't answer my question. How do you know about spy networks and all that?"

"Um, can I tell you later?"

He gave Deli a silent, pleading look. Then, with both hands in his lap, he pointed to the front seat. The cab driver cruised along in the jolly chaos of the road, whistling a carefree tune punctuated by short bursts of jubilant profanity. His eyes routinely flicked to the rearview mirror and their conversation. Deli understood why Carl was playing the Cold War hush-hush.

She stared into the mirror until the cabbie looked at her again. Then she glared at him until he looked away. He stopped whistling, but the smile never left his face. She gave up trying to grill Carl and settled for looking out the window.

Outside the cab, buildings crowded in on both sides. Deli watched, wide-eyed, as the glory and guts of Hong Kong flew by. Women, melting in the evening sun, carried umbrellas as they crossed roads, shopped street vendors, even hailed cabs. Deli wanted to get out and explore.

She also wanted to get out so she could breathe again. Turning away from Carl had been an odiferous mistake, and she was getting light-headed from lack of oxygen.

The cab driver pulled through a crowd of people passing on the sidewalk without hitting a single one. He tore through the roundabout, stopping only when the front tire was securely over the curb. No one flinched, not even the door attendant standing a mere two feet from the grill. Deli couldn't help but be impressed.

In the rearview, the cabbie grinned.

"The Four Seasons, Mister and Miss. Three hundred Hong Kong, *please.*"

Carl pulled a wallet from his back pocket and paid the man without hesitation. The cab driver pouted as he pocketed the cash.

Carl reached in his wallet for another note and handed it over. Deli didn't stop him, but she was disgusted all the same. She shoved Carl out the door with her elbow as soon as the transaction was over. Once he was out of the way, she turned to the cab driver and growled.

"I could *rent* a car cheaper than that, *asshole.*" She pushed herself out of the backseat as the cabbie revved the engine. He gave her barely enough time to shut the door before he zipped away through the throng of people and out onto the street.

"Good riddance!" Deli shouted into the exhaust fumes. She turned to Carl and sighed. "You should learn currency conversion. That guy just charged you an arm and a leg."

Carl was curiously calm about the transaction. "Yeah, I figured he would. That's why I asked him to take us to the Four Seasons. It's a pretty swanky hotel."

He swooped down, grabbed the bag from Deli's hand, and slung it across his shoulder. Then he turned to the woman attending the front entrance and nodded smartly as she pulled open the heavy glass door. A welcome rush of conditioned air greeted them. It smelled pleasantly of nothing.

FOUR SEASONS HOTEL LOBBY

"WAIT, ARE WE NOT STAYING HERE?" Deli asked as they walked into the lobby. It was gigantic. A waterfall of stairs cascaded around a colossal marble pillar, spilling its travelers onto the sparkling marble floor. Seriously, the floor shone brilliantly. What was it with shiny floors here? It was beginning to freak Deli out a little.

"No," Carl said over his shoulder. He marched steadily up to the front counter, a walk of maybe three or four miles. Deli skipped behind him, trying to keep up with his long strides.

"If they followed us from the airport, I want to throw them off."

"Wow, that's actually a good idea," she said. Then she realized what she sounded like and tried to look less astonished. Carl cleared his throat with a small cough.

"Thank you. I did some planning on the plane."

The woman at the concierge desk smiled with all of her teeth as they approached. Carl stepped up and put Deli's bag on the floor in one efficient movement. He returned the concierge's smile with one of his own (no teeth; he wasn't that kind of guy) and pulled a folded-up sheet of paper from his pocket.

"May I ask you for some help with directions?"

The woman's teeth sparkled at the suggestion. "Of course, sir!"

Carl unfolded his little square of paper with a dramatic gesture. It turned out to be a map from a travel website; printed on an anemic printer that had run out of cyan ink. Several arrows dotted the more populous areas. Random notes colonized the margins.

"Can you tell us where we went wrong? It says on my map here" — leaning over the desk, Carl pointed to a spot on the map rendered almost entirely in yellow, making the streets impossible to decipher—"that we should be at the Sheraton Hotel. But, this is the Four Seasons, correct?"

To her credit, the woman's eyes flashed with concern for only the briefest of moments. She stayed calm while politely explaining to the bewildered Carl that he was many miles away from where he needed to be. The beauty of Victoria Harbour must have enchanted him, making him follow the road well beyond his exit. This, she assured him, has been known to happen from time to time.

"Fortunately, it is easy as sunshine to make this problem better. I will call a taxi for you." She picked up the phone, but Carl held up his hand to stop her.

"No thank you, Miss...Ming," he said slowly as he read the name off her lapel pin. "I would rather not tempt the beauty of Victoria Harbour from another taxicab today."

Then he turned to Deli. "If *you* don't mind? Because if you'd rather go by taxi, we can certainly do that. I just thought..."

He trailed off, and Deli realized he was serious. He was *literally* asking permission. She didn't know the plan, but Carl had gotten them this far without mistake. "Ugh, I don't want to take another cab. Isn't there a more relaxed way to get there?"

Carl smiled and turned back to the toothsome Ming, who, at the suggestion of scenery, lit up like a carnival.

She exchanged Carl's smudgy map for a glossy one of the building complex explaining how the Four Seasons hotel was only one part of the upscale adventure. The Star Ferry could take them across the harbor. To get there, they would pass many beautiful and trendsetting shops in the mall, to an expertly engineered walkway on the other side. She outlined this in ink so they would not miss it. Then she produced another map, less glossy but much more pedestrian friendly, from her prodigious resources and detailed the route they needed to take to the Sheraton.

"Thank you so *very* much, Miss Ming. I'm sorry we didn't make reservations here instead."

Carl looked truly sorry. Deli wondered how much of it was an act. He was always so sincere about everything. He picked up Deli's bag and took two steps toward the door before stealing back to the counter.

"Miss, I'm sorry to trouble you again, but can you direct us to the restrooms before we go?"

Ming had not stopped beaming. "Of course, sir!"

She took one of the maps from Carl's unresisting hand and circled the appropriate spot. Then she handed him back the map and pointed, just to make sure he knew.

"Enjoy your journey, and enjoy Hong Kong!"

Carl strolled away. When he caught up with Deli, he quickened his pace until Deli had to pull on his arm to get him to stop. "Could you please slow down? I don't walk as fast as you."

"I'm sorry." He stopped in front of the elevator and bounced on his heels until it arrived. "I wasn't walking *that* fast, was I?"

"Probably not for *you*, but my legs are a lot shorter than yours." Carl held the door with his hand as she tucked herself into the elevator car. "And I have to walk twice as fast to cover the same ground you do."

He focused on the elevator buttons, selecting the one for the floor above with abnormal care. Deli waited for the doors to close before turning to glare up at him. It was a long way to glare.

"At some point, are you going to tell me what the hell is going on?"

"As much as I can, yes. But if we *were* followed—and I have every reason to believe we were—the next…" He glanced down at his watch. "…seven minutes are very important.

The elevator dinged politely for their floor, and the doors slid open. Again, Carl held the door for Deli. She walked out, peering sideways at Carl as she did so.

His eyes focused on a point far away, giving Deli the feeling that Carl knew exactly what he was doing, except for the fact that he had never done it before. It was an unsettling dichotomy.

When they arrived at the bathroom, as pointed out by the ever-helpful Ming, Carl slowed to a stop. "I'm not saying you have to use it, but you should at least go *into* the bathroom for about ninety seconds. Then, come out and meet me over there."

He pointed at a store selling expensive watches. Deli nodded, made a step toward the bathroom, and whipped back around to face Carl. He jumped backward slightly.

"Do you promise to tell me what's going on?" She pointed her finger directly at his nose. Carl's hands shot up to either surrender or shield his face, she wasn't sure which.

"I promise! But can we wait until we're safe?"

"I'm going to hold you to that." She waggled a finger in his face.

Deli didn't like being strung along, and she hated being lied to. If Carl didn't come through with the information soon, he was going to find out exactly how seriously she took these things.

After a beat, she nodded at him, then lowered her finger. Though she would never admit it, she really did have to pee.

Eighty-five Mississippis later, Deli was drying her hands under the air blower. She counted off five more Mississippis on the way out. A man in a cheap suit with gel-slicked hair had just passed the restroom, and Deli followed him down the promenade to the watch store. She ducked into the store half a second before the slick man turned around. An upright display case hid her from view.

Carl stood in the back corner, bent over a glass case of watches designed for ladies with expensive taste. He nodded in her direction but did not look up.

"Look at the diamonds on this watch," he said as she approached. He put his hand on her back and almost pushed her over. Deli smacked his arm away.

"What the hell is *with* you?"

"I'm sorry. You need to put your head down."

"All you had to do was *say* so." Deli leaned over the case. She spoke through the side of her mouth, foot tapping angrily on the carpet. "Is Johnny following us or not?"

"Yes, he is. And he's got help. Another guy passed the front of the store right before you walked in. He very nearly saw you."

A sales lady walked past to check on them and Carl busied himself pointing out another watch. He and Deli squinted at the case and mumbled until the she went away.

"I'm waiting for an opening to leave. When we go out, we'll need to get to that escalator quickly."

His eyes flashed toward the entrance of the store, indicating a direction. Deli glanced up to see where they were headed.

"If we can get down there without notice, we'll have about three minutes to get to the walkway. We should try to get as far down the walkway as we can manage in that time. I don't exactly blend in here."

Carl's eyes strayed out into the mall where throngs of people milled about. The people may have been dressed in French clothes, Swiss watches, and German shoes, but most all of them had one thing in common: Chinese physiques. Compared to the average Hong Konger, Carl looked like he should be wearing fur boots and wielding a magical hammer.

"Christ, Carl, how are we going to get down there? You're a freak of nature compared to everyone around us." She hadn't meant to insult him, and he didn't take it that way.

"I don't know. But if we don't get out of here, Johnny's friends are going to find us."

"I like that one."

"Did you hear what I said?"

"I heard you." Deli's left eye squinted, giving her a halfhearted sneer. "I still like the watch."

Out in the mall, three women, each pushing a baby carriage the size of a small town car, chatted their way past the store entrance. In the lead stroller sat a baby-shaped marshmallow, festooned with lace and ribbon roses, happily gnawing through a pink party hat. Tied to the front of her stroller, a small flotilla of balloons bobbed and swayed in the air.

Carl touched Deli's arm lightly. "Let's go," he said.

This time, she followed without comment.

CENTRAL TRANSIT STATION

THEY WOVE THEIR WAY THROUGH THE MALL to the transit station. Mostly Carl tried to stay to the walls, ducking in and out of shadows to appear less monstrously huge. It wasn't working. People stared. People pointed. Lots of people shouted. At one point, Deli thought she saw a camera flash. Carl was definitely a big hit in Central Transit station.

They made it across the main floor before catching sight of Johnny again. He was struggling to pass an ancient woman with abundant suitcases. Of his partner, they had seen nothing. It was not a good sign.

They bounded onto the walkway, scaring a group of schoolchildren into excited peals of laughter as they tore past. The walkway was covered, so they weren't directly in the sun, but the sides were open to the elements and the current element was a humidity level of roughly seven thousand percent. Carl still wore his suit jacket. He also had Deli's bag slung across his chest.

"Come on, Carl! You need to move your ass!" She grabbed his hand to pull him along. Carl immediately sped up.

They ran on, leaving a trail of excited looky-loos in their wake. Deli didn't care. She didn't want to go to prison. Even if it was fake prison. She didn't want Carl to go to fake-prison, either. She continued to run.

With the ferry terminal in sight, they made a last push to reach it before Johnny and his unseen accomplice caught up with them. Up ahead, people scattered. A hole began to form in the dense crowd. She pointed at it with Carl's hand, and he headed in that direction.

Unfortunately, Deli only saw a clear spot to cross through the crowd. She didn't stop to consider the reason the spot was clearing. In a matter of seconds, she understood both why the crowd was dispersing, and where Johnny's accomplice had gone.

It wasn't the size of his gun that was the problem. It was the fact that he was pointing it at everyone and shouting. Since Deli didn't speak Chinese, she could only guess what he was saying, but it certainly didn't sound very nice.

He stood in the middle of the concourse, blocking the path for new passengers to get to the ferry. A knot of wary people milled about the turnstiles near the entrance. No one wanted an angry gunman pointing and shouting at them, but everyone wanted to board the ferry before it left the harbor. As they approached the bottleneck, Deli yanked hard on Carl's hand. He slouched over obediently. She squatted down with him and whispered in his ear.

"Let me take care of this. I know what to do. You just stay down." Without another word, she slunk away. Carl stayed down.

She crept under the nearest turnstile and up to the edge of the open circle where the little man stood. It was the same man from the front of the watch store. He had removed his sports coat to reveal a blue dress shirt. Dark patches of sweat bloomed down his sides as he waved a large pistol in the air. His eyes searched the crowd frantically.

"Yoo-hoo! Are you looking for me?" Deli waved her hands. One brave woman took the opportunity to scuttle across the open field to the waiting ferry. Deli waved hard to draw his attention away from the fleeing woman. The people nearest Deli melted away.

"You! Come with me! You are *arrested!*" His eyes lit with a manic glow.

"Um, no. I don't think you can do that, can you? Thanks all the same." She giggled but stepped closer to the man as he waved his arms around.

"You are *arrested!* You come with me!" Spit flew from his mouth as he shouted.

Deli didn't know much about guns, never having the passion for weapons that some of her training partners did. She knew enough to keep the end with the hole in it pointed away from her and that anyone with a gun was dangerous, whether they looked it or not.

Not only was this gun pointing in her direction, but the man doing the pointing looked crazier than a shithouse rat. She needed to get closer to make it a fair fight.

He stood straight and kept his gun pointed at Deli. She put her hands in the air in front of her and waved them to show him she had no weapons. Keeping her hands up, she stepped forward, shortening the gap between them.

"When I get close enough to you, little man, I'm going to break your hand."

The man brandished, waved, and spat some more but showed no other signs of recognition.

"You don't understand a word I'm saying, do you?"

The man, mistaking Deli's words for surrender, pushed his shoulders back. "You are *arrested*! You are *criminal*!"

On the fringes of the spectacle, Deli sensed people pushing and jockeying to get around them. Some people watched the show, but most just wanted to catch the ferry before it was too late. The gunman noticed this, and thinking he had Deli cowed, turned to scream at them. One person made a break for it, running toward the ferry at full speed. The man retaliated by shooting off a round into the ceiling.

Everyone fell to the ground at once. Several people started screaming. The man looked as scared of his gun as the rest of the crowd, but he was on the trigger side, so he stuck his chin out and screamed crazy things at them. Shortly, the real police would arrive and compound their troubles. It was now or never.

"*Hey!*" Deli shouted at the gunman, taking a final step forward. "You are *really* starting to piss me off."

As he turned back to face her, Deli kicked her foot sideways in a roundhouse that connected squarely with his knee. It made a terrible, crunching sound. The man staggered around, trying to regain his balance while he held his leg.

Deli did not stop. She became a flurry of arms and legs that, for a split second, appeared to contain more than the usual number of hands and feet. Carl watched the fray with his mouth hanging open.

Within seconds, the man was doubled over on the floor, clutching his jaw. His gun, tossed aside to use his hands for protection, lay just out of reach. Deli leaned over and grabbed it.

"Carl, let's go!"

He was already beside her, running to the ferry with the rest of the crowd. Deli detoured to the edge of the dock and tossed the gun out before diving back into the crowd to the ferry.

Deep golden rays from the setting sun glinted off the barrel in a sentimental way as the turquoise waters of Victoria Harbour swallowed it up.

THE STAR FERRY

THEY DID NOT EXPECT HELP, and, officially, they did not receive any. But seconds after the gun splashed into the harbor, Carl and Deli found themselves surrounded by a crush of curious people. Most spoke at them in Chinese. A few smiling faces commented in English. The dominating opinion was that Deli had fought well, probably because she had a lucky giant.

They jostled and snatched at their clothes and hair, pulling Carl forward and pushing from behind. Soon, he found himself on the upper deck of the ferry with no recollection of having paid the fare for crossing. Delilah appeared next to him, smoothing down her hair where someone had run a hand through it. And just like that, the deck was empty. Carl and Deli were left wondering what happened.

Carl straightened his suit coat and tucked the tail of his shirt back in.

"I feel like I've been wrung out." Deli said.

She inspected the buttons on her shirt and frowned. The center-most button was missing, making a large gap where common decency dictated none should be. Carl tried not to notice anything too…well, anything at all really.

"Dammit! What the hell? Don't look!"

Carl turned toward the water and studied the cityscape with intense interest. "I think perhaps our friends back at the dock were not operating with the consent of the state," he said to the skyline. "It's the only explanation I can come up with for the lack of police back there."

"Well, what do you call that tiny little bastard with the big shiny gun? If he wasn't police, then what *was* he?"

"If I had to guess, I'd say mafia. Possibly Tong but since it's Hong Kong he's probably Triad. Honestly, he looked more scared than anything else."

He watched as Hong Kong Island grew smaller, a jewel drifting off into the sea.

"You can turn around now."

Carl turned. He opened his right eye first. Deli stood in front of him like an inflamed gnome. She was so short, it almost made him laugh. He didn't laugh, though, because he'd just seen her kick the crap out of a guy with a semiautomatic. Instead, he opened his other eye.

Deli scowled up at him. Her brown hair was smooth and shiny again. He tried not to see where the button was missing on her shirt but looked anyway because her fix was ingenious. She had unbuttoned the entire row then fastened it back up skewed, so that the buttons didn't line up correctly. This made the gap poke out somewhere near her navel. She compensated at the throat by tucking the collar in.

"That's a smart idea," he said, pointing to Deli's navel. He appreciated ingenious fixes. He also appreciated navels. But not Deli's, because he didn't want to get yelled at again.

"Where to now?" she asked.

"I've been thinking about that." He turned back toward the water to avoid any more appreciating, and relaxed into the boat railing. Deli moved forward and joined him. Together they leaned out over the water. "The way I see it, we have three choices. Option A"—he held out his thumb as a counter—"we can double back to the airport from the Kowloon side. When Jake booked me through on the Alzona flight, he set up two return flights for tonight, just in case."

Deli's eyebrows puckered. "How are we going to do that with Johnny and the Hong Kong Maniacs on the loose?"

"I haven't figured that part out yet."

"What's the next option?"

Carl stuck out another finger.

"Option B," he said. "We go on to the hotel and lay low for a while. Together, Jake, Sacha, and I can probably get us back home in about forty-eight hours. Longer if the airports are being watched, which they might be by now."

Deli didn't comment on Option B. Instead, she said, "What's Option C?"

Carl stopped counting and ran his hand through his hair nervously. He was of two minds about Option C.

Part of him wanted nothing more than to go home. He was completely out of his element here. They hadn't been hurt so far, but that was pure luck. If the guy with the gun really *was* mafia, then they were in more trouble than he had anticipated.

But another part of him—the part that secretly resented dry-cleaning bills and thought goat-cheese appetizers were stupid—the private part of him that thought Paul was an arrogant jerk who didn't know beans about his own sister, *that* part of him became increasingly optimistic about Option C.

He exhaled a long slow breath before meeting Deli's eyes. "Option C is that we keep going."

THE MAXWELL HOTEL

THE FRONT ENTRANCE TO THE MAXWELL HOTEL twinkled in the Rolls Royce–colored twilight. Inside, the lobby set a scene leftover from the British Empire: high columns with intricate detailing, door attendants in white tunics and matching cotton gloves, potted palms strategically arranged to afford the maximum in privacy for whispered conversations. The floors were *incomparably* shiny.

The lady at the concierge desk was so thrilled at the prospect of helping them that Deli was afraid the poor woman's head might fall off if she attempted to smile any more broadly.

"May I help you, sir? Madam?" she purred at them, showing as many teeth as decency allowed. Carl looked genuinely pleased to see her, but it occurred to Deli that she did not like concierge ladies with lots of teeth all that much.

"Hello, you are expecting us. The name is Harrison. Mr. and *Mrs.* Harrison."

He gave Deli a goofy grin and leaned sideways. Deli almost didn't catch the implication. When she did, she tried simpering. It was awkward at best.

The concierge's fingertips, armored with metallic pink polish, flew over her keyboard in a subtle attack on the hotel's computer system.

"Of course, sir! How perfect! You are in the Garden Suite. It is very pleasant room. You will stay in comfort. And I see that we already have your luggage, is that correct?"

"Just one bag. I had it sent over earlier."

Deli raised her eyebrows at Carl, who shrugged. He frowned and shook his head to show how unimportant and trivial this tiny detail was.

The concierge disappeared for a few seconds and came back with Carl's messenger bag, full to bursting, and did her best to place it on the counter with grace. There was a small note attached to it. Carl grabbed for it, but Deli was much quicker.

I'm at the Marriott if you get done early and care to join me for a drink.

—Jenny

She looked up from the note to see that Carl had turned a pinker shade of red than before. He focused intently on finalizing the reservations with the concierge and didn't look back at Deli until they were well and truly checked in. Deli spent the intervening time studying the lobby in an effort to keep herself from giggling.

"So, you have a hot date tonight, then?"

"No." He shook his head. "Definitely not."

"Why not? Her note seemed pretty nice." The elevator dinged for their floor. "I would hate to be the reason you didn't get any action this trip."

The doors opened and Deli stepped out into the hallway. Carl didn't follow immediately. He was busy having a small coughing fit.

"She's not really my type," he said at last, but rather quietly, and Deli was already halfway down the hall.

The room looked a lot like the lobby: full of expensive ambiance and potted plants. Thick white shag cuddled her feet, which was good because Deli didn't know if she could take much more glare. The entryway wallpaper was embossed with a subtle fleur-de-lis pattern. She ran her hands along the bumps as she walked but stopped as soon as she realized what she was doing.

Carl followed her in. Together they stood in the large living room, surrounded by windows overlooking Victoria Harbour. The black mirror of water reflected a shimmering image of the city's nightlife.

The room itself was no less spectacular. A couch, overstuffed and inviting, sat next to a peacock-themed wing-back chair so richly upholstered that Deli was afraid to sit on it. Over the mantel hung the largest television she had ever seen.

Behind her, a set of French doors led into another room. From where she stood, she could see a bed, lonely and inviting. The fluffiness of it all drew her in, and she realized how much her feet hurt. Her head hurt, too. And, if she were to be brutally honest, her butt still hurt from the plane trip. She stared longingly from the doorway. There were so many pillows, she could build a fort.

"Are you going to take a nap?" Carl called after her.

Deli grunted at him.

"Only, it's probably not a good idea to sleep just yet."

Her back was to him, so he didn't see the disappointment on her face. But Deli wasn't seriously thinking of sleep. For one thing, if she lay down now, she probably wouldn't get up until tomorrow. No, she had other things in mind. Not the least of which was getting Carl to talk.

"Don't worry, I'm just looking."

"Would you mind if I used your computer?"

Out in the living area, Carl was uncoiling cords from his bag. On the couch next to him lay a laptop, another black, boxy thing, and his fancy phone. Where did all that hardware come from? Did he forget to pack clothes?

"It's not *my* tiny computer, Carl, it's *yours*. If you need it, take it. It's in my duffel bag." Deli never intended to use it, anyway. Hell, she only brought the damn thing because he insisted.

Though her bag was next to him on the floor, he didn't move. He sat there, looking hopeful, until she realized he wasn't going to search through her stuff. She crossed the room, unzipped her duffle, and rooted around until she found the little computer tucked within a nest of underwear. She unraveled it from her unmentionables and handed it to Carl, who was trying not to look.

"Don't think I've forgotten—you owe me an explanation."

Carl nodded as he carefully took the laptop from her. Deli would have forced the issue, but she was too tired to be angry or even upset. Besides, she was still impressed by his rescue effort. If he hadn't shown up when he did, Deli would have punched someone, she just *knew* it. And then she would *really* have been in trouble. Diplomacy had never really been her strong point.

Thanks to Carl, she wasn't hanging from a meat hook in an abandoned warehouse or whatever the Chinese mafia did with people it didn't like. She was in this fabulous room with Victoria Harbour in the front and Fort Pillowmere in the back. That alone entitled him to a little bit of slack—say, about the length of time it would take for her to check out the tub and wash the travel grime off before she grilled him. She wandered toward the bathroom, wondering what kind of shampoo they had.

"I need to take a shower. I feel like I've been scraped off the bottom of someone's shoe. How about we meet at the table in half an hour?"

She pointed across the room to an antique dining table. It had chairs for six, though the table had only been set for two. At least, it *looked* like it was set for only two. There was a surprising amount of cutlery involved.

"That's a good idea. I want to make sure Paul isn't still here." Carl picked up his laptop, and headed for the table, tentacles of tangled cords trailing in his wake.

"Uh, this may be a stupid question, but *how?"*

"Their reservation system should be easy enough to access."

"Won't they have it like, password protected or something?"

For a second, Carl looked as though he didn't understand the question. Then he snapped his fingers and pointed at her.

"Probably," he said and flipped open the laptop. Deli shook her head. They had been on a plane for thirteen hours, in "police" custody for two, and on the run since. She was beat, but Carl didn't even seem fazed. He was either made of steel or excellent at faking it.

The bathroom was too large to be anything other than majestic. The counter stretched from one side of the country to the next. It ended in an ornately tiled shower stall, somewhere near the Vietnamese border. In the opposite corner sat a marble pedestal crowned with a bathtub and polka-dotted with extravagant French soaps.

Deli wondered if people could see up to the seventh floor, then decided it didn't matter. Her feet wanted to soak in hot water; they didn't mind who saw the rest of her naked, and the rest of her was too exhausted to care. She had enough things to worry about, most of which were Carl-related.

That guy knew *way* more than he let on.

She was slightly embarrassed to have mistaken him for a security guard now, but that wasn't her fault. Paul *told* her he was a security guard. She remembered him distinctly bragging about how nice he was to let the firm's security guard rent out his extra room.

Why the hell would he say that?

But Deli already knew the answer. It was the same reason he didn't invite her to parties unless he absolutely had to. He didn't like Deli to know his friends. More specifically, he didn't like for his friends to know *her.*

He worked so hard to present himself as one thing—surrounded himself with people who thought a specific way about him. Ten minutes with Deli and most people had an entirely different view of him. Paul never came across quite as honest or compassionate when she was around.

If he weren't so slick all the time, people would think differently about him, she thought, because that's what she always thought, even though it never helped. Deli doubted Paul would ever change.

But never mind that now. Paul had been missing for at least four days, possibly longer. If he had been kidnapped for money, then it was by the world's stupidest kidnappers.

"It's not like they don't know how to find me. So where's the ransom note?" She said this aloud without thinking, then blanched and looked at the door. Had that been loud enough for Carl to hear? *Oh God, did he think she was talking to herself?*

Deli stayed extra still for a few moments—so Carl wouldn't think she was crazy—and concentrated on the problem.

The more she thought about it, the more she realized one very important detail: Paul being kidnapped for money sounded just as ridiculous *outside* of her head as it had on the inside. This was no tourist kidnapping and she had a hard time imagining that anyone who knew Paul would kidnap him on purpose. For one thing, they'd have *Paul* on their hands.

Did he do this himself? Deli couldn't imagine what purpose Paul would have for kidnapping himself, but she didn't rule this out. He'd done sleazier things.

But Johnny puzzled her. Try as she might, Deli couldn't get him to fit. Someone like Johnny wouldn't work for Paul. They wouldn't give Paul the time of day, let alone take *orders* from him. Johnny was a higher class of criminal than Paul could ever hope to be. Deli almost laughed at that thought. She didn't, though, because Carl might hear her.

No, if Johnny was involved—and Deli was pretty sure he was—Paul had gotten himself into some *serious* trouble. Now she had to decide if it was the kind of trouble that required her to rescue him, or the kind that might finally teach him a lesson. And was she prepared to go up against more tiny men with big fucking guns to find him?

Deli lathered her hair in uncomfortable introspection.

Yes, Paul was a self-centered little goblin, but he didn't try to make bad things to happen to people. It was simply that, by being himself, bad things often happened to people anyway.

Take all the crap with Augie Terkle, for instance. If Paul had *thought* about the consequences of what he was doing, that whole thing probably never would have happened. But of course he didn't think that far ahead. He never did. Well, not unless Nana was concerned.

Deli shook the whole mess out of her head and wondered again what Carl saw in her brother. He seemed so intelligent, so *likable* compared to the rest of the meatballs that hung around Paul. They definitely didn't have much in common.

She rinsed the shampoo from her hair and thought about Paul's business endeavor. That was the key. What did he bring here to show off, and how much of a stake did Carl have in it? Deli didn't give a rat's ass about non-disclosure agreements. When she got out of the bathtub, that guy was going to *talk*.

THE GARDEN SUITE
(NOT THE BATHROOM)

CARL TRIED TO FOCUS ON HIS COMPUTERS but no matter how much he pressed his concentration, he could still hear the rush of water from the faucet.

That must be a huge tub, he thought. The water ran on, and he forced himself back to work.

He didn't like being away, but there were no other options. Someone was *definitely* after Deli. If he hadn't shown up, she would certainly be in prison by now, probably worse. Carl shuddered. It would be entirely his fault if Deli ended up being murdered by the Chinese mafia.

How could he have let her go in the first place? He had *wanted* to go with her, but then he got nervous and opened his big stupid mouth about the Euro-Stock drop. And she sounded so confident about finding Paul on her own that it seemed like a jerk move not to believe her. After the lecture about their uh, *relationship potential,* he had been too fearful to even joke about it.

Carl sighed deeply and felt like an idiot. At least he'd showed up when he did.

What's done is done, he thought. *I'm pretty sure she doesn't mind that I'm here now. Mike will take care of everything back home. He won't let me down.*

Mike was Michael Thorston, Carl's apprentice and right hand man. Secretly, Carl had been training him to take over his position as head of security since the day after he and Heather had broken up. Without Carl there to supervise, the Euro-Stock security upgrade would be in Mike's lap. That was a major step for everyone.

Carl didn't think Mike understood the intricacies of the double blind firewall any better than his dissertation committee had, but he was proving to be quite adept at some of the other security protocols. Certainly, this phase of the upgrade was within his range of abilities. If he came through the project well, Carl would recommend him as the only suitable candidate for his replacement.

Once the Euro-Stock security revamp was out of the way, he planned on checking out his options on the other side of the water. He'd been in the suburbs for too long. Maybe he would even move back to Horsey House—temporarily, of course.

For now, he put his faith in Mike and hoped that everything went okay. No one was going to notice a difference at the user end, anyway. Heck, no one but Carl and Mike really *understood* this stage. Things weren't going to get messed up. Mike could take care of it.

Plus, he reminded himself, *there's always my backup.*

Not even Jake knew about that. It definitely wasn't the most legal step in his plan, but at least, if everything went ass over teakettle, he could reinstall the old system when he got back without too much fuss. No one from the Euro-Stock team would ever see the difference.

He continued to talk himself down from the panic that always set in before a big project. It might have been worse this time, being thousands of miles away from his workstation, but the occasional splash or trickle from the next room kept his mind tethered to the problem at hand. He logged into the hotel's reservations system without incident.

DELI'S COUCH, SEATTLE
4:00 A.M.

JAKE SLEPT ON THE COUCH with an awful-looking cat curled up on his chest. How disgusting. It was a filthy, mangy animal, and it probably had fleas.

It would be easy to wake him up, tell him why this was all happening. It would be enjoyable to watch his face as he realized the truth. But there was a slight chance that he had bugs on him, and nobody wanted a recording of this. So the expensive shoes crept *quietly* over the multi-carpeted floor, avoiding creaky floorboards when possible.

The man snored like a pig. Being up close to him gave one pause, it really did. He was just so…*gross*. There was no other word for it. His stringy yellow hair was as filthy as it had ever been. He needed a shave. His pants were torn on one knee and he still wore that stupid black t-shirt. How *pathetic*. Humanity would be better off without this bum.

Seeing him again, knowing he hadn't changed *at all*, made this even easier.

The gun clicked softly. Jake's eyelids fluttered open at the noise. His eyes widened in recognition, and he opened his mouth to say something, but it was too late.

The gun went off with a muffled pop.

THE GARDEN SUITE, HONG KONG

CARL CLEARED HIS EMAIL CACHE in a sparkly pink cloud of euphoria. If what Jake said was true, then half of their problems were already solved, and *that* was no minor miracle. Deli's cat had given them the first lucky break since they'd dreamed up this project back in college.

It had started out as another stupid idea. They'd spent the weekend high on caffeine and Cheetos, building the basic platform for *TerrorCity*. Jake was coding super-abilities into random characters, and together, he and Carl hypothesized what it would take to create them in real life.

They hadn't expected anything to come from it. It was just a mental exercise to have fun with while they worked. Each assumed the other had forgotten about it until a few weeks later when Jake presented Carl with a schematic drawing for vibrational sound activation. The theory behind it was ephemeral at best, using sound waves to generate a low-level energy cascade for biological enzymes. Jake thought he could get it to work if only he could figure out a programming language. That's when Carl stepped in.

Within a month, Carl developed the quaternary, positive/negative coding matrix and adjusted it to fit within the limitations of the human body. If the energy was there, his little machine could create human proteins using the positive and negative charges of amino acids to draw them close and paste them together. It was tedious work, especially since each protein had to be hand-coded in relation to its genetic sequence.

They called them Elevators. Basically, they were tiny robots that used your voice and ambient sound energy to enhance the biologic functions of your body. They had prototypes specialized for muscle and bone regenerative proteins as well as some basic blood/brain proteins like L-dopa and serotonin.

They also had…uh…the *other* one.

Carl blushed when he thought about the other one.

It was Jake's idea. Paul loved it. He called it their "money-maker" and slogged through all the protein-structure research by himself. Carl consented to code it just to shut them up. So far, it hadn't mattered because none of the Elevators had ever worked.

Huh, Carl thought. *I wonder if that one works, too.*

"I feel almost human again," said Deli.

Carl jumped slightly as he turned toward the bathroom. Steam poured from the door, spilling out a fresh pink face and short, soggy hair. The rest of Deli was lost in a white terry-cloth bathrobe many sizes too big.

"Hey!" he said and winced at how lame it sounded.

"Hold on a minute," she said, ripping a comb through clumps of hair. "I'm almost done."

She finished her hair with a flourish and disappeared for a second to stash her comb. Her feet, constricted by two layers of bathrobe, shuffled across the room to the table. He tried to watch her with studied indifference, but a strong smell of honey and almonds followed her around, and he had to shut his eyes for a moment to get back on track.

Carl had to tell her something about the Elevators, but he was unsure how much detail he needed to go into. *No one* knew the extent of Carl and Jake's involvement except for Paul. And Paul's ego would never let him acknowledge that Carl and Jake were anything more than minor players. That was why they'd hired him in the first place. He was a perfect front. Smart enough to know the project's worth but too arrogant to admit that he knew nothing about it. If Carl learned anything from the last five years, it was to keep a low profile and never tell anyone how much you knew—not even your girlfriend.

But Deli *wasn't* his girlfriend. Carl sighed. He didn't know the protocol here. He didn't want to lie to Deli, but he couldn't tell her everything even if he wanted to because of the damned contract.

She settled into the chair next to him in a veil of lightly scented steam. Carl wanted to assure her that everything would be fine. They would catch the flight Jake reserved for them. When they got home, he would report all of this to the CIA. Then he would leave her alone.

But they were too late to catch the flight home and even if they did, he wasn't going to tell the CIA that he and his friends could (theoretically) make super-powers. That just sounded stupid.

He *would* leave her alone if she asked him to, but he really hoped she wouldn't ask him to. Maybe he should leave that part off. There was no call to bring up the subject needlessly, was there?

She sat down at the end of the table and kicked her feet up to the chair next to him. Heat radiated from her bath-watered skin. It made Carl's ears itch inside. Her toes stuck out from under her bathrobe, wiggling happily. They mesmerized him into confusion.

"Let's start with the part where you tell me what's going on." She pierced him with a stare, intense and very hard to ignore. "*All* of it, please."

Carl opened his mouth to tell her the truncated version of his story but realized that he still didn't know which parts to edit out. He looked down at her happy feet and could not think of a single reason to keep the truth from her. He brought his head up, looked into her naked blue eyes, and told her everything she wanted to know.

It was easier that way.

TWENTY-FIVE MINUTES LATER

DELI GAVE HIM A WITHERING LOOK that no novice could pull off. Something in the way she wrinkled her nose (up and ever so slightly to the left) told Carl that she didn't buy a word of what he'd said.

"I thought you said you were in security," she said.

"I am."

"No, Carl. Security guys wear uniforms and carry nightsticks. *You* are spying for the CIA." Her blend of sarcasm and exasperation was incredible. She was good at this.

"It's not spying," Carl gently corrected her. "And it's not the CIA."

Deli had moved over to the couch. She sat with her legs curled beneath her, following him around the room with her eyes as he paced. Every time he neared the couch, the smell of honey and almonds became too strong to ignore, so he turned and headed back to the table.

"You break into computer systems and gather information. If that's not spying, what the hell do you call it?"

"*Research*," Carl said, then hastily added, "It was just the one case for the CIA, and that's only because I was already involved. Usually, it's just banks."

Deli's expression had not changed. Carl had no defense against towel-damp withering, so he sat down in one of the wing-backs and tried looking trustworthy.

"Okay," he said. "I admit that I spy on their subsidiaries—but my clients either own those companies or are in the process of purchasing them. What I do is not illegal, it's smart business. If I'm going to orchestrate their security, I need to know their weak points first."

"And you do that for them? You give them security?"

There was a lot more to it, but Deli's explanation was as good as anything he'd come up with so far. "Sure, you could say that," he said.

"That doesn't explain the CIA."

"No, it doesn't." Carl lowered his eyes to his lap. "That *was* a surprise. Turns out, I knew the person involved. I helped the CIA build a case for prosecution, but the suspect fled the country. When they took the case overseas, I helped as much as I could. That's how I got the Department of Homeland Security clearance. But the suspect went underground somewhere near Antwerp, and I'm not really sure where the case stands right now." He sighed quietly, then lifted his head to meet her gaze.

"Honestly, I'm glad to be out of it. They always had some sort of paperwork that needed to be filled out."

"So you *were* spying for the CIA, but you aren't anymore."

Carl nodded and shrugged at the same time.

"What about the mutant ninja robots?"

"*Nanobots*," he said.

"Nanobots, whatever. Are you Dr. Frankenstein, too?"

"What? *No.* They enhance the body's natural functions, they don't make zombies."

"Carl, the last time I checked, I couldn't grow an extra arm at will."

"That's only *theoretical*. Nothing like that is going to happen."

Deli squinted at him. "Are you certain? You said the sound battery thing didn't work, either. My cat proved you wrong."

"Yes, I have been bested by a cat. Thank you for wording that so simply. I would like to point out that it was the vibrational sound activation fuel cell that was faulty. Until now, it hasn't worked."

"*Which means the rest of your little robot is completely untested.*"

Deli huffed and stood up from the chair. For a girl who spent most of her time punching things, she had the vexing habit of direct, logical reasoning. Carl wasn't sure if that was a good thing or a bad thing.

"If you look at it that way—"

"I do look at it that way! And now, my brother is gallivanting around Asia with a—what did you say it was?"

"Hormone-stimulating nanobot."

Deli glared at him.

"It's for when you need"—he looked at the floor—"hormones or something."

"He has a Spanish fly robot in his pocket? This is what you're telling me? You realize that could be considered an act of war against every single woman in the known universe, right?"

"Actually," Carl said. His voice had grown very small. "He's got two."

Deli simply shook her head and walked over to the window.

"I'm not sure which ones he has, though. It could be the androgen, but it might be the BMP/muscle complex. There were a few versions of that one."

Deli waved his explanation away with an aggravated flick and turned to look out the window.

"And because of these nanobots, people are trying to kill him?"

"I don't know if they're trying to *kill* him, exactly. They probably just want to steal the technology."

Carl watched her reflection as he spoke. Reflected-Deli rolled her eyes at him. He wasn't surprised. Even to Carl it sounded stupid.

"Are you *mental*? Anyone holding that guy hostage for longer than three hours is going to kill him. Hell, I would probably kill him just to shut his—" Deli stopped short. She stared intently out the window. "Carl, what's our next move?"

"Well, I was getting to that. I have a few ideas of where we might start looking. I've been mapping some of them out. Would you like to see?"

He stood up and offered her the chair in front of his makeshift network, but Deli didn't turn around. Her eyes were still locked on the street, seven stories below.

"No."

"Oh." Carl's heart stopped beating for a second, and he struggled to appear calm. "Well, if you'd rather rest, we could probably leave this alone for a few hours."

"No, that's not what I meant."

"Oh?" Carl's heart started beating again, and he struggled even harder to appear calm. "What did you mean?" No matter how hard he tried, his voice would not stop shaking.

"I *meant*, my brother is an insufferable pig, and I am *starving*. Are you going to take me to dinner or not?" She emphasized this statement by whirling around to face Carl and pointing an accusing finger at him.

Carl shut his mouth in an attempt to avoid saying anything stupid. But Deli kept looking at him, and he realized that she wanted an answer.

"If you want to?"

"I do!" Deli said enthusiastically. "And I've found the perfect little place."

"You have?" His voice cracked. He hoped she didn't notice.

"Yes!"

Deli went back to the window and pointed to the street. Carl edged his way over to her, trying not to make any sudden movements.

Down below, across a four-lane sea of taxis, a row of shops and restaurants lined the opposite shore. Deli pointed toward the end of the sprawling retail empire at a small pub-like storefront. A sign in the window proclaimed it the Silver Hammer.

"I fucking *hate* the Beatles," she said.

DELI'S LIVING ROOM, SEATTLE

SOMETHING UNEXPECTED HAPPENED. The bean had been monitoring its environment and churning out proteins at a merry clip when suddenly the titanium of its outer shell cracked and a warm oozy substance filtered in.

0.2 picoseconds later, the bean had a preliminary survey of its new environment. It found the ooze to be rich in iron and amino acids. It also read and stored several of the host's baser DNA sequences. Unfortunately, it could not analyze any further due to a buildup of complex proteins along the crack in its casing.

The bean deflected damage to its internal programming by triggering lipid production. It was not a sentient bean, so there is no way it could feel smug about its quick mastery of the host's genetic code. All the same, when it came across a rogue endorphin, embedded within the prehistoric code of introns, it overrode seventeen logic circuits and began translating endogenous morphine across the blood-brain barrier every 1,298,467th program cycle. It felt like the right thing to do.

The host's heart rate fell off drastically after the change in environment, so the bean increased endorphin transcription to stabilize it. Soon, the heart started beating again with a shallow thump.

It was getting the hang of the host's full genetic complement now, kicking the regenerative powers into overdrive. The endogenous programming included several basic protocols for creating bone structure. Unfortunately, most of those protocols required excess calcium, which had become scarce after the recent trauma event. The bean conferred with its previous findings and recalled a splice variant for that particular code that could be optimized by using something with a slightly heavier atomic weight.

As luck would have it, the bean was surrounded by the *exact* material it needed.

THE SILVER HAMMER, HONG KONG

"DID WE HAVE TO TAKE *ALL* THE GADGETS?"

Carl did not reply. He was unsure if Deli was teasing or if she really didn't understand the danger of their situation. It was likely that whoever had tried to kidnap her at customs knew they were staying at the Maxwell. After all, Paul had referenced the hotel directly in his last email, and of course, he hadn't encrypted it. Paul never encrypted anything, even though Carl constantly reminded him. Carl suspected he didn't know how.

"I would rather be safe than sorry." It was all he could think to say, most of his brain function being dedicated to getting them across the street without dying.

The curb was short but impeccably clean. Deli hopped it with gusto and headed straight to the door of the pub. Carl followed, his excitement mounting in anticipation of the next hour. Maybe Paul left a message or something. Perhaps he would be here to greet them.

No, Carl had to admit that did not seem likely.

Deli reached the door half a second before Carl, but his arms were longer, so he opened it anyway. The air inside the pub was cold. It froze the roots of his hair and the base of his skull. It was glorious.

Walking into an Irish pub is like coming home. The cracked leather barstools, the Guinness button sign, the pockmarked dart board tucked unceremoniously in the corner. From Cork to Cuzco, no other establishment can rival the quaint, intoxicating familiarity.

Carl certainly felt no more awkward than he normally would walking into the George and Dragon back home. Except for the fact that he no longer went to the George and Dragon because Heather usually went there on trivia night. He missed trivia night, but not enough to risk running into Heather.

They shivered up to the bar. The man behind it stood at ease, polishing glasses with the ghost of a rag. He had a full-moon face and smiled at them with his eyes as they approached.

"Is your kitchen still open?" said Carl.

The barman nodded in his own time.

"Please, sit," he said. His hands took a break from polishing to sweep the dining area in a grand gesture. "Anywhere you like."

They chose a table near the window. As they settled in, a group of drunk businessmen swaggered through the door and crowded around the far end of the bar. The barman greeted them with a nod as he followed Deli and Carl to the table.

"Take your time," he said, dealing out menus. "Menu is very good."

"What's the special today?" Carl asked.

"Very good special! Beer soup with potatoes. Very good. Very healthy for you, especially!" He pointed at Deli. "Makes you strong and tall, like me!" He barked out a laugh, slapping his knee to punctuate his joke. Deli laughed along with him. She didn't know what else to do.

"Want beer?" the barman said. "Very good beer. Guinness! Makes you strong and tall, like me!" He pounded his chest and laughed as though the joke were funnier the second time around. Carl and Deli each ordered a beer and the special before the man could make his joke a third time.

As the barman walked away, Carl turned to Deli and gave her a look of intense puzzlement. She tried to keep a straight face by arching her eyebrows, but the way she screwed up her mouth to keep from laughing struck Carl as hilarious and he chuckled before he could get his own mouth shut. This caused Deli to break into tiny fits of giggles.

They both lost it at the same time. They laughed about the absurd situation. They laughed about the detective. They laughed about the taxi driver and his homicidal aromatherapy.

Through a jumbled exchange of snorts and hand gestures, they shared the intimacy of knowing the other's thoughts. This is because they were both thinking the exact same thing. Namely, *What the hell are we going to do now?*

Deli caught her breath first. "I'll bet you five dollars that he comes back here and makes that joke again."

Carl stopped laughing at once. His face went slack as his mind calculated numbers. Then his eyes widened and he looked at Deli. "You're on."

"Easiest five bucks I ever made."

"It seems likely that he will. But in actuality, it is improbable that he will make that joke again."

"Oh, come on! He's going to keep doing that all night. I've seen his type. They do that to bump tips."

"Okaaay," he said, but took a few seconds before elaborating his thought. "You think the bar tender is going to continue making the same tired joke all evening. If you're right—let's say even if he makes it one more time—you win. I owe you five dollars. If, however, he comes back here in a good mood and merely refers to his joke, but does not attempt to repeat the hilarity, I win."

"And I owe you five dollars," said Deli. Then she rolled her eyes, in case he didn't understand sarcasm.

Carl shook his head. "I don't want your money. How about this? If I win, I get to sleep in the bed and you have to sleep on the couch."

"But the bed has all those pillows." She said this mainly to herself, but Carl was paying attention. Then she mumbled something that sounded like *pillow fort,* but it was much quieter, and he couldn't be sure if he heard her right.

"I will give you fifty percent of the pillows," he said.

Deli did not answer right away. "No," she said at last. She looked straight at him, eyes sparkling. "You assume that I get the bed, whether or not we made the wager, so if I *don't* bet, then I still get the bed. So..." She crossed her arms and sat back in her chair. "I choose not to wager anything."

"Oh, come on! You can't back out, that's cheating."

Deli responded by crossing her legs. Her foot bounced up and down, daring him to one-up her. Carl ummed and ahhed until a thought occurred to him. Their laughter had given him a rare sense of confidence, and he wasn't going to squander it. He leaned forward across the table.

"Okay, then, how about this? You win, I give you five bucks. If *I* win, you come to dinner with me." He sat back and smiled the least mischievous smile he could manage.

"I hate to point out the obvious, Carl but we are literally doing that, *right now.* I was supposed to change some money at the airport, but because of Johnny the Thug and Detective What's-His-Butt, I missed that opportunity. This one is on you, whether I lose or not."

She smiled back, twice as un-mischievously.

"Yeah, but *this* doesn't count. We're here to figure out what happened to Paul. I meant when we get back home."

Deli's eyes turned to slits of suspicion. "That sounds suspiciously like a date."

Carl didn't hesitate before answering. "Not at all. We'll pick the most un-date-like place we can find, like a hospital cafeteria or something."

"Who's paying?"

"We'll go Dutch."

"That's supposing we get back to Seattle okay."

He noted that she did not say no.

"Good point. If the bar tender comes back here and doesn't make his joke, and we get to Seattle okay, you come to dinner with me."

"Also supposing, of course, that we find Paul."

"Fair enough," he said. "If the bar tender comes back here, does not make his joke, then we find your brother and make it back to Seattle safely, you come to dinner with me."

"And it won't be a date," she said sternly.

"Absolutely not. Just two people sharing some soggy fries and red Jell-O."

He put on his most innocent and chivalrous smile so Deli wouldn't get the wrong idea. Friends could meet and have soggy fries and red Jell-O. Friends did stuff like that all the time.

"Fine." Deli didn't move a muscle.

"Good." Neither did Carl.

At that point in the negotiations, a tray wandered over to their table, arresting their attention and giving them a convenient way out of the conversation.

Carl bent over to find the tray steered by the tiniest person he had ever seen. She looked like an elf, if elves were elderly Asian women that worked in Irish pubs.

The food elf sat her tray down on the empty table next to Deli and ferried their plates to the table one by one. Carl was deeply disconcerted by the idea of being served by Chino-Celtic elves. It was all he could do to keep himself from jumping to help her with the tray or maybe carry her back to the bar so she didn't get lost. He sighed in relief when she left.

They ate. They hadn't eaten for some time and the soup was thick with potatoes. Not many words were spoken, although Deli made several yum-yum noises. Carl tried to concentrate on other things.

Up at the bar, the businessmen spoke in loud, drawling voices. Occasionally, they shouted something in unison, then drank the remainder of their glasses. Carl wasn't paying them enough attention to figure out the rules to their game.

In the back, a woman sat low in a darkened booth. She jumped every time the businessmen shouted and glared at their table with fresh disgust. Near the pool tables, a group of glittering women drank cocktails and gossiped loudly in a rolling language that was definitely not Chinese. He thought it might be French. But then again, Carl assumed most foreign languages he overheard were French even though he had no basis for such assumptions.

The women kept ducking in and out of the bathroom, so Carl couldn't get an accurate count of them right away. But after two minutes of observation, he put their number at seven.

He scanned the room three more times but saw no one else.

"Do you suppose he's here?" Carl had been concentrating on the people around them so much that even though Deli spoke in a whisper, it made him jump. He recovered quickly.

"I've been looking, but I don't see him anywhere."

"Do not see whom? For whom are you looking?" The barman reappeared at their table like a magic rabbit. This time, Deli jumped, too.

"We are looking for her brother, Paul. He ate here last week."

"You are familiar! Very strong and healthy!" He swept the air in front of Deli and smiled wide. She grimaced. Lots of the same words were there, but he hadn't made the joke.

"Do you remember him?"

"Brown hair, like yours?"

Deli nodded and the barman's face lit up.

"Yes, I remember. He is Majestic Constellations!"

"He's *what*?" Deli said.

"Majestic Constellations! Big Spender *and* Little Tipper!"

Carl snorted into his beer.

"Did he leave a message or anything?" she said.

"Message?" The barman tapped his head in an exaggerated gesture. The businessmen erupted again, shouting and whooping, then finishing their drinks.

"No, no message. But you sit next to him. He sat here." He motioned to the table next to theirs and held his hands out wide. "Ate big lunch, strong and healthy!"

Carl glanced over at Deli. He held up two fingers and smiled. *Twice now, and still no actual joke.*

Deli scowled at him and shook her head softly. "Where would I find the bathrooms, please?"

"Down hall, in back," replied the barman and pointed at the gaggle of women. Beyond them, in the corner, a green canvas curtain hung across a doorframe.

Eyes still shining with glee, the barman gathered up their empty dishes and wandered back to the bar. Deli turned to Carl, a plastic smile plastered to her lips.

"Excuse me a moment, I have to use the little girls' room."

She stood up, somehow managing to step on Carl's foot in the process. He looked at her, unable to decide if she'd done it on purpose.

"Sorry about that," she said. "I slipped."

Her contrived look of innocence answered his question. As she walked away from the table, Carl stretched out his foot in the wrong direction, tripping her up.

"Sorry about that," he said. "I slipped."

She shot him another plastic smile and walked toward the bathroom, middle finger held high behind her back. Carl watched her go, smiling to himself. Deli could certainly be bratty when she wanted to be. Paul never said anything about that.

After she disappeared behind the green curtain, he stood up and quickly switched to the table where Paul had sat. They knew from his credit card information that he'd gone to the post office that same day. Had he mailed the Elevators to Deli? Paul wouldn't be that stupid, *would he?*

Carl's heart sank. If he answered that question truthfully, he would have to say yes, Paul might just be that stupid. It was entirely possible that he thought mailing the Elevators home would be a smart idea. He exhaled slowly. Even if they somehow made it through customs, someone could simply walk up to the mailbox and steal them. Carl didn't think whomever orchestrated all of this cared much about the illegalities of mail fraud. He took his mind off such a depressing scenario by searching for clues.

Pictures on the walls boasted crew teams rowing down the Liffy and cricket teams smiling uniformly from Gothic front steps. Nothing stood out as unusual. The floor was hardwood, scarred and pitted from years of drunken revelry. If it held any secrets, Carl could not read them.

He ran his fingers through his hair in frustration before hunching forward to bang his head against the table two or three times. He couldn't think of anything.

Another explosion of laughter came from the businessmen's table, followed by more shouting. The shouting sounded more urgent than before and Carl looked over in time to see one of the men lean sideways and vomit all over the floor. Two of his friends jumped up, took him by the arms and started hauling him across the room. Slowly, they made their way down the back hall toward the bathrooms.

Carl shook himself. He was getting sidetracked. Soon, Deli would come back from the bathroom and ask him what the plan was. He didn't have a plan. He needed to think. He folded his hands, tucked them in his lap and began to rock back and forth, trying to force an idea out of thin air.

Rocking and thinking.

Thinking and rocking.

Nope. It wasn't working. For one thing, he was too tall and his hands didn't fit very well in his lap. They hit the underside of the table and scraping across something bumpy. The second time his hand hit the bumpy spot, Carl realized it was bubble gum. He gagged.

He unfolded his hands and tried extracting them from his lap without touching the gum but misjudged the height of the table. His wrist scraped against it, unexpectedly giving him a small electric shock. He flinched.

Chewed-up bubble gum shouldn't do that.

As much as it grossed him out, Carl ran the pad of his finger over the wad of gum. It was roughly the size and shape of a kidney bean.

This is completely disgusting, he thought and poked a stubby thumbnail into the lump. It sank in slowly as Carl fought back nausea. Then it hit against something hard.

DELI'S LIVING ROOM, SEATTLE

TOESY WOKE UP PISSED OFF. One of his back legs had stiffened up during his nap. He wanted desperately to stretch it out but for some reason, it refused to move. His back itched fiercely, but his neck had a crick in it that caused him to wince in pain when he tried to scratch. The air smelled funny, in a familiar way. Bass notes of fear and revulsion throbbed through his whiskers. It reminded him of that time at the animal hospital.

If he'd had another one of *those* operations, he might have to murder something. This time he would make sure his victim was more than just a stupid metal bean.

Slowly, Toesy stood up. His hind legs stretched out reluctantly, as though they still slept.

Wake up!

His stomach lurched forward and he experienced a momentary flush of nausea, different from the normal hair-ball induced variety. It felt more as if he'd swallowed a fat spider that was trying to crawl back out.

When the feeling had gone, Toesy's back legs felt better. He stood up carefully but it proved unnecessary. His legs now moved with an ease he had not felt since kittenhood. He still stretched, though. It is important to limber up properly, *especially* if you might have to murder something. You never know who was going to play the hero.

Toesy looked down at the great man and noted that he looked very white compared to Deli. She was much pinker when she slept. And she usually breathed with more enthusiasm.

He stepped farther up the man's chest, toward his face. When he did so, the weight underneath his feet shifted and the salty aroma of stale tortilla chips filtered past his whiskers.

The man's breath was definitely there, but it was wrong somehow—too *small*. Toesy looked down at his chest and for the first time acknowledged the other smell—the pervasive scent that his instincts had recognized, even if his nose had not.

It was blood.

He studied the spot where he had slept. The man wore a black shirt, which hid the wet spot effectively, but Toesy could smell it now. There was a lot of it to smell. In his experience, blood in those quantities usually came from the animal that didn't win.

He leaned down toward the sticky mess and sniffed three times. The scent filled his brain, and Toesy drew on all the cogitative powers he possessed. After a moment of consideration, he was certain of three things:

1. The Great Man had bled real, human blood.
2. He'd bled enough of it to consider him the loser in whatever fight had taken place.
3. Toesy was *incredibly* angry about this.

He jumped down gently so he would not disturb the shallow tortilla breath of the man and sprinted to the front door. Yet even before he reached the end of the hall, he knew it was in vain.

Damn his useless thumbs! All they were good for was getting stuck in the ratty old couch. He could not turn the front doorknob.

This was ridiculous and maddening. Toesy's whiskers began to shake in frustration. Deli had sent the Great Man to feed him all of the Seafood Flavor and nap with him on the couch. Now he was covered in blood and breathing shallow salty-corn breaths. *Who would do such a thing to him?*

Faint *tick-tick* sounds broke his concentration. He looked to the coffee table, where the vial of metal beans had stood before they napped, but it was gone.

More *tick-ticks* came, this time followed by a cooing sound. Outside, birds were waking up the sun.

The indigestible birds!

He ran to Deli's bedroom. High on the west wall sat a window that opened out, instead of up and down like most other windows.

Toesy always thought of this window as the door window. Indeed, the curly-headed man often used it instead of the front door.

Toesy never minded when the curly man came in that way because he always forgot to latch the door window behind him. The first time the man had come crawling through that window, Toesy had a whole month of freedom before Deli noticed. He hoped, for the sake of the Great Man, that he had freedom now.

He jumped up to the sill and leaned against the corner of the sash. The window swung open effortlessly. Toesy huffed with satisfaction and stepped sideways to the end of the exterior windowsill. There he steadied himself before jumping the five-foot gap to the fire escape.

The man knew the importance of Seafood Flavor! He understood the napping protocol! Toesy did not want the Great Man to die. That kind of nonsense might be all right with that stuck-up calico from B6, but Toesy was part *Maine Coon*. He would not stand for these shenanigans.

* * *

A brief moment of antigravity disrupted the bean's processing. It was followed by an impact event that would have been catastrophic had it not been for the previous hour of diligent bean-work. The bone it had cobbled together wobbled furiously and threatened to break but the bean had designed its new scaffolding with attention to detail. After the energy from the impact dissipated, it found the new titanium framework, built from the remains of its own exoskeleton, held its shape admirably.

The bean started cycling endorphins through the processing menu at a higher frequency. If it were more self-aware, it might begin to think it was having fun.

WOMEN'S BATHROOM,
THE SILVER HAMMER

THE BATHROOM HAD TWO STALLS. Deli headed for the nearest one, but that door was closed. She ducked down and saw a set of stockinged feet on the linoleum. The farthest stall would have to do.

She didn't really have to pee—that was just an excuse to leave the conversation with Carl. She'd made her position clear back at her apartment: Paul was her brother. Carl was his roommate. That was all. There would never be anything more to it than that.

But that was before he flew to Hong Kong, impersonated a US government official, and sprung her from custody. For someone as embarrassingly awkward as Carl, that was a pretty slick move. She wondered if she might have made a mistake about him.

The toilet in the next stall over flushed, and the stockinged feet walked out to the sink. Deli leaned over and peered through the crack in the doorframe. A glamorous-looking woman with black satin hair stood in front of the mirror, applying lipstick.

The woman was still dabbing and daubing as Deli walked out of the stall and stepped around her to get at the sink.

As she waved her hands beneath the automatic faucet, the woman turned to face her.

"Do you think this looks right?" she said. Her voice was much deeper than Deli had expected.

Deli normally had a not-unless-there-are-expensive-dinner-plans-involved policy about cosmetics, which ended at pink lip gloss and maybe some mascara. This woman's makeup was … generous. It amazed her that someone would apply so much makeup *willingly*.

She did notice that the woman's neck looked weird, but that wasn't something cosmetics could help, so she smiled and offered her best guess.

"Sure?"

"Well, you might be right."

The woman zipped her lipstick back into its tube and dove into a designer purse the size of a small battleship. She resurfaced in seconds with a torpedo of hair spray and turned back to the mirror to primp a few more times. Deli concentrated on washing her hands and tried not to look at the woman's neck.

"There," she said as Deli dried her hands. "That's better."

She held the hair spray up to the subjugated hair but did not use it. Instead, she turned to Deli.

"Don't you think that's better?" She didn't wait for an answer before plunging down on the spray nozzle. Deli had opened her mouth to agree, when part of the spray caught her in the cheek. She coughed.

"Sorry about that!" the woman tittered and held up the bottle again, this time, spraying Deli full in the face.

"My aim is a little off today."

Deli heard her titter once more before blacking out.

DINING ROOM,
THE SILVER HAMMER

CARL PRIED THE GUM LOOSE from the table and shoved it into his pocket without looking. Until now, he had thought of the entire trip as a null exercise. Paul wasn't really missing, he was just hiding somewhere ready to jump out and yell *surprise*! He half-expected him to show up at the Dungeon tomorrow and demand to know why his roommate had run off with his sister.

But when he felt the Elevator under his thumbnail, the reality of their situation hit him hard. Paul thought the Elevators were his meal ticket, especially the androgen stimulator. He would have eaten the dratted thing before squishing it into a wad of bubble gum. He'd been itching to since the day Carl explained how they worked.

But he hadn't eaten it. He'd left it here for Carl to find.

Where was Paul now? Was he okay? Was he even alive? Questions bubbled up through his thoughts, boiling his concentration away like steam. It irritated Carl that he could not control his mind. Something felt wrong.

A chorus of song started up from behind the green canvas curtain. Everyone in the bar turned to watch as the men who had hauled their drunk friend to the bathroom now hauled him back to the table. Carl watched the unconscious man's left shoe slip off as they dragged him across the restaurant. He waited for one of the lush-bearers to stop and pick it up, but neither of them saw it happen and they left the shoe where it lay.

They paused only briefly to shout their good-byes to the rest of the group before lugging their charge out onto the street. The barman shook his head sadly as the door closed.

When the clamor died away, Carl went back to thinking up a strategy for finding Paul. The demons in his head went back to questioning him. Was it his fault that Paul was in danger? Should he have warned him somehow?

Something's wrong.

If he could have warned him, what would he have said? "Hey, Paul, don't go to that secret business meeting in Asia with the rich guy who wants to buy our product because you are going to be kidnapped."

What was wrong?

A twittering exclamation pointed his thoughts in a different direction and he turned to study the women near the bathroom. Carl watched as they gathered up designer purses and tailored coats. The women looked different, but for a second, he could not figure out why.

Then it hit him. There should be *seven* women near the pool table. Counting them now, Carl discovered there were *eight*. The original seven and one that Carl hadn't seen before. Had he missed her? She must have been in the bathroom.

Carl checked his watch. Deli had been gone for almost ten minutes. She wasn't sick, was she? Carl didn't feel unwell, and they'd eaten the same thing.

He looked at the discarded shoe in the middle of the dining room. The short black lace was tied in a bow. Why did that seem odd?

Carl slid back to their original table, fiddled around with his wallet, extracting a bill large enough to cover the meal. He gathered his gear as casually as possible. Anyone watching him saw a man getting ready to leave while waiting for his date.

He sauntered past the bar, dropping the bill at the register on his way toward the back of the pub. It took him years to get to the green canvas curtain. When he finally slipped behind it, he ran.

Carl knocked only once before throwing open the door to the ladies' room and rushing in.

It didn't matter. Deli was not there. He found her red high-tops stuffed in the garbage can.

THE DUNGEON, SEATTLE

HER PLATINUM HAIR SPILLED OVER her shoulders, skimming the porcelain skin of her neck. Sacha refrained from looking farther down since he always had a difficult time forming words when her cleavage was involved.

"I missed you last night," he said, not quite meeting her eyes.

"Aren't you just the sweetest thing?"

She swept across the room, leather pumps clicking against the plastic with a hollow, *tock-tock* sound. She searched for somewhere to put her handbag, finally settling on the empty chair next to him as the cleanest spot available.

She faced Sacha and peeled the tailored coat from her arms, making sure to bend over seductively as she folded and stored it next to her handbag. Sacha gulped and ran a hand through the mass of curls clinging to his head.

"I missed you, too," she said.

She leaned over again, letting the neckline of her low-cut blouse fall open as she slipped off one of her shoes. Sacha reached out and touched her shoulder nervously. She jerked her head up. Her hair, stiff with hair spray, whipped him in the face. He let go of her shoulder.

"Sowwy, sweetie. You supwised me. I wasn't expecting such a *manwy* touch."

Sacha thought her baby-talk voice was creepy, but didn't dare admit it.

As she slipped the other shoe from her foot, she studied the monitor in front of him. He squirmed in his chair for a second before reaching up and clicking it off. The movement caught her attention, and she slithered into his lap. His arms fell around her waist with surprising ease. He knew this was a terrible idea, but the smell of jasmine in her hair overpowered his senses and he couldn't help himself.

"What have you been doing?"

She whispered into his ear with just enough breath to tickle his brain. A flush started near the base of his spine and headed upward. He was glad to be sitting down and doubly glad she was sitting in his lap.

"Does that matter?"

"Not at all."

She looked deep into his eyes and Sacha wondered, for the millionth time, why she was here. He'd asked her that very question a few weeks back. She'd responded with a shrug and half a smile. He hadn't found the nerve to ask her again.

Sacha blinked and looked away. She enjoyed making him look away. She enjoyed making him do all sorts of things.

"What have *you* been doing? You said you were coming over last night."

He tried to sound disinterested, even though he was dying to know and disgusted with himself for caring.

"Sorry," she said, not sounding sorry in the least. "I had this stupid project I needed to get done before I could come over. I only just finished it about an hour ago. I'm sorry I didn't call to tell you I'd be late. Are you mad?"

Her fingers began to fiddle around the collar of his t-shirt, pulling on a curl near his ear, tracing little lines down his neck. Her breath was hot and close, and even though she'd said that last sentence directly in his ear, he hadn't heard it at all.

"Have you been up all night?" she said.

He nodded slowly. She breathed into his ear again and his brain went all fuzzy. Her fingers fiddled around his collarbone.

"You know, I've been up for hours and *hours*. I feel positively *dirty*."

"Um..." was all he could say because he'd stopped breathing some time ago and didn't have any more air to speak with.

"I need to take a shower," she said. Her fingers found more interesting bits of clothing to tease apart. Sacha almost blacked out from lack of oxygen. He closed his eyes tight and breathed in deeply. Jasmine swirled around his thoughts, and he was grateful that Jake had decided to stay at Deli's.

SEARCHING FOR A CROSSWALK, HONG KONG

CARL DISCONNECTED THE CALL after the seventeenth ring in order to pay attention to the traffic. Jake wasn't answering.

He checked the GPS tracker. It blinked and pointed him in the opposite direction *again*. The satellite signal bounced all over as he ran. He was having a devil of a time trying to pinpoint it. After the direction stayed steady for ten full seconds, Carl veered appropriately and called Sacha.

"Hey, Carl! How's it going man? You find anything yet?"

"Do you know where Jake is? I've been trying to reach him for twenty minutes." Carl spoke fast and slightly out of breath.

"What's going on?" Sleepy morning noises emanated from Sacha's end of the conversation. Something else in the background made Carl's ears perk up. It sounded like giggling.

"I'm in the middle of a huge city that doesn't seem to believe in crosswalks, and I need Jake to help me triangulate a satellite signal." He kept his answer vague in case there really *was* giggling. "Can you see if he's remotely logged in to the server?"

He rested briefly at a red light, though his foot never stopped tapping. When the signal changed, he dodged a taxi and ran on.

"Probably, but that don't mean—*ouch!*"

Another noise, *definitely* a giggle this time, and the phone connection went mumbly as Sacha put his hand over the receiver.

Sacha was with a girl—or at least someone who sounded an awful lot *like* a girl. Carl knew he shouldn't be shocked, so he settled for being embarrassed. He should *not* have called. An unwelcome thought sprang to Carl's mind: *What if he'd interrupted something?*

He cringed and waited for Sacha to stop mumbling.

"Sorry about that. I stubbed my toe. As I was saying, he's probably logged in, but that don't mean he's awake. Last time I talked to him, he said he was gonna sleep at Deli's on her couch. Get this: He says it's because her bathroom smells better than ours. Can you believe that shit, man? I cleaned that bathroom last week!"

"Oh, uh… Right. Listen, I don't want to bother you," Carl said, because he didn't. He really, *really* didn't. "But, uh, if you get a chance, can you do me a gigantic favor?"

"No worries, man. What do you need?"

"Well, uh, if you have a spare moment, could you go over to Deli's place and check on him? No rush. I'm sure he's just sleeping. So like, you know, whenever."

"Sure thing. Anything else I can do for you? I *do* have the power of the internet at my beck and call." Sacha said it in his usual deadpan. Behind the unfunny joke, Carl heard another of the trilling noises. It was undeniably female.

"It's cool. Don't worry about it. Jake knows all the details. I just need him to answer his phone." Carl's voice was tight with anxiety, but there wasn't much else Sacha could do. He didn't know about the Elevators. And Carl certainly couldn't tell him now, especially if there was *giggling* involved.

"Sure, Carl. I was gonna go get some coffee, anyway. I'll go over there soon."

"Thanks, Sash. You know where Deli lives?"

"I'll find it, man. You know you can count on me."

As Sacha disconnected, Carl turned his attention back to his screwy GPS unit in order to shake the past three minutes from his mind. The buildings of the city blocked his satellite feed, sending him in several different directions, but he was nearing open space, and the compass soon made up its mind with resolute magnetic assurance. Deli's tracking signal was definitely coming from the waterfront. Carl jogged toward the harbor.

The tracking device in the watch that Carl gave Deli was an excellent performer. It used minimal power, and even if you turned it off, it would send out a short signal if it came within fifty meters of a cell phone tower. It led Carl right up to the gate of the Lucky Fortune

Marina. Carl's only real complaint with the gadget was that it was no longer around Deli's slender wrist.

He found it in a clump of weeds right outside the gate. Her smashed-up cell phone littered the ground nearby. As he gathered the pieces and stuck them in his bag, a deep watery rumble caught his attention. He looked up in time to see a yacht pull away from the dock. His heart sank.

Deli was on that yacht.

He just *knew* it.

Damn.

SACHA'S BEDROOM, SEATTLE
7:00 A.M.

SACHA DISCONNECTED THE CALL with a shiver. She had been running her fingers up and down his back, listening to every word of his conversation, though he pretended like she hadn't heard. He didn't like talking about Carl with her.

"I have to go," he said. Her only response was to snake her hands forward so that her fingers trailed along the inside of his thigh, just above his knee.

"I don't want to," he said, which was entirely true. "But it's kind of important."

Her fingers trailed higher.

"My, uh, friend needs me to do him a pretty big favor. So, uh, I have to…"

At this point, her fingers reached an intricate part of his anatomy and Sacha forgot what he was going to say for a while. There were definite plans hatching in his brain, and none of them had anything to do with Jake.

"Are you sure you have to go, just now? I'm *so* cold," she whispered and nibbled on his earlobe. "Can't you just warm me up a little bit?"

By nature, Sacha had a difficult time with women. He liked them very much, but none of them were ever inclined to give him anything more than the time of day. Not only had *she* given him the time of day, but she'd also given him five hickeys, a few scorch marks, and several leg cramps. Her straightforward lust shocked him. It made him do things that his brain didn't want to do. Things he knew were wrong. Things he knew that *she knew* were wrong.

And he knew she enjoyed it.

He couldn't stay. He had to go check on Jake. Her fingers went back to massaging his inner thigh.

"Stay with me, Sacha. I promise to make it worth your time."

He closed his eyes and tried to find the will to leave. She must have guessed as much because as soon as he opened his mouth to say no, she pinched his left nipple *really* hard.

The rest of his body quickly overruled the morality conflict on the grounds that his brain *always* got to make the decisions, and just this once, would it please shut the hell up because it was remarkably close to having sex with this girl again.

And, his body insisted, *whatever trouble you get in for this will totally be worth it. Especially if she keeps doing that.*

DELI'S COUCH

JAKE HEARD THE PHONE RING, but had a difficult time trying to reach it. The damn thing was miles away on the table, and he could not move his arm. His eyes resisted any attempt to open them. He thought about cursing. It seemed appropriate for this situation, but he lacked the energy to do it. He wanted to sleep some more. Fluffy, warm thoughts clouded into his mind, and he began to drift peacefully back into the void.

Somewhere in the back of his mind, though, a muffled voice barked out a command that woke him up briefly. He began slipping away again almost immediately, but before his thoughts fuzzed over, the voice cleared its throat and shouted at him.

Get your ass off this couch! The voice, finally getting his attention, turned up the volume. *Listen to me, man, some very bad juju is about to go down if you do not MOVE IT. I mean it. Get up! You! With the fat ass and the stinky feet, get up! For the love of Pizza Girl, GET YOUR ASS UP.*

It was the idea of Pizza Girl that did it. She was so pretty. He wondered what she liked to eat when she didn't eat pizza.

It doesn't matter! You will never have pizza again if you do not MOVE!

He tried opening his eyes. Wow, his head was kind of swimmy. In fact, his whole body felt swimmy.

Jake would be the first to admit that he was incredibly out of shape. But even *he* should be able to sit up without getting winded. This must be what his grandma felt like all the time. She couldn't light a cigarette without exhausting herself.

The voice didn't care. It continued screaming. *Get your ass UP!*

Jake dropped his feet to the ground and scootched his hips around so that he was not as horizontal. He became aware of how cold it was in Deli's apartment and wished he could reach the blanket off the back of the couch.

By the time he shifted himself into a sitting position, Jake concluded that something was seriously wrong. He was dizzy and weak. He could hardly catch his breath, and his left arm wouldn't move at all. Plus, his shirt was cold against his skin, almost like it was wet.

Using his right arm, Jake ran his hand over his chest. It *was* wet. Did the cat pee on him or something? Because that would be so *gross*.

LUCKY FORTUNE MARINA, HONG KONG
11:30 P.M.

CARL HELD HIS MESSENGER BAG in front of him like a shield of nerdiness and walked straight through the gates. There weren't a lot of people around, but there were some, and one tall, sandy-haired *gweilo* definitely stood out in this crowd. It was better to look confident, like he belonged, even if he clearly did not.

The yacht motored away, as nonchalantly as possible. Carl could almost hear the captain's carefree whistling as the boats in the marina danced in his wake. He groaned again, but to himself this time on account of the short guy leaning against the mailboxes up ahead.

He was smaller than Carl by at least a foot. What he lacked in height, he made up for in squint. He wore a shapeless hat and a neckerchief. Fat drifts of smoke issued from the cigar in his mouth. He even had a tattoo of an anchor on his arm.

Carl walked up to marina guard and smiled his best dopey grin. "*Nihao!*" he said. "*Zen...uh...zenyang?*"

"What you want?"

"Oh, you speak, uh..."

The man squinted at Carl with disapproval.

"Right, I'm here to calibrate the Sat-Nav equipment on the...*Wind Dancer.*" Carl patted the bag at his hip to indicate the delicate computer equipment inside.

"I need to get a reading from the dock and a reading from the deck of the ship once an hour for the next six hours. Are you the captain?"

A thin smile stretched across the man's face, and his cigar stopped puffing out smoke.

"No," he said.

"Well, can I talk with the captain?"

"No."

"I'm supposed to get a satellite reading from the deck at the zero hour. Can I go up on the deck at least?" Carl asked.

"No."

"Why not?"

"Because I not captain. No captain, no boarding." The marina guard squinted at him with both eyes to show he was serious. Carl looked affronted for the half second it took to come up with an alternate plan.

"Okaaay, well, if that's the case, then don't worry about it. Anyone can do the readings. Here, I'll show you how. It's not very difficult."

He pulled his fancy phone out of his messenger bag, then the notebook computer and a cable that had three strange plugs on each end and one in the middle. He moved his hands quickly, plugging the cable into his fancy phone and a notebook computer, which booted up as soon as Carl opened it.

"All you have to do is place the computer on location for three minutes. Wait for the gyroscope program to calibrate its location on the y-vector and then move it over to the x-vector." He typed in a series of numbers and the computer did some technical bloop-blooping. He waited for it to bloop twice more before typing in another command.

"See? It's easy!" Carl offered up the computer and phone setup enthusiastically. "You only have to do it once an hour, but make sure it's at the same exact time, okay? Also, it has to be in the exact same coordinates, so try to not move the main computer, because that will throw off the satellite coordinates, and if the satellite isn't calibrated properly, it could mess up the entire navigation system." He arched his eyebrows and shook his finger in a preemptive warning. "And in a harbor as busy as this one, that could be dangerous." Carl continued grinning like an overly intellectual idiot. It came naturally to him.

The guard glared back, but one eyelid seemed less squinty than it was before. "No," he said.

"I know it looks complicated, but you can do it! It's not that hard. I can do the main calibration from the cabin tomorrow, when we test out the system for real, but we can't do that without the preliminary data."

"You here tomorrow?" This time, the man's eyes definitely opened half a squint wider.

"I put it in, didn't I? I gotta make sure it works. You have no idea what kind of trouble I'm going to be in if it doesn't. If you'd help me out here, that'd be super."

"No."

"Come on, man! This is one of our premier clients. If you can't let me on board, then at least help me out! I need to analyze the calibration differential before tomorrow, and I can't do that without taking measured readings." He tried handing the rigged-up computer system over again, but the man wouldn't touch it.

"No." He stepped forward and tapped Carl in the chest with a dirty finger. "You do it."

Then he stood aside and let Carl onto the dock.

*   *   *

Pleasure cruisers lounged along the dock in arrogant stupor. Carl didn't need a big boat. All he needed to do was catch up with the yacht that had Deli. A small ski boat would probably be good enough.

He marched past the first few ships with determination. A smaller dock split off to the left. Carl turned, eager to get out from under the watchful eye of the marina guard.

When he was out of sight, he slowed down and paid more attention to the boats in their slips. Mostly they were huge, white bathtubs, built for mixed drinks and open ocean—not the type of boat one could easily steal for a rescue mission. He searched for something smaller.

Tucked between two hulking fiberglass leviathans, the *Doris Day* bounced in her mooring like a kid sister. She had sleek lines and an aerodynamic hull that Carl thought looked fast enough to be a drug runner. However, everything Carl had ever learned about boats came from outdated *Miami Nights* reruns, and easily half the boats in the marina looked suspiciously like drug runners to him. He climbed over the rail as quietly as he could, hoping that the owners were law-abiding people.

A tidy canvas canopy covered the captain's area above the cabin, leaving the controls accessible. He climbed the few steps up to it and took a minute to familiarize himself with the various buttons and dials. Carl had never hotwired anything before, though the concept was easy enough. He wondered if he should worry about an alarm system, but when he set his bag down, Deli's high-tops flopped out, and he decided it was worth the risk.

DELI'S LIVING ROOM FLOOR, SEATTLE

DAMMIT! THIS WAS HIS FAVORITE SHIRT, TOO. Now it was soaked with blood *and* there was a hole in it. He remembered seeing someone familiar, but when he tried thinking about it, his head got all swimmy again. He didn't know a single person who hated him enough to want him dead.

Wait…

Yes, he did.

But why *now*?

He should be angry, but he couldn't breathe well enough to get a simmer going. Standing had definitely been a mistake. On the plus side, his arm was responding a little better now that he'd fallen to the floor.

The floor had its advantages, too. For instance, he could *almost* reach his phone. If he scooted closer to the coffee table, he might be able to knock it off somehow. But after a frustrating minute, his strength tapped out. He gave up.

With his face smashed into Deli's shaggy living room floor, Jake thought about what was happening and came to the only conclusion available: he was going to die. Right here, on Deli's crappy rug, without ever having said more than two words to the delivery chick from Pizza Joe's.

That sucked donkey balls.

He brooded as only an overweight man, who has been shot in the chest but is miraculously still alive, can. Pizza Joe's seemed miles away, and the more he thought about the delivery girl, the broodier he got. He'd been working on an opening line and *everything*. She had such nice hair.

Jake sulked and wondered when the end would come. It should be any moment now, if all the blood was any indication. He went back to thinking about Pizza Girl. She always smelled nice, like basil or rosemary or something.

He was waiting for his life to flash before his eyes when the phone started up again. From the floor, he could feel the vibration through the table leg.

I'm here! Jake thought. *Don't hang up! I fed the cat! He purred on me and the Elevators worked! He's purring now, can you hear him?*

Jake could hear him purring, louder and louder.

Suddenly, the phone vibrated itself off the table and fell, with a solid *thwack*, onto his head. He shook thoughts of the Pizza Girl from his mind and came back down to reality long enough to see a silver flash beneath the couch. If he hadn't fallen to the floor, he would never have found it, so at least he had that going for him. The phone went on ringing.

Using his more responsive arm to search, Jake came across a pen, a few bottle caps and something else he couldn't identify, before his fingers lit upon the familiar bean-shaped object. The phone buzzed. The bean had another sound-induced seizure.

He rolled the bean along with his fingers, slowly teasing it from underneath the couch. When he finally fished it free, He had just enough strength left to do the one thing he'd wanted to do since the whole damn project started: He ate the bean.

It tasted like metal, carpet fuzz, and blood loss.

It also tasted like hope.

VICTORIA HARBOUR, HONG KONG
THURSDAY, JUNE 6TH, 12:10 A.M.

THE BOAT'S ENGINE REVVED LOUDER than Carl expected, but that couldn't be helped. He eased the throttle forward slowly. The boat responded by tugging against the dock.

Nuts! thought Carl, *I knew I forgot something.*

He cut the gas and jumped from the bridge onto the deck. Carl fumbled at the dock cleats, untying the ropes and throwing them onto the deck of the boat.

No longer tethered to the dock, the *Doris Day* began to float gently away. Carl jumped back up to the bridge. He maneuvered her from the slip in a wide arc, following the lazy, reluctant motion of the water. When it came to the physics of motion, Carl was a fast learner. He soon had the boat cruising slowly down the waterway.

He could see lights far in the distance, moving steadily away. He aimed the front of the boat at the kidnappers and increased its speed.

So focused was he on the moving lights that he forgot to keep an eye out for danger.

"*Zhaohu.*"

Carl jumped straight up and smacked his head on the aluminum frame of the awning.

He turned to see where the voice came from, but the moon was bright and it lit the man up from behind. All Carl could make out was the figure of an older gentleman in boxer shorts and a slouchy sweatshirt, brandishing a nasty-looking weapon. Silver light glinted off the pointy end. It was probably a harpoon, but Carl didn't feel it was entirely appropriate to ask.

The man spoke, then waggled the probable harpoon threateningly. Carl was not inclined to argue with pointy weapons and put his hands up. As soon as his hands came off the wheel, however, the boat turned sharply. This caused both Carl and the man to stumble.

The man jabbed his weapon toward the controls, indicating that Carl should feel free to steady the boat as long as he didn't get any funny ideas. Carl emptied his head of any funny ideas and cut the throttle back down to a crawl. He kept his hands on the wheel and made placatory gestures with his shoulders at the ostensible harpoonist. He tapped and dipped in profound sincerity until the business end of the man's weapon jabbed a few cringe-worthy inches away from his stomach. After that, he stood still. It was definitely a harpoon.

The man studied his face, barking out more Chinese words that Carl did not understand. He tried explaining.

"I'm sorry, sir, but my friend's been kidnapped and..."

The shining tip of harpoon justice jabbed at him once more and he stopped.

This time, instead of shouting, the man spoke in the long, slow drawl of someone talking to the incredibly stupid. He even made a few hand gestures. Carl listened attentively and understood. He was to step out from the shadow so that the man could get a better look at his attempted burglar.

Carl ducked his head and stepped sideways, out from under the canopy.

The moonlight was bright, and as Carl's pale Norwegian frame slid into view, his features glowed. The harpoon wielder gasped, then did something totally unexpected.

He started laughing.

DELI'S APARTMENT BUILDING, SEATTLE

NEAR THE ENTRANCE TO THE BACK PARKING LOT, Toesy heard Stupid the Rat. He knew its name was Stupid because he'd heard it shouted many times. He was less sure about the rat status, though. It certainly looked more like a rat than anything else Toesy had ever seen, but occasionally, it barked. In Toesy's opinion, barking was suspiciously un-rat-like behavior.

Stupid was in its yard, running in circles. As Toesy stalked past, it stopped the frantic running, sniffed the air and exploded in a frenzy of teacup-sized snarling. Toesy watched it rocket to the fence, shaking with rage and excitement. It barked out a battle cry, focused on *cat*-related death or at least bodily harm.

It was a good battle cry, as far as these things went, but Stupid was remarkably outclassed. The mammoth cat merely looked at it with the curiosity of one studying an appetizer menu in a cut-rate restaurant.

Two feet from Toesy, Stupid's basic instincts finally took over. It stopped running. It stopped barking. It almost stopped breathing. A look of bewildered terror gathered on its furry face as it realized that the only thing now separating it from sudden, cat-*related* death was a flimsy length of chain link fence.

Toesy's claws dug into the ground. His fangs jutted out angrily. They pushed his lips apart to reveal the straight rows of needles behind them. He opened his mouth, pointed his whiskers back as far as they would go, and hissed loudly.

The pseudo-rat panicked. It defecated in fright before turning around and running, full tilt, into the trunk of a tree, knocking itself out cold.

Until that moment, Toesy had been feeling rather despondent about the whole mess upstairs. But watching Stupid's paw twitch unconsciously in the air cheered him up considerably.

He turned his attention to the drifts of grass flourishing between the cracks in the pavement. The green blades smelled juicy and sweet. A long snuffle of the fence yielded countless layers of urine: dog, cat, rat, raccoon, and—was that an *owl*? Toesy wasn't surprised. An owl could make a good meal out of a rat. Pity that it hadn't succeeded with this one.

Farther down the driveway, he smelled the oily, blue heat of exhaust and moved on before it imprinted his nose. Out on the sidewalk, the smells were more confused. Sweet, heavy, acrid, dusty—his brain churned through the new information, connecting those smells to places and people.

At the front stoop of the apartment building, he caught a whisper of almonds and honey. Visions of Deli bubbled into his mind. Then came the sharp odor of cheese and stale sweat, very much like the funk from the Great Man's shoes.

Toesy had another sniff. Yes, that was it exactly!

He followed the scent down the sidewalk, paying no attention to the sudden outbreak of creatures fleeing for their lives in his wake.

The great man's shoe funk trailed along steadily for three blocks. As it neared a park, Toesy could smell layers of wood bark and rubber. He looked up to see a pit full of tiny, sand-crusted humans.

Toesy stood absolutely still. If one were to make a list of all the things that frightened him, it would be a short list indeed. But right on the top, in italicized letters, would be *tiny humans*. He did not like them.

They were unpredictable and malicious and often smelled like urine. As a result, he made it his business to keep out of reach when tiny humans were around.

Toesy darted underneath a nearby laurel hedge to avoid being spotted. Creeping through the tangle of branches, he hoped to duck out the other side but stopped abruptly because he ran headlong into a garbage can.

What damnable sort of idiot puts a garbage can in the middle of a hedge?

He shook out his ears then chanced a peek out the top of the shrub. The garbage can sat a few feet from the sidewalk. It may have started out in the park at one time, but the hedge had grown up, engulfing it in leaves and branches. If you were unaware it was there, you might never know it.

Before he ducked back into his foliage foil, Toesy noted that the hedge surrounded the park on three sides. If he kept to the inside, he could skirt the sandy pit of tiny humans and avoid being seen or, worse yet, *petted*.

He studied the hedge intently for any kind of gap. Later he would tell himself this was why he didn't hear the little girl. In his defense, the sound of her approach was dampened by the sheer volume of ruffles. Her legs were lost in a sea of purple frills.

"Scary doggie!" she said, squeaking in a mixture of dread and delight.

Toesy's reflexes had a remarkable response time, and before the last syllable left the cherubic lips of his beruffled admirer, he darted to a more secure section of hedge.

The child wailed at its mother and pointed to the spot that, seconds earlier, had been full of Toesy. "There was a scary doggie!"

"For God's sake, don't pet it!"

Presumably this was shouted by the child's parent, but Toesy didn't turn around to see. He focused on keeping himself completely still to avoid giving away his position.

The child reached out a braceletted arm and used a juice box to push the swinging lid of the garbage can open. She did this slowly, searching the surrounding hedge for the scary doggie. Toesy tried not to blink.

"Amelia Delores, get your hands out of that filthy garbage can at once!" The tone of voice suggested that a spanking would soon follow should the fluffy little girl not comply. For a moment, Toesy disliked the adult more than its kit.

The girl complied. She let go of the juice box, trapped now between the lid and the can, and ran back to her parent. Toesy waited another ten seconds before moving.

He was halfway to the inner sanctum of branches when an acrid smell hit his nose. He *remembered* that smell.

Making sure the ruffles were out of sight, Toesy stood up on his back legs to investigate the garbage can. He didn't have to reach far. His whiskers, shivering with anger and curiosity, poked through the opening. They led his nose into the belly of the can. The sweet miasma of rotting fruit assaulted his senses but it was nothing compared to the odor of burnt metal and oil. He pulled his head back sharply and sneezed.

Toesy didn't know the word *cordite*, but he knew what smoke from the fourth of July tasted like, and this was both the same and not the same. This was a dangerous smell.

He stretched his back legs farther, reached down with a spiked paw and snagged the limp, smelly thing.

BRIDGE OF THE *DORIS DAY*, VICTORIA HARBOUR

THE MAN'S NAME TURNED OUT TO BE JIN. The last time Carl had seen him, he'd been trying not to laugh as his wife stormed away in a profanity-laced huff.

Through a combination of choppy English, hand movements, and vigorous nodding, Carl eventually came to understand that after he'd stolen their cab, Jin's wife had been very upset indeed. But— and this seemed to be the important part—*she was not upset at Jin*.

When he finally caught up with her, she'd been fuming like a bull, ready to lash out at anyone. Jin suggested that the *gweilo* was at fault for being so stupid, and for once, his wife agreed. In fact, she was pleased he understood.

Not one to miss an opportunity, Jin suggested that it might calm her nerves if she invited her sister over for a long stay. She happily obliged. Then he kindly offered to sleep on the boat for the next few nights so they might play mahjong in peace. His wife had been so taken with him at that point that she had kissed him—on the cheek, of course. Before he left, he bought them a bottle of plum wine, for which his wife almost *thanked* him.

Or something like that. Carl wasn't too sure about the sister thing. It could have been a cousin. It hardly mattered, though, because in the end, thanks to Carl, Jin had gotten a three-day reprieve from his formidable wife, and if there was *any* way he could repay the favor, he would do so unhesitatingly.

Carl wove his hands in the air, trying to explain the ship that took Deli, but there was no need. Having been a longtime denizen of the

Lucky Fortune Marina, Jin knew the ship immediately. Her name was the *Marty-Lu*, and she was well known for being captained by a squad of ill-mannered hooligans. Judging by the way his lips curled back as he spoke, Carl assumed that *ill-mannered hooligans* was not a direct translation.

He had a bit more difficulty trying to explain the Deli situation. Jin remembered Deli from the airport and jumped to the same conclusion as everyone else, that she was Carl's girlfriend. Carl spent a full minute stammering out a refusal, but Jin would not be persuaded to believe something so ridiculous. Carl dropped it and moved on.

When he got to the part where he found Deli's shoes in the bathroom, the little man jumped in the air with rage. Those gangsters would pay for this indiscretion! They cannot get away with this! This time, they have gone too far!

He hip-checked Carl away from the controls with startling strength and captained the boat closer to the *Marty-Lu*. His expression grew angrier the closer they got.

Carl tried talking him down. They didn't need to go in with harpoons blazing. All they needed to do was get Deli and get out. But the more Carl explained, the more Jin worked himself into a lather of righteous indignation. Carl did not understand the words, but fist-pummeling meant pretty much the same thing in most languages.

As they neared, Jin extinguished the lights. Unfortunately, they could do nothing about the engine noise. But as The *Marty-Lu* loomed larger on the starboard side, the sound of her own huge engines made the *Doris Day* seem almost quiet in comparison. She was so large, in fact that her deck was easily twelve feet or more above them.

"Uh, Jin?" Carl said, immediately feeling silly for pointing out something so obvious. "How am I supposed to get aboard?"

Jin just smiled at him. Then, with one hand still on the wheel, he raised the harpoon and shot it directly into the hull of the *Marty-Lu*, six inches below the floor of the deck.

The rope attached to Jin's harpoon sailed through the air with a whisper. Carl reached out and grabbed it the moment it slowed down. Jin tucked the boat alongside the *Marty-Lu* matching her speed, so that Carl could shimmy up to the deck. It was a gangly minute with lots of elbows and knees involved.

Once aboard, he looked down to Jin and waved. Jin smiled back and called out the one English phrase he knew well: "Right in the frickin' nose!"

TOESY'S DIGESTIVE SYSTEM, SEATTLE

AFTER SEVERAL FAILED ATTEMPTS to breach the blood-brain barrier, the bean finally found a hack into the main logic circuits of the dynamic biomachine using a shortwave frequency. It spent four thousand nanoseconds interpreting and translating alpha waves, then built a crude generator out of iron and zinc found in the support medium. Once this two-way communication system was in place, things really took off. It learned a staggering amount of information in a very short time.

The first lesson was the Cat.

The Cat was its Overlord. The bean would follow the commands of the Overlord with accuracy and aplomb because that was the bean's job. It existed to do the Overlord's bidding and the bean was *nothing* if not professional. It did not think about how much fun it was having with the Overlord because fun is not in a bean's job description. However, were the bean ever to become self-aware, it is probable that the first autonomous word it uttered would be *Wheee*!

Even though the bean could not think on its own, it had grown an appreciation for a good challenge. Its job, so far, had been difficult, but the bean had succeeded masterfully. It looked forward to the next challenge with an eagerness not usually found in machinery, bio- or otherwise.

Toesy wasn't sure when the voice started or if it had been there all along. He thought maybe it was a new addition, but it was getting hard to tell. Either way, he listened because it told him things he wanted to hear. For example, it currently told him that resting in the sunshine was an excellent idea.

It's not that he was trying to be lazy, Toesy was dearly concerned for the Great Man. But the voice was adamant that there were internal problems that required fixing. And that it would behoove him to supply the voice with as much nutrition and sunlight as possible.

Toesy, tired from all the snuffling, was in no mood to argue.

He had yet to make up his mind about the smelly thing from the bottom of the garbage can. It seemed to be some sort of glove but it was very thin and the smells on it made no sense. The outside of it reeked of bad, sulphury smells yet the inside was nice and flowery.

Which smell should he hunt down? The bad ones would certainly know what happened to the Great Man, but the good ones might not try to kill him again.

Eventually, Toesy decided to find the flowery smell. It might bring him back to the Great Man. Plus, it hurt his head much less.

VICTORIA HARBOUR, HONG KONG

THE OVERHEAD LIGHT WAS ON, illuminating the room through a layer of dust. Some enterprising decorator had tried to turn it into a chandelier by hot-gluing loops of plastic beads around the edge. It hadn't worked. The poor light fixture looked like it belonged in a brothel.

Deli stared at the beads swinging gently back and forth. Their hypnotic motion soothed the pounding in her head, lulling her back to sleep.

She was nearly asleep again when a blunt *thud* hit the wall of the room, followed closely by a muffled *oing-oing-oing* sound. She jerked awake and immediately regretted it, as her head exploded in pain.

Damn it, how much did I drink last night?

She tried thinking back but gave up. It felt like there were angry dwarves inside her skull, hammering their way out. She needed some water and about twelve aspirin.

Carefully, to avoid provoking the skull-dwarves, she tried sitting up. It didn't go so well. Her arms were stretched out over her head, and one of them was completely asleep. She couldn't get enough leverage underneath her body to hoist herself upright.

She tried flipping over to let gravity do the job, but shifting her weight off her dead arm caused it to wake up. Now, in addition to the angry dwarves, there were hot needles stabbing her in the arm.

Keeping her head as still as possible, she scanned the room to see what she could see.

She lay on an overstuffed couch. From what she could tell, it was as ugly as the makeshift chandelier. Her shoulder was bare, which was worrisome. And a quick glance down the length of the couch told her that most of the rest of her was bare, too.

This can't be good, she thought.

Across the small room, a queen-sized bed lurked in the corner. It had a pink satin duvet and black leather throw pillows, which matched the horrible couch. Deli cringed and decided that whoever had decorated this room should be bludgeoned to death with their own hot-glue gun.

The beads of the chandelier clacked together as the room swayed up and down with renewed enthusiasm. Deli watched them clack, wondering why they kept doing that.

Pieces of the previous night were coming back to her: Carl, the Silver Hammer, the funny little bartender...

Oh, sweet merciful crap, she and Carl hadn't... *Had they?*

Deli decided they hadn't. She would *definitely* remember something like that. Plus, try as she might, she couldn't remember drinking more than one beer.

The needles in Deli's arm were fading. She tried sitting up again, only to realize that she wasn't just lying on the couch, she was *attached* to it. There was a shiny set of handcuffs on her wrists.

I am nearly naked and tied to the world's ugliest couch. This is all sorts of not good.

By wiggling herself around, she managed to sit up without dislocating her shoulder. The sudden gain in elevation made the dwarves in her head scream, but she pushed on. The handcuffs were clipped to a brass hoop set into the arm of the couch. Fortunately, the hoop had a spring latch on it. After three attempts, she jimmied herself free.

She tore through the room, looking for anything that would tell her what was going on. The pain in her head weakened now that her body was moving around.

Three minutes spent rummaging through drawers produced several items of—well, it had to be lingerie, because what else could it be? Deli grimaced. If you have to dress up *that* much for sex, then you're either doing it wrong or getting paid a lot of money.

There were other drawers, stocked with other *things*. She tried glossing over much of what she found by sitting back down on the couch. Apparently, the designer had been spot on with the chandelier.

She worked her way through the events of the previous night. They'd sat at the table, making fun of the quirky little bartender. Carl made a bet and everything went awkward for a while. Then Deli got up to go to the restroom.

She remembered the woman in the stall next to her, and how her neck hadn't looked right in the overhead fluorescent lighting.

Then she remembered the woman saying something in a deep voice and holding a small bottle that was definitely not hair spray. Deli looked around the swaying room.

Oh hell, she thought. *I've been shanghaied by a transvestite prostitute with obnoxious taste in interior decorating.*

There was a knock at the door, followed by the jingle of keys, and then the door opened an inch. A set of hairy knuckles curled around the door frame. Deli quickly arranged herself in a helpless position. An observant person might notice that her arms now rested in front of her, still bound together with cuffs, but far from useless. She hoped Hairy Knuckles was not very observant. She wanted time enough to size him up before she hit him.

A tall man with curly black hair and a deep bronze tan followed the knuckles through the door. From the hairiness of the knuckles, Deli assumed the man would have a beard. Surprisingly, this man didn't wear one. He *did* have bushy eyebrows, though. They were very enthusiastic about being on his face. When they saw her lounging on the couch, they jumped halfway up his forehead.

"You are awake," he said, rolling his Rs like a pirate. Then he stepped into the room and closed the door behind him.

"Can you tell me where I am?" Deli tried to sound helpless. Most people thought she was too tiny to be a threat. Hopefully this guy would, too.

"Do you *not* know where you are? The contract is already signed, my dear," he said in a gentle voice.

Deli pondered that before replying. "I'm sorry, I meant—what ship am I on?"

"Oh!" he laughed. "I see. You are on the *Marty-Lu*. She is *most* beautiful ship in harbor." He spread his arms wide, as if presenting the world to her. His accent was hard to pin down. If Deli had to make a guess, she would say it was fifty percent Russian, fifty percent Greek, and one hundred percent fake. She smiled. A plan began forming in her head.

"And you are the captain?"

"Most definitely." He walked across the room beaming and sat down on the couch so close to Deli that she either had to scrunch her legs up or drape them over his lap. She scrunched, but in a polite way. She wanted to make him comfortable.

"I am Captain Viktor Korunzch," he said, and beat his chest with his right fist in an uncanny impersonation of an orangutan. He even gave a little, half-crazy smile at the end.

"And you," he murmured, "are a very beautiful woman."

He probably meant it to be more of a purr than a murmur, but purring in a fake Greco-Russian accent was an act too perilous for even the captain, so he whispered low and inched closer to Deli's side of the couch.

She closed her eyes to keep from rolling them. When her sarcasm reflex subsided, Deli opened her eyes wide in puppy-dog fashion. She held her hands up for him to see the handcuffs so cruelly biting at her wrists. She might have even whimpered a bit, who can say?

Captain Korunzch shook his head slightly. "But, what is this? Are you in a *bind*?"

His eyebrows, which had been waiting like patient caterpillars, launched themselves into a complicated knot as he laughed at his own joke. Deli gave him a timid smile, her wide blue eyes shining with fear.

"They told me not to trust you. It says in your contract that you are here by choice, but Leonardo, he tells me—do not trust you. He says you are very cunning. It is a pity I do not know your name. I like to know the names of my friends. Friends are important to me. I *trust* my friends."

Now it was the captain's turn for puppy-dog eyes.

To his credit he did *try*. But eyebrows like that will not be upstaged, and his simpering went from likable to laughable so fast that Deli had to throw her head back in a mock swoon to keep from cracking up. But Captain Korunzch had a significant weight advantage, and she still had the handcuffs on, so she redirected her giggles into small hiccoughing sobs.

"I have no idea what I'm supposed to do here, Captain. I woke up tied to this couch. I didn't even know what boat I'm on. And you are the only person that has even spoken to me."

She rubbed her eyes, poking a few eyelashes inward as she did so, then bowed her head in despair.

144   TIFFANY PITTS

With her head hung low enough that Viktor couldn't see, Deli squeezed her eyes shut until the out-of-place eyelashes made her tear up. Then she lifted her head and blinked several times in succession. One solitary tear fell down her face. She paused to let the light from the cheap chandelier glint mournfully off her cheekbone.

As the tear splashed down on the couch, Deli sniffed loudly and made a show of wiping her eyes.

"My name is Delilah," she said. She held her hands out daintily, so as not to inconvenience him with her cuffs.

"It's nice to meet you, Captain Korunzch, sir."

The captain didn't stand a chance. He could not bear tears from a woman, especially one so delicate and nearly naked as Delilah. He fell to his knees on the floor in front of the couch and fumbled through his pockets.

Deli frantically curled herself into a ball. "What are you—?"

The captain paid her no attention, and continued to search his pockets. He soon produced a tiny silver key.

"Oh, I apologize! I thought you were..." She uncurled. Drawing her hands from her lap, Deli offered her right wrist to the captain. He unlocked the cuff. She looked into his eyes and hooked the right half of her mouth up into a mischievous grin. He stood up on his knees.

"Never mind what I thought," Deli said as the cuff fell away from her wrist. The captain took her left wrist in his hand but did not unlock the cuff.

"I leave this one on. We might need it later," he said. His hand fell from her wrist to her knee. Deli put both feet on the ground and leaned into him. Together, they stood up.

From one angle, it may have looked as though Deli was coming on to the captain. Anyone spying through an appropriately placed keyhole, might have excused themselves at that moment to go use the bathroom or get a bag of chips, maybe even a sandwich.

But from another angle, the scene looked exactly like Deli getting a solid footing before kicking someone's ass. Any weapon in an unfair fight is better than no weapon at all, and sex, as the captain was about to learn, is a very powerful weapon.

Before he stood up all the way, Deli's right hand whipped around and punched him hard in the gut. After he doubled over, she roundhoused him in the cheek with the other fist, hard enough to incapacitate him but not hard enough to break anything. The captain dropped to the floor.

Deli fell on him, splaying his arms out and pinned each to the ground with a bony knee. She applied pressure to a specific spot on the inside of each arm and watched as his hands fell dead at the wrists.

"Where are you taking me?" Deli said, dangerously calm. The captain stopped struggling after a second or two and glared at her. He had no reason to lie. She would know soon enough, anyway.

"The Rig. I take you to the Rig." His voice held on to a certain amount of pride. Deli would not intimidate him, even if she was currently cutting off the circulation to his hands.

"Where is this Rig?"

"The middle of the ocean! We are on a boat, no?"

"Who owns the Rig?" Deli said.

The captain whined. The feeling in his arms would be sharpening from tingles to uncomfortable sparks right about now.

"I do not know! It is called just *the Rig*. I take supplies out there once a month. No one tells me who owns it. I never ask. I am on need-to-know basis, and I do not need to know! They pay me. This I know. Now get off me, *bitch!*"

The strain in his words became acute when Deli, unsatisfied with these answers, rolled forward on her knees and applied more pressure to the inside of each arm, turning the sparks into needles.

"These supplies, what are they?" she asked.

"Food mostly. Sometimes girls. They want to go. Money is good." His face turned a semigloss red and his breathing quickened.

"So, you're a pimp?"

"They give me rent for this room, that's all! I do not ask for a cut. They meet Leonardo, he brings them here. They don't complain. Is glamorous!"

Deli *really* wanted to slap him now, but needed him to talk, so she gritted her teeth instead.

"Who the hell is Leonardo?"

The captain must have sensed the ease in her demeanor because the tiny edge of bravado showed back up in his voice.

"I told you. Leonardo, is recruiter for girls like *you*. He brings them to me, I bring them to the Rig. They profit, I profit, Leonardo profits."

"Exactly what profession do you think I'm in, *Captain*?"

The look in her eyes could cut through steel. She jabbed her left knee into the man's arm so hard he squealed. Words tumbled out of him, no longer accented by anything but good old New Jersey goon.

"You're like the rest of them! All of 'em's been call girls. Lenny said you were the same! He handed me your contract and everything!"

"Was it Lenny who tied me up?"

"Sure it was. It's in your contract, ain't it? Said you like all dat stuff. Said you get off on it."

She had a contract with a bondage clause? That was interesting. She'd have to find out more about that later.

"Do you sample all the girls who come through here, then?" She jammed her right knee down some more. The captain gasped.

"No!" He screamed, this time for real. "I'm not allowed to touch any of them. You're the first one that's ever given me the time of day."

Deli didn't want him yelling too loud, so she eased up on his arms a tiny bit. "You are a terrible liar."

The captain, who until now had indulged Deli out of deference to her age, and the fact that she was almost sitting on his face, snapped. "What the hell are you going to do about it? You ain't that big, and you can't pin me down here for the rest of the voyage. Do you think you can arrest me or something? I'm the captain of this ship, and we'll be in international waters in less than ten minutes. You ain't goin' nowhere without me."

He was right. Eventually, someone would come looking for him. She couldn't sail a ship, especially not one this size. Fortunately, there was a very simple solution.

"Oh, I'm not going to *arrest* you, Captain," Deli said. She gave him her best come-hither look, which, for such a violent little woman, was quite come-hithery, and eased up on his arms slightly. "I want to make a *deal* with you."

The captain's eyebrows registered her intent immediately. They wiggled in lascivious anticipation. Deli traced her finger lightly along his cheekbone up to his brow. She stopped there and leaned over him, letting her half nakedness fill his field of view.

"I'm not going to go easy on you, just because you're the captain." she said and ran her hand down his chest, toward his belt. The captain relaxed and tensed at the same time.

Her fingers reached his waistband and crawled sideways, slipping into his pants pocket. His eyebrows arched into hyperspace and he started making weird kissy faces. Deli pretended to shut her eyes in ecstasy so she wouldn't have to watch the twitching specter of Captain Horn-Dog.

She fished around his pocket for a minute, accidentally bumping into the little captain. This caused his eyebrows to launch into an elaborate mating dance that could give an Australian bowerbird a run for its money.

She found what she needed, and pulled her hand out of his pocket before any more accidental grazings could ensue.

Deli smiled and held up the tiny silver key so he could see it. Then she winked and dropped it into the cup of her bra. The captain growled. He probably thought he was being sexy.

"I must warn you," he said. His fake Greco-Idiot accent had returned. "I drive a hard bargain."

He emphasized how hard his bargain would be driven by thrusting upward with the little captain. Deli slapped him hard in the face. It was a natural reaction.

"So do I," she said.

Then she slapped him again.

THE MARTY-LU

CARL OPENED THE DOOR TO THE ROOM quietly, not understanding what he saw.

Deli was...

And there was a guy...

"Oh," he said. "I am terribly sorry." He blinked twice and took a step backward, meaning to shut the door behind him, but as soon as he moved, the shouting started.

"*Carl!*"

"Who is this? What are you doing here? What is going on?"

"Carl, *come back here!*"

Carl stopped when he registered what Deli had said. Still holding the door open, he walked back into the room.

The scene was mayhem; specifically, half-naked mayhem pinning a screaming man to the floor. Carl wanted to scream, too. He refrained.

Deli gave the man a hard look and did the only thing she could to shut his mouth: she sat on it.

"Shut *up*, asshole!"

The man shut up. He kind of had to.

Over by the door, Carl stood in stunned silence. He tried not to think about what she was doing.

"Shut the door, Carl," she said.

Carl shut the door.

"I need you to help me," she said.

Carl walked forward, but he had no idea what to do. Deli appeared to have everything under, uh, *control.*

"You're, uh..." He stammered over the rest of his sentence and gave up. She probably knew she was half-naked.

"I know. I woke up like this. Apparently, it's in my *contract*. Give me a second."

The man, who was slowly suffocating under Deli's purple striped panties, glared up at her in a kind of ecstasy. He was angry *and* horny, which would have made him dangerous except that he was also lightheaded from lack of oxygen. Deli leaned over to talk to the man quietly, causing Carl to inspect the ceiling out of politeness.

"I'm going to get off of you in a moment. If you keep your mouth shut, you won't have any problem from me."

The man did nothing but glare.

"If you give me any shit," Deli spoke slower, in order for her words to sink in. "You are going to have a very bad day. Do you understand me?"

The man continued glaring.

"I'll take that as a yes," she said. "Don't say I didn't warn you."

Deli shifted her weight around so that she could move quick then she sat back. The man kept his mouth shut for the length of time it took him to inhale. Then he opened it and began to bellow.

"What are you gonna do? You signed a contract! You ain't going nowhere!" He tried to hit her by swinging his head around, but Deli still had his arms pinned down, and he did little more than give himself a sore neck.

Carl stepped in to help. He contemplated where exactly he might hold on to her as the man's shouting built to a crescendo. Deli silenced it by rearing her head back and delivering a great thwacking blow to his forehead. The screaming stopped abruptly and the man's feet went limp.

"Oh thank *God*," said Deli. "I've had just about enough of that guy." She stood up (still half-naked) and looked at Carl. "What took you so long?"

She grinned at him. Carl opened and closed his mouth a few times, but no sound came out. He was having a hard time focusing.

"What's, uh, what's going on?"

"This here"—Deli pointed to the unconscious man—"is the captain of the *Marty-Lu*. He was trying to woo me with his manly eyebrows. I was trying not to kill him. What did it look like I was doing, *boning* him?"

Carl swallowed hard against the way Deli pronounced *boning*. He never heard a word with so many connotations before.

"What? No, of course not." If she was going to be nonchalant about it, he would, too. "It was, well...he didn't, um, do that to you, did he?"

"What, strip me half-naked and tie me to a couch? What would you do if he had, Carl, punch him? I already did that." She looked directly at Carl. It took courage, but he didn't look away.

He wanted to say something indignant because that's how he felt when he found them struggling on the floor, but she stood in front of him wearing purple striped underpants and a matching bra, which had a tiny bow that moved up and down with her breath. If he said something stupid right now, he might have to curl up into a ball and die. He chose his words carefully.

"Yes, I would have punched him." *Right in the frickin' nose*, he added—but he didn't say that part out loud.

"Well...thank you, Carl. That's very...chivalrous of you." She cleared her throat. "Now, would you mind helping me get the captain on the couch so I can tie him up?"

Carl jumped to do her bidding because it gave him something besides tiny bows on which to focus. He grabbed the captain by the waist and threw him like a sack of hammers onto the couch. Deli's eyes bulged out slightly, but not so far that anyone would notice.

"Do you have something to tie him up *with*?"

Deli stuck one hand in her bra and rummaged around. Carl took a moment to study the light fixture on the ceiling. It was very ugly.

From the jersey-knit nether regions of her underwire, Deli produced a minuscule silver key. She used it to unlock the handcuffs still attached to her wrist and handed them over to Carl.

"You know how these work," she said and handed him the cuffs with a sly grin.

Carl blinked. He heard the roll and crack of drawers being opened and slammed shut as he zipped the captain's wrists together.

The captain fluttered back to consciousness. He opened his mouth to scream, but at the same moment, Deli slithered under Carl's arm and popped something orange into his mouth. The captain gagged instead.

"Hold his head up for me?" she said to Carl in a chipper, business-like manner.

Carl grabbed the back of the captain's head and hoisted it into the air. He watched as Deli fiddled with a strap on the orange thing and realized it was a ball-gag. Where did she find *that*?

She fastened the gag and moved to the other end of the couch, drawing a length of silk cord out of nowhere.

"Where did you...? You know what? Never mind."

"Hold his feet for me?"

Carl held the captain's feet steady and tried to concentrate somewhere besides the omnipresent bow. It was so tiny, how could it be everywhere he looked?

"If you haven't already guessed," Deli said, kneeling down to bind the captain's ankles together with the cord, "this is a floating whorehouse. This here is the number one pimp."

She gave Carl a disgusted look, finished with the ankle truss, and stood up. The captain was helpless to do anything, although his eyebrows looked ready to attack. Deli leaned over, just out of reach, and spoke slowly. "Sorry, Captain, I don't mean to leave you in such a *bind*. Get it? *A bind*? Ah, I crack myself up."

The captain sat up, as far and as menacingly as he could, which was not far and not that menacing, unless you counted the eyebrows. Apparently, he did not enjoy the joke.

"Oh, Honey-Bear!" Deli said and gave him her plastic smile. "I hate seeing you like this, all cozied up on the couch. I should have shown you what I do for a living. I think you would have found me very *thorough*."

Carl didn't need to see the malicious glint in Deli's eyes to know she would have beaten him senseless.

THE MARTY-LU

DELI DRAPED A BLANKET OVER THE CAPTAIN, which made him somewhat easier to take. He was still grunting and thrashing about, but at least they weren't being menaced by his eyebrows any longer.

"Carl! I'm glad you're here. Have I said that already?"

Carl looked pleased. He did not look directly at Deli, but he looked pleased all the same.

"Happy to help," he said. "But we should be going soon, if that's okay with you."

Deli looked at him sideways. "Can you at least help me find my pants?"

Carl snapped his head up.

"Of course! I'm very sorry. I should have guessed you would want to find your pants. Everybody needs pants." He stepped to the other side of the room and started rummaging through drawers.

Deli watched as he opened and closed the same handful of drawers three times in succession. There was a full mirror on the wall next to him and she saw his glassy eyes search without seeing. Then she looked at herself and noticed with relief that she had at least managed to match her bra to her undies today. If worse came to worst, maybe she could pretend it was a bathing suit.

Carl searched the same trio of drawers once again, still babbling about how people tend to want to wear clothes, pants most especially. Deli figured he was down for the count and searched the rest of the room on her own. She found her clothes shoved into a storage locker under the bed.

* * *

Deli stood there, half-clothed, arguing with the fly on her jeans. Carl didn't want to watch, but his eyes had stopped listening to his brain ages ago and refused to move. He closed his eyelids enough to blur the scene, but he could still sort of see her dressing. The bubbling, itchy feeling inside his ears almost made him sneeze.

Over on the couch, the captain was not making this any easier. Carl usually opposed violence but watching the blurry form of Delilah Pelham wiggle into her rumpled t-shirt made him want to march over to the couch and kick that guy, *repeatedly*.

"Dammit all to hell! Where are my high-tops?" Deli said. Her sudden expletive took Carl surprise. His hand shot up to his ear and began to rub at it with a knuckle.

High-tops. They were red. A vision of empty red sneakers shoved into a garbage can floated up from the recesses of his overwrought brain and Carl followed it back down to earth.

"I found them!" he said. "I had them! Where did I have them?" He looked around the room, trying to remember where he'd put her shoes.

"I think I shoved them in my bag!" He found his bag just inside the door. It must have dropped during all the yelling. When he picked it up, Deli's shoes flopped out.

"My high-tops!" she squealed. She ran over and grabbed them off the floor. She looked up at Carl as if he'd just saved a puppy from certain death.

"Thank you!" She threw her arms out and hugged him, reaching up on her tiptoes to give him a kiss on the cheek. Because of her height (or rather, lack thereof) she ended up kissing him on the neck instead. Carl stopped breathing for a while.

"I'll just, uh, go see if the coast is clear, shall I?" he said. He cleared his throat and stepped across the cabin in two long strides to a small door near the closet. He opened it and disappeared.

* * *

The captain still thrashed around on the couch, so Deli sat on the bed to lace up her shoes. She wondered how long it would take Carl to notice he was in the bathroom.

"That is the bathroom," Carl said, stepping back into the cabin. "In case you need it."

"Thanks," Deli said. "Can we go now?"

Carl looked relieved at the very idea and was across the room, peeking out the door, before Deli had her second shoe on.

"The hallway is clear," he said quietly.

"Gangway," said Deli.

"What?"

"Never mind. Let's go."

They left the door locked with the Do Not Disturb sign on the handle. Deli thought a little peace and quiet might be good for the captain right now.

GANGWAY

"WHERE ARE YOU GOING?" Deli hissed at him as he headed down the gangway toward the deck.

"The bridge," said Carl. He motioned with one hand for her to follow. Deli stopped short and put her hands on her hips.

"But what about Paul?"

"I don't think he's on the ship."

"That's what I'm saying." She gave him a look that said he was kind of being stupid. "Let's get the hell out of here while we can." She smiled and nodded encouragingly.

"I want to check something out first."

"I don't think these people would take kindly to finding uninvited strangers on their boat."

Carl just stared at her.

"Fine. But you better know what you are doing."

Carl *did not* know what he was doing, which was specifically why he wanted to look around. The bridge might hold some clue as to what was going on. He couldn't quite remember everything back there with the captain, and when he shut his eyes to try, tiny green bows dominated his thoughts. But he thought they might have a solid ten minutes if they got going now.

* * *

They snuck down the gangway, which was silly because there was no one around to sneak away from. After a few yards of tiptoeing, Deli stopped. She stood straight and faced Carl, hunched over and looking suspicious.

"Why are we sneaking?" she said.

"Because we don't want to get caught," Carl said as he heel-toed to the door at the end of the hall. It looked promising.

"Carl, stop," Deli said.

Carl stopped.

"There's no one here to find us," she said.

Carl stood up straight. He looked around to confirm this. There was no one in sight. He breathed deep and relaxed his shoulders. Then he walked confidently over to the door at the end of the gangway. It was a pocket door, designed to slide open. Instead of a window, it had an ill-fitting piece of plywood, soggy and green around the edges. Carl grabbed the latch and slid it open with authority.

The man standing on the other side of the door was not as tall as Carl. He was, however, *wider* than Carl and twice as angry looking. In his right hand he held a gun, shiny with murderous intent. His left hand hung in the air, amazed that the door had opened by itself. He looked from his hand up to Carl. Carl smiled brightly.

"Lovely day, isn't it?" he said. Then he punched him. Or at least he tried to punch him. Later on, Deli would give it an A for effort but a D minus in execution. Unless, of course, he'd actually been aiming for the wall. In that case, he scored full marks.

Before the burly man could punch back, Deli stepped underneath Carl's outstretched (and very sore) arm and stood up, forcing Carl backward. To solidify her intention, she pushed him out of the way with a short bump from her backside. Carl got the hint and stepped aside to nurse his hand.

"Hey!" Deli matched Carl's chipper attitude. The man's scowl dismissed Carl as incompetent and adjusted itself lower, toward Deli. He grunted once.

"Are you Lenny?"

Recognition sparked a slight reaction, and he grunted once more.

"I said, are *you* Lenny?"

"What da fuck are you doing out here?"

"So, you *are* Lenny?"

"Fuck you, bitch, get back to your room. You ain't supposed to be out here." His sausage arms moved slowly, but carried the gun with them. He aimed it at her.

"That's not very nice," Deli said. "If I'm supposed to be prostituting myself for you, the least you can do is be nice to me."

"I ain't gonna argue with no whore," Lenny said, somehow making the word *whore* sound even more degrading than normal. "You gonna do what I say or I'monna teach you a lesson you won't soon forget."

"No, I ain't," Deli said, mimicking his accent. She scowled and stuck out her chin in defiance, giving him a target on which to focus, while distracting him from her feet.

Behind her in the gangway, Carl sucked on a bruised knuckle. He stood back like she told him to, but the words being thrown around were upsetting. He was just about to say something when, to his absolute horror, Lenny lowered his weapon and smacked Deli hard in the face. Reflexively, he jumped at the man, intent on punching him in the nose this time, only to be kicked backward by a tiny red high-top that came out of nowhere.

"Back!" she screamed.

Carl stayed back. He watched as Delilah Pelham turned into a whirling dervish of fists and feet. It reminded him of the Tasmanian Devil from the old cartoons, although he had to admit, she made more lady-like noises.

Lenny did not get up afterward. Deli stepped lightly over him and looked at Carl.

"Sorry I hit you. I didn't want you to step into the kill zone." Carl didn't know entirely what a kill zone was, but he had a good idea and he wasn't about to question her strategy.

"No worries," he said. He shook his fist out behind his back so Deli would not see.

"Give me your hand."

"It's okay." He stepped over the Lenny-heap while surreptitiously trying to check if he was still breathing.

"No, it's not."

She grabbed Carl by the arm to stop him then turned him around to face her. It took both of her hands to hold his one injured paw, but she pored over it, looking for signs of a fracture. Her delicate fingers tickled his arm and Carl hung his head, feeling awkward.

"You're not a good liar," she said.

Carl hung his head lower. She continued to manipulate his hand, bending each finger lightly. He kept silent. He didn't want to say anything to break her concentration.

"Well, nothing is broken. It's going to be sore for the next few days, though. And it will probably bruise up pretty good." She tilted her head sideways to look up into Carl's eyes but he hung his head lower.

"Hey," she said. "You're going to live. It's not the end of the world." She didn't let go of his hand immediately.

"I'm sorry for jumping in. I just…well, I couldn't just stand there and watch him hit you." He squeezed his eyes shut and rubbed his forehead with his good hand.

"Carl, I set him up to hit me. It was the quickest way to distract him." Still Carl could not look up.

"I know how to take a punch, Carl. I do it for a living."

"I *know* you can. But knowing something is different than seeing it happen right in front of you. He *hit* you, Deli. In the *face*. On *purpose*." Carl hung his head again. He would never forget the last ten minutes.

"Yes, but then I hit him back. Like, *seventeen times*." She turned slightly so Carl could see the Lenny-heap, now snoring softly behind them. "Did you miss that part? Because that part was awesome."

That did it. He looked up at Deli. She did a fake little karate kick and Carl couldn't help but laugh.

"Yes, his ass appears to have been well and truly kicked," he said.

Deli beamed at him. Moonlight sparkling off the water made her hair shine. Her bottom lip was a mess. Blood dripped from where Lenny split it open. Carl wanted to wipe it away, but he didn't. Deli probably wouldn't want someone wiping her face like a child.

"And *you*." She tapped him on the chest. "Certainly showed that wall who's boss."

"Well," said Carl, shaking his hair back in mock triumph. "It was getting kinda uppity."

Deli laughed so hard she snorted.

THE PILOTHOUSE

DELI WASN'T EVEN SURE she wanted to find Paul anymore. She'd already been semi-arrested, mostly kidnapped, and definitely manhandled. He may be her brother, but that didn't stop him from being a dickish liability.

"So, what are we looking for?" she asked.

Carl shrugged. "I have no idea. Maybe we can find out where this ship is headed. I mean, it's worth a try, don't you think?"

"Okay, Einstein. But I go first. In case anyone else needs an emergency ass-kicking."

"You got it, boss." He gave Deli a small salute with his wounded hand.

"Shut up and move it."

They slunk up the stairs and almost made it to the pilothouse without incident. As they approached, the door slid open and out stepped a woman done up in military style. She wore an olive green dress with brass buttons that flashed in the moonlight. Her black hair was done up in a matronly bun and topped with a narrow hat that defied logic. When she turned her back to close the door, Deli used the opportunity to push Carl out of sight before the woman saw him.

"What are you doing here?" She did not sound amused.

"Trying to find some help! I don't want to cause any alarm, but the captain has passed out in my, um…bedchamber."

"What have you done to him?"

"I didn't do anything. He's had too much to drink, if I'm any judge."

Carl found the steadiness of Deli's voice amazing. He could never pull off such an outrageous lie in front of those brass buttons.

"Viktor is drunk?" The woman's voice dripped with disgust. "What am I saying? Of course he is drunk. You"—she pointed at Deli—"come with me. This area is restricted."

"Right you are!" Deli said and waited for the woman to cross in front of her before following.

Carl heard them coming his direction and ducked farther into the shadows. The woman passed his hiding spot and marched downstairs in a bureaucratic huff. Deli rolled along behind. She walked with a confidence that Carl appreciated, even if he didn't share it. As she passed, she kept one hand behind her back in a sly okay sign.

He watched her go. It wasn't easy, but she'd given him an opening, and he wasn't going to squander it. She could look after herself. He hurried to the door.

A square table stood against the back wall of the pilothouse. Leather stools blocked two of its three sides. On it sat a mess of papers and maps. Carl made a beeline toward it.

The maps were of Victoria Harbour and surrounding seas—*that* much he could figure out. Everything else was in a jumble of Chinese symbols. Carl couldn't tell what was important and what was trivial, so he swept everything into a stack and shoved it in his bag. They could sort out the important bits later. He poked around for another twenty seconds but found nothing of interest.

He had one thing to do before leaving. It would take about a minute and a half, but it was worth the risk. He found the ship's guidance system and set to work.

Carl was in the middle of explaining to the ship's computer that north was south and west was east when he heard footsteps. The bridge had no real hiding place unless he scrunched down below the map table, in between the leather stools, so he did just that. He had to bend over in addition to scrunching down to keep his hair from sticking out. He pulled his elbows in and hoped for the best.

The door slid open. Carl tucked his elbows in more and doubled his efforts in the knee department. The shoes clicked around the controls a few times, then left. Carl relaxed long enough to take a breath before going back to making himself as small as possible, just in case.

He stayed like that, crunched into a medium-sized Carl-ball, while he finished convincing the ship's guidance system that true north was

180 degrees away. Technological shenanigans pulled, he hazarded a look out the window.

No one was there. He straightened up his head. After seven seconds of empty deck, Carl decided to make a break for it. He stood up and walked out of the pilothouse with the gait of a man who knows what he has done and is afraid someone else might know too.

The punch came out of nowhere, followed closely by an awful crunching sound that felt exactly like his nose breaking. Then the pain hit him. The crunching sound had indeed been his nose. Carl fell to his knees and grabbed his face.

"Who are you?"

"Carl," he said.

"Who do you work for?"

When he didn't answer right away, a searing pain shot through his knee, exactly as if someone kicked him with a pointy shoe.

"I dode know whad you mead," Carl said around his dripping nose. The view in front of him was coming into sharper focus, though he wished it wouldn't. The military woman was huffing and spitting like a rabid badger. She scared the crap out of him.

"Do not lie to me. You work for that Vory bastard! *I will kill him myself!*"

The woman grew more and more agitated as she screamed. Carl edged backward as much as possible but she came at him anyway. She brought her arm up to strike. He flinched, curled into another ball, and prepared to get the stuffing beat out of him.

It never happened.

Instead, she flew backward with a ripping sound as Deli yanked the improbable little hat from her head. Carl had barely enough time to marvel at the strength of Deli's attack before the two women turned into a jumble of fists and *hai-ya*s.

He didn't see much of it on account of them moving too fast, but in the end, Deli stood panting and victorious. She leaned down and grabbed the unconscious woman's arms, dragging her to the shadows behind the pilothouse. Carl heard a metallic zipping noise followed by the quiet din of water sloshing against the hull. Then Deli was beside him again, still panting.

"Carl. Look." She pointed out across the deck. Carl followed her finger to a ship cutting its way across the water. At the prow stood a heavyset man, his moonlit silhouette bristling with guns and bravado.

It was Johnny.

* * *

Deli helped Carl to his feet while he held one hand protectively over his nose. They stumbled down the stairs as fast as gravity would allow. The ship was still far enough away that Johnny couldn't shoot them, *yet*. But every second brought him and his homicidal dreams closer. Deli could already smell cheap aftershave.

"Carl," Deli said at the bottom stair. "How the hell do we get out of here?"

"Jin," he said, wiping the blood from his nose and pointing to the spot where the harpoon of justice pierced the hull of the ship. It was not far from the stairs.

"What?" she said. Deli understood the mumblings of broken-nose victims better than most, but it sounded to her like Carl just said *Jen*.

"Jin," he said, louder this time, and pointed with more enthusiasm to the harpoon.

"Who the hell is Jen?"

She focused on Carl. A deep red bruise formed on his cheek where he'd taken most of the punch, making his eyes puffy and swollen. Several clumps of his hair had banded together to form tight factions of cowlicks. The two largest ones wavered threateningly at each other in the breeze.

Despite the dissension in his appearance, Carl looked more confident and happy than she'd ever seen him. He took Deli's hand and pulled her to the opposite side of the ship. Below the railing, a boat bobbed in time with the *Marty-Lu*. On the deck stood an older man in an overlarge sweatshirt and no pants that Deli could see. He was smiling and waving.

"Jin," he said, pointing at the man.

"Ni hao!" said Jin.

* * *

Deli shimmied over the railing, then turned back to Carl. She gave him a strange look which he could not interpret, sort of happy and angry at the same time. Then she leaned forward. Carl assumed she was bracing herself against the fall, so he shifted his weight in anticipation of lowering her down.

But she kept leaning, well beyond a suitable distance, and continued looking at him strangely. Carl got the feeling that she wanted him to do something, but he wasn't sure what. He smiled enthusiastically and nodded his head in the direction of Jin and his getaway boat. This time, Deli smiled back.

"Thanks," she said. Her voice was low and intense as if they were sharing a secret. The bubbling sensation returned to Carl's ears. The heat from her skin made his head swim, or maybe that was from the blood loss, he didn't know. They were dangerously close together now.

"I'm glad you're here," Deli said in the same low voice. He watched the perfect line of her lips form the words, and his heart started racing. His self-control couldn't handle any more words from such adorable lips and Carl's willpower buckled under the strain. He bent toward her. A lock of her hair draped itself across her brow, and his free hand reached up to brush it away.

Though he managed to do this smoothly, the movement of his arm caused his overstuffed messenger bag to slide off his back where he had been holding it, and nudge its way between them.

Then it started vibrating.

Deli inhaled deeply and stood up as straight as she could without falling. Carl dropped his hand back to his side and straightened up, too, somewhat grateful now for the convenient position into which his bag had fallen. It still vibrated.

"You're ringing," Deli said.

"Yep," said Carl, but he made no move to answer his phone. "Dat appears to be the cade."

"We should probably get out of here before they start shooting at us or something," Deli added.

"Yep. We chould probably do dat."

And then, because bad guys have no sense of romance whatsoever, a fizzy sound boiled past his shoulder and smacked the water beyond with a flat *thwip*.

"Shit," Deli said. "I was only kidding about that part! Carl, *move your ass*." Carl moved his ass.

He grabbed Deli by both arms and lowered her as far down as he could. She aimed feet at Jin and let go, falling gracefully to the deck. Bullets zipped past without so much as a crack to announce their presence.

"How are you going to get down?" Deli shouted up to him.

"I'm going to jump."

"I don't think that's a good idea, Carl!"

"It'll be fine," he said, but Deli did not look convinced. She rocked back and forth on her heels.

Jin came back and stood at the ready, arms outstretched for Carl to jump into if he needed. Carl hoped he wouldn't need to. He had already stolen the man's boat, he didn't want to break his legs, too.

Another bullet zipped by, ripping a path through the wooden handrail before ricocheting off toward the water. Carl grabbed onto the railing, hoisted himself into the air, and swung his legs over like he was hopping a fence. But instead of landing on the other side, he twisted in midair, allowing his hands enough room to switch places as his legs swept back to a small shelf of deck beyond the railing. He caught the shelf with his toes and hung on.

Then he threw his feet outward and jumped in a controlled arc to the deck. He bent his knees on landing and would have stayed on his feet—but at the last minute, his sore knee gave way. His arms shot out instinctively, and he pushed himself backward. This caused him to sit down hard instead of falling forward on his face. Unfortunately for Carl, his messenger bag had shifted around to his back during his leap, and he sat down with an expensive-sounding crunch

"Wow, that was...astonishing."

"I wad priddy good at gymadtics in junior high," Carl said, bowing his head slightly. "Undil I got doo dall."

*   *   *

From the deck of the *Doris Day*, Jin watched the pair of them and finally understood what the poor *gweilo* meant about the girl. *They would make a handsome couple, though,* he thought, because deep down, Jin was a hopeless romantic.

Then a bullet hit the right windscreen of the upper deck, cracking the glass. Jin jumped to the controls and revved the engine. Romantic or not, he knew what came next. Actually, he'd been rather looking forward to this part.

He threw open the throttle and tore away from the *Marty-Lu*. Once the bullets stopped snaking past them and started hitting their wake, he took his eyes off the controls long enough to find the missing piece of the getaway scene.

Reaching down to the catch-all between the captain's chair and the passenger's seat, he dug out his sunglasses. They were the same style that Tom Cruise wore in that movie with all the fighter jets and the flashy women. Jin loved them more than anything. And even though it was still dark out, he snapped them in place, smiling from bow to stern.

This was turning out to be quite an exciting week.

FRONT LAWN OF
HORSEY HOUSE, SEATTLE
10:45 A.M.

TOESY SNIFFED AT THE AIR and found the flowery thread he needed. It wound around the back of the gigantic building, down a short flight of stairs, to a door. He approached it cautiously, but it was just a door, and a closed one at that. His thumbs, as he so often lamented, were useless against rotating technologies. After a minute, Toesy gave up and went in search of a window.

He found one, nestled within the leafy confines of a gigantic rhododendron. It was small, rectangular and latched shut in its wooden frame. The glass was ancient, making everything in the room behind it all wavy and deformed.

Inside the room, a woman sat on a very messy bed. She was putting on the same kind of see-through sock pants that Deli sometimes wore. Toesy hated when Deli wore those things. Something about the sock pants made her vulnerable to his claws and he wasn't allowed to sit in her lap while she wore them, even if he felt extra cuddly. It was his good fortune that Deli only wore them occasionally. If this was the flowery woman he sought, then he would have to be wary of her sock pants.

Toesy leaned against the window, hoping to push it inward. It did not budge. Inside, the woman finished with her sock pants and left the room. He leaned against the window with more force. It still did not budge.

When the woman did not return after a few minutes, Toesy became worried that she might leave. Instead of panicking, he did the most sensible thing he could think of. He tucked his head down and ran at the window.

The impact cracked a clean diagonal line through the center of the pane. Toesy punched one furious paw through the top pane. It came away smoothly, breaking into two pieces when it hit the carpet. Toesy barely heard it; he doubted if the sock-pants woman did, either.

He punched the second half of the pane in much the same way. It made more noise than the first, but still not enough to draw attention. He sighed, a feral feline snort of air that made several of the smaller, creepier denizens of the rhododendron bush scramble away in fear. Toesy took no notice of them. He wanted Sock Pants to come back. She was not coming back. *Rats.*

He squirmed most of his bulk through the now empty window frame and aimed himself at the bed, leaping as well as he could through the broken window. Eventually, gravity took over and he landed with a thud and a *tink* on the carpet. The little voice told him not to worry about the lacerations to his exterior, it would take care of them. Toesy began to purr.

He stood up and shook himself to get rid of the glass shards but his belly and back fur were thick with a grisly paste of blood and dirt. The glass stayed stuck.

Completely unaware that he was now covered in blood, mud *and* razor sharp pointy bits, Toesy trotted off to find Sock Pants.

THE DUNGEON

HEATHER WAS UP AND DRESSED within minutes of Sacha leaving. There was no one in the apartment, but she tiptoed anyway. It was strange being there.

She sat down at a computer, typed a few key phrases and slipped a thumb drive into the socket. It sat home with a click. Transferring the files would be easy, but because of Carl's stupid double blind firewall she had to do everything twice. It would take almost five minutes to erase her tracks. She sat down at the command center and went to work.

There were notes and scribbles everywhere, most having to do with the oceanic signals. She shook her head and continued typing in commands until the computer beeped a request back.

Please enter password for access to Sector Nine.

She smiled and punched in a string of numbers and letters. The computer thought for a brief second and then beeped.

Password Incorrect. Please try again.

She punched in the letters and numbers again, exactly how they were coded. The computer thought for another second before beeping again.

Password Incorrect. Please try again.

She frowned and typed in another string of characters.

Password Incorrect. Your account has been locked. Please contact Administrator.

Heather Drury, Carl's ex-girlfriend and current love interest of the idiot-brained Sacha, swore loudly and punched at the keyboard. The screen blinked once, then displayed a complicated table of numbers. She skimmed down the list and swore again, louder this time. The password, which had taken her three weeks to get, had been changed yesterday.

Dammit!

She extracted the thumb drive from the computer and threw it into her purse, slipping into her shoes in one graceful movement. As she bent to pick up her coat, something in her peripheral vision moved. She turned to get a better look.

In the doorway to Sacha's bedroom sat the ugliest cat Heather had ever seen. How could people live with those things in their homes? It easily weighed fifty pounds. And it was a mess. I looked like it rolled in some sort of goopy brown paint. The paint had all sorts of stuff stuck in it like lint and dirt and, for some reason, glitter. The more she looked at it, the closer she came to gagging.

Heather put her hands up in the air, afraid to touch anything that had come in contact with such a repulsive animal.

"Shoo!" She waved her arms at it and made get-away-from-me noises. "Get out of here!"

The monster did not budge. Instead, it regarded her with its intelligent but wary eyes. She kicked a high-heeled foot and repeated herself.

"Shoo, you disgusting thing! Get out of here right now!"

It was still disinclined to move.

Heather was not afraid of cats, especially not this one. All the same, she decided to leave immediately. She grabbed her coat from the chair where she left it and started walking toward the front door.

This was apparently the right thing to do since the monster started to make low chittering noises and followed her to the entryway. She did *not* run the last ten feet. She may have walked very fast, though.

Heather turned to the creature, ready to kick it if necessary. She hoped it wouldn't be necessary; these shoes had cost her six hundred dollars. If that cat got so much as a speck of mud on them, she would —

Mrrrrreeeeoooooowwwwwww.

It screamed at her! Heather did not stick around to find out why. She slipped through the door as fast as her pencil skirt would allow and slammed it behind her. Then she shimmied up the stairs sideways and clopped out into the sunshine of the day.

After a few hundred feet, she slowed her pace to a canter, which was not easy to do in five-inch platform heels. She could have worn tennis shoes and sweatpants last night and Sacha would never have noticed. But she wanted to make sure he'd be blindsided, so went with the traditional sexy — red lipstick, high heels, and a tight skirt. At least it worked fast.

Just like Sacha, she thought, and rolled her eyes.

And all for nothing because someone changed the fucking password. *Damn it all to hell.*

Now she was going to have to find Sacha and get the new password from him. And of course he still regretted giving her the *last* password, so a blow job probably wasn't going to persuade him this time. She needed something more *convincing.*

Thankfully, she still had just such a thing in the glove box of her car.

*   *   *

As the door slammed shut in his face, Toesy thought again how handy it would be if his thumbs worked. The bean, not knowing any better, checked the muscle capacity for the sixth and seventh digits on each arm and set to work bringing them online. For now, though, Toesy was forced to run back through the bedroom and jump precariously out the window. He shot across the yard to the front door and picked up the flower scent immediately.

Why had Sock Pants shooed him? He thought females were supposed to be nice. He was confident that she would help him if only she would listen.

The trail grew stronger and Toesy heard the rhythmic noise of clicky shoes on pavement. Ahead of him, he spotted Sock Pants hurrying across the street to a parking lot. Toesy had to act quickly. The bean upgraded adenosine triphosphate production to red alert.

DELI'S APARTMENT BUILDING

THE DOOR OPENED TO A CLOUD of green smoke. The kid stood in the doorway wearing a pair of cutoffs and the nappiest dreadlocks Sacha had ever seen. His eyes were exceedingly bloodshot.

"Hey," said Sacha. "Sorry to bother you. Are you the super for this building?"

"Gill out now, mon," said the kid. "Aye and aye Clarence, his brotha. What can aye and aye do for da big mon?"

It took Sacha a second to decipher what he'd said.

"Uh, Delilah Pelham is out of town for a few days, and she wanted me to look after her cat. But she left before giving me the key. Did she leave a spare key with you?"

He wasn't sure if the kid heard. His eyes were almost closed, and he was bobbing his head up and down slowly. Sacha was trying to figure out how to wake him when suddenly Clarence's eyes opened wide and he shouted. *"Oh ya, mon!"*

Sacha jumped. He was still nervy from this morning's activities. Clarence didn't notice. His eyelids slid back down.

"Gill school aye and aye bout dat," he mumbled and walked away, leaving the door open behind him. Sacha didn't know if he was supposed to follow, so he stayed put.

"Um..."

"Aye and Aye tink Gill left a note here somewhere. Aye and aye saw it dis beautiful marn did we now?" Clarence hollered from somewhere in the apartment.

Sacha interpreted this as "Please wait, I must go find something," so he waited patiently at the front door, counting off by hippopotamus.

Twenty-eight hippopotamus...

Twenty-nine hippopotamus…

He got to fifty-two hippopotamus before Clarence wandered back, singing something in Bob Marley cadence. When he saw Sacha, his eyes opened almost all the way in shock.

"Oh sheet, mon!" he said. "You be waitin' and I be late on da beat!"

"Look, all I need to do is go in and feed the cat. I won't be long; you can come in with me if you like."

"I don't find dat note, mon," Clarence said, rubbing a hand over his grubby dreads. Sacha didn't get angry. In his experience, arguing with a poseur Rasta sporting blond dreadlocks was a complete waste of time. Plus, he was still trying to figure out what language the kid spoke.

They stood in uncomfortable introspection for a few seconds until the kid shrugged, turned and grabbed a gigantic set of keys off the table behind him.

"Aye and aye say fook it. Less go. Aye and aye let you eeen."

Sacha smiled and nodded. After a few hand motions, he eventually understood that he was supposed to follow the kid up the stairs.

U-PARK PARKING LOT

HEATHER CUT THROUGH THE PARK to the U-Park lot across the street. She hated to see her car sitting out like that where anyone could touch it. There was no telling what the people in this neighborhood would do to a car. She scanned the side for dents as she unlocked the doors by remote.

Usually, she would smooth her coat out over the passenger seat before getting in, but she caught a glimpse of a suspicious feline-shaped shadow lurking behind her so she threw the coat in the backseat with complete disregard for wrinkles. She was still not afraid of cats. But that one was dirty and ugly, so it would probably be best if she just waited in her car until it went away.

She held her purse close to her lap, faced outward and fell back, neatly tucking herself into the driver's seat without having to hike up her skirt. She drew her legs into the car, shut the door and locked it. Then she double-checked that it was locked.

Safe in her car, Heather forced herself to relax in order to catch her breath. The visor was down so she checked her reflection in the mirror. *Not too bad,* she thought, snapping it back in place. She was leaning over the passenger seat to unlock the glove compartment when something landed on the roof with enough force to rock the car on its axles.

Heather did not scream. She reminded herself that she was not afraid of cats—especially not overweight, mucked-up, sorta-familiar-looking ones. She had to remind herself two or three more times of this as she looked at the roof of her car. It bowed inward.

* * *

Sock Pants seemed a little upset by something, so Toesy made sure to perk up his whiskers in goodwill. He didn't want to frighten her away a second time. He tried to think of a way to introduce himself without her screaming but settled on the just-get-it-done method. He hopped lightly from the roof of the car to the hood.

She was inside the car, staring at the roof. As soon as the car stopped rocking again, Sock Pants lowered her gaze to the hood. When she got to the part that was mostly Toesy, she went all white and opened her mouth. Toesy noted that no sound came out, so he tried to say hello.

That was when Sock Pants started screaming.

* * *

The thing was sitting on the hood of her car, growling at her. If she were dreaming, there would be probably be more flying monkeys and definitely a few talking appliances, but she didn't see any of these things. All she saw was a pissed-off, glass-encrusted demon cat spitting and hissing at her.

She screamed some more to make up for lost time. Then she panicked.

Jamming the keys into the ignition, Heather dropped the car into reverse. She tried shaking the cat off the hood by driving a few inches and slamming on the brakes as she backed out of the parking lot. The cat swayed with the car but otherwise held fast. She couldn't be sure, but it looked like there were small holes in the hood where its claws dug in.

She swallowed back bile and drove forward, zigzagging her beloved Volkswagen through the parking lot. It wasn't a big lot, and the space between cars was kind of tight. If she hit a few cars in her absolute terror, she never noticed.

Still the cat-thing held on, so Heather tried one last tactic. She hit the gas and raced toward the opening of the lot, slamming on the brakes at the last minute.

This had the intended effect of launching the demon cat into a wide arc across the street. Unfortunately, it also caused a landscaping truck, which had been trying to merge into traffic from the previous block, to veer wildly out of the way.

The truck turned sharply into the oncoming traffic then over-corrected too soon. This caused the ass end of the truck to slam into her front bumper before hurtling off down the street in a shower of rakes and hoses. The traitorous light at the intersection turned green just in time for the truck to zip through and disappear down the road.

Heather took a minute to shake the birds from her head and come back to reality. She wasn't hurt, but the airbag had deployed, and there was probably one fuck-all of a dent on the front end. She contemplated the damage to her car and seethed.

Toesy hit the side of the building at an incredibly high rate of speed, but was able to tuck his head down before impact. He bounced when he hit the ground and managed to whip his hind legs around so fast that he was standing upright and in attack mode when he landed for a second time. The little voice congratulated him on the fabulous landing and gave him a nine-point-eight for making it stick. Toesy was pleased.

He shook himself off in a shower of tinkles. The glass spikes matted into his fur had shattered into smaller shards as he bounced, which also stuck to the lumpy mess of his blood-soaked fur. The overall effect made him sparkle in the mid-morning sunlight like a scruffy, vampire-themed disco ball.

Sock Pants didn't move much, she just sat in the broken car and yelled. Toesy felt that her anger was well executed. He liked the way she punched the dash. It showed the proper level of commitment. Also, he had never seen a car balloon before; they were very surprising.

He waited for the woman to see him, yet she did not. She appeared to be looking for something. Toesy thought she might be ignoring him on purpose, which was rather rude.

A minute turned into two and the Great Man was still in mortal danger. Toesy decided to take the matter into his own paws and walked over. The car door had popped open in the accident and he got close enough to stick his nose inside so he did. The woman shrieked.

"Stay away from me, whatever you are!" Sock Pants kicked a foot out at him, grazing his spikey exterior.

"Ouch!"

Toesy marveled at Sock Pants' dedication to being loud. He wouldn't have guessed it from her diminutive stature.

Perhaps she is part Siamese, he thought and moved closer to see if he could smell any Siamese on her.

"Get away!" She flailed a heavy looking bag at him.

Toesy backed up. She certainly had a Siamese demeanor. Shakily, she stood up, holding her handbag out threateningly in front of her. She brushed herself off with her free hand and wobbled forward on her heels, which were now quite scuffed.

"Shoo, you monster!"

Toesy shooed backward about a foot, giving Sock Pants room to scoot around him. She left her car where it was and started walking. As she did so, an eerie calm came over her. She moved steadily toward Deli's apartment building without distraction, growing cooler and more resolved with each step. She must be going to help.

But her resolve had a familiar feeling to it that made Toesy's whiskers twitch. He could not think why that should be. He watched her go and wondered where he had seen such stillness before.

It would come to him.

DELI'S APARTMENT BUILDING

CLARENCE SAID SOMETHING TO HIM on the first landing but Sacha didn't understand a word of it. He repeated himself on the second stairway.

"Aye and aye say, dis you lady, mon?"

"Is Deli my girlfriend, do you mean?" The kid nodded in time with the bobbing and the stair climbing. Say what you will, he had rhythm.

"No, she's not my girlfriend," Sacha said wearily. "She's my friend's girlfriend."

Either the kid didn't hear him, or he was too stoned to care. Hell, he probably forgot Sacha was even following him, he was so engrossed in the internal beat he had going. But Sacha needn't have worried. Clarence crested the last flight of stairs and headed down the hall. Sacha stumbled over the last stair and hopped down the hall after him.

The door lock was sticky from a shoddy re-key job. Clarence jiggled the lock a few times and finally got it working with the master key.

"Dem cat, him no bite, ya, mon?" he asked as he opened the door.

"Did you just ask me if Deli's cat bites?"

"Ya, mon," said Clarence. His head stopped moving as he waited for the answer.

"Nope," Sacha said, not at all sure.

Clarence motioned for Sacha to go in first. Sacha looked at him closely as he walked past and saw the bloodshot eyes of a twenty-something stoner, scared to death of cats. He laughed silently at that. Who would be afraid of a cat?

The door swung open. Sacha got as far as the bathroom door before he felt it. Something was wrong. He walked to the middle of the living room and gaped.

Deli Pelham owned the ugliest couch in the world. But that wasn't half as worrisome as the blood stains now covering it.

In the twenty seconds that it took for them to realize something terrible had happened, Clarence magically transformed from peacenik to punk-ass. He paced back and forth, tromping all over the bloody floor.

"*What the fuck, man? Who the hell is this chick? Is she dead?*" Clarence's voice climbed an octave in fright. Sacha found himself missing the Poseur-Rasta by comparison. At least that guy was chill.

"Calm *down*, Clarence." He gave the kid a gentle push toward the door. "Go downstairs and call the police."

Clarence turned immediately, jittering with fear. But as he walked away, Sacha watched his shoulders relaxed.

"Don't go down there and smoke pot, you twit! Call the police *first*."

Clarence's shoulders tightened again as he stepped into the hallway. Sacha let him go without another word. There were cords on the floor but no computers anywhere. Broken glass twinkled on the carpet, but there wasn't enough of it to make sense. Also, the apartment was suspiciously lacking in any sort of dead or dying Jake. Sacha had no idea what was going on, so he did the first thing that came to mind. He called Carl.

APT. 2D

CLARENCE WASN'T BORN YESTERDAY. He knew enough to call the police and then get the hell out. He didn't want nothing to do with no dead bodies, even if they were the bodies of dead hot chicks.

Wait, did that even make sense?

Screw it. He had to go.

The last thing he needed was for the police to show up at Gill's apartment. If Gill's little secret got out, Clarence was going to be up shit creek without a paddle. Gill would never speak to him again, and worse than that, he would probably tell Mom on him. He was always such a pussy about shit like that. *If you don't get a job, Clarence, I'm gonna tell Mom. If you don't stop stealing shit, I'm telling Mom.* Fuck it, he didn't need that bullshit.

Bill and Linda Rogers in 2D were out of town for the week, so Clarence stopped off on the second floor and used the master key to break into their apartment. He went straight to the kitchen, took the phone off the hook and placed the receiver on the counter as he dialed 9-1-1. Then he ran.

If he had chosen any other apartment in the building, things might have turned out differently. But Linda Rogers is superstitious about leaving things plugged in when they go on vacation, *especially* the phone—because you never know who might use it to make a long-distance call.

Bill Rogers loves his wife dearly even though he thinks the phone thing is a little over the top. Still, he always unplugs it for her because *you never know*, do you?

DELI'S APARTMENT

CARL'S PHONE WENT STRAIGHT to voice mail. That was bad. Sacha's anxiety took over, and he found himself pacing the floor, just as Clarence had, only being more careful about it.

This was his fault. If Jake was dead, Carl would never forgive him.

Shit, shit, shit, shit, *shit*.

He searched every spot he could imagine for a clue to Jake's whereabouts. Underneath the coffee table he found several large drifts of cat hair but nothing else. He stuck his arm under the couch. A shoe, a few cat toys, several pens, and *bump*, his hand knocked against something small and heavy. His fingers told him it was a phone. He grabbed onto it and drew it out from beneath the couch. Sacha recognized the trademarked blue and red web pattern on its casing. It was Jake's.

He got the password right after the second try only because it was pizza*girl*, instead of just plain *pizza*. With the recent upsurge in Canadian bacon and pineapple-centric dinners, Sacha should have guessed that sooner.

He opened it and found the most recent block of texts, all to Carl. They talked about code, they talked about Paul, a few of the later ones even talked about Deli. But there was nothing on it to tell him where Jake might be.

This was very bad. Sacha stared at the floor, trying to come up with an idea—something, *anything* that would help him find Jake.

The rug twinkled with tiny shards of glass. There were blood splotches everywhere. Some were cat-paw shaped; others were just drips. Drips here and there and over there and…

Oh.

Sacha followed the concentration of drips through the living room, through the kitchen, and into the bedroom. The spots became more regular near the bedroom. Some of them even smeared into streaks. They led through the room toward an open closet door.

When he got to Deli's closet, Sacha cringed. Inside sat the most gigantic pile of dirty laundry he had ever seen. It was gross and probably stinky, and there were at least three pairs of underwear and a couple of bras that he could find.

Something about her closet made him uneasy. He'd seen lacy underwear a few times before, and he was not so easily frightened at the sight of Deli's. But he couldn't shake the feeling that he was being watched.

He studied the drips of blood on the carpet and followed them halfway up the pile. Then the blood drained from his face and his heart stopped.

He *was* being watched.

Within the heaping pile of dusty jeans and sweaty t-shirts, a set of eyes stared back at him. Sacha stifled a scream as a small laundry-quake erupted. When it was over, Jake sat in front of him, holding an aluminum baseball bat and glaring like a sharpened knife.

Sacha opened his mouth to speak, but before he could, they heard a muffled knock at the door. Both men looked confused.

"Are you expecting someone?" Sacha said.

Jake gave him a one-fingered answer.

"It's her," he wheezed.

"Who?" Sacha said, trying to be coy. He was not convincing.

"That psycho bitch, Heather. Who do you think?"

"Shit. Is the door locked? What do we do?"

"I don't give a rat's ass what you do, just make sure she doesn't find me or I swear to god, Sacha, *I will ruin your life so hard.*"

Sacha was close to panic. "What about the blood?"

Jake responded by grabbing some of the clothes next to him and throwing them in the middle of the room; not very far, because it was hard for him to move, but far enough to give Sacha the right idea.

Sacha ran over to Deli's dresser and pulled open the middle drawer. He tore all the clothes from it and threw them everywhere. Then he pulled open the top drawer and did the same, sprinkling the floor with an even layer of underwear, socks and pajamas.

Another knock, louder this time and Sacha turned to the kitchen. Jake hissed at him. He turned back around.

Phone.

He mouthed the word at Sacha and made threatening gestures with his bat. Sacha looked confused. Jake mouthed it again, shaking the bat with one hand while waggling his other hand, pinky and thumb stretched apart—the universal sign for *give me my goddamn phone, or I will hit you with this goddamn bat.*

Sacha tossed Jake's phone over to the closet as quickly as he could. It landed near a pair of cast-off pajama bottoms. Jake snatched it up and melted back into Deli's laundry.

I'm sorry, Sacha mouthed and high-tailed it to the kitchen.

Another knock, much louder now, and Heather called from outside in the hallway. "Sacha?"

Shit, shit, shit, shit, *shit.*

Instead of answering her, he ran to the living room as quietly as he could and did his best to tidy it. He grabbed the rag rug between the dining table and the kitchen and turned it over so the spatters of red were no longer visible. Then he moved the couch forward a few inches to hide what stains he could before flipping over the couch cushions. If she looked hard enough she would find bloodstains, but on the outside, it looked just like a regular living room.

The floor in front of Deli's room was smeared with bloody paw prints, so Sacha grabbed the blanket from the back of the couch and spread it out like a rug. It looked kind of funny to be a rug, but there wasn't anything else to use, so he went with it. Then he ran to the bathroom, grabbing the soiled hallway rug as the knocking grew more insistent.

Sacha threw that rug into the bathtub as he tried thinking up a plan. He always knew Heather was unbalanced, but he had no idea she would turn homicidal. No wonder Carl ditched her.

He thought all of this from a crouching position behind the bathroom door because he still couldn't remember if he'd locked the front door earlier, and he was terrified that she had a gun.

"Sacha!" Heather called again. "Please open the door!"

A note of fear crept into her voice, but Sacha didn't trust it. The only way she could have found him is if she'd followed him here, or she already knew where the apartment was. Damn his stupid sex drive.

"Please, Sacha! There's a…" She sounded terrified now. "There's a monster out here and it's going to get me if you don't open this damn door!"

Something hit the door hard. The noise scared the crap out of him, almost literally. That gave him an idea. He reached out and closed the bathroom door with a quiet *snick*.

Another thump shook the door. He heard plaster break as the front door flew open and smashed into the opposite wall. Sacha had a very bad feeling about the next thirty minutes of his life.

"Sacha!"

She stood just inside the front door, shaking with rage and fear. Sacha could see her through the keyhole in the bathroom door. He had about five seconds before she found him, so he set to work unbuttoning his pants.

"Sacha, where the hell are you?"

The toilet belched a great rumble of noise as he flushed it. He opened the door, flicked off the light and started buttoning his pants in a comically exaggerated moment.

"Sacha!"

He knew she was there, but he almost pissed himself when she shouted. Thankfully, he managed not to pee in the face of her unbridled wrath, as that would have ruined his alibi *and* his pants. He probably deserved some sort of combat medal for that.

"I've been standing out there for nearly two minutes trying to get your attention! *Why* didn't you answer the door?"

Her platinum hair, usually sprayed and combed into submission, quivered in resignation. Small frizzy tendrils danced around her like a dust cloud. Red lipstick smudged up her right cheek and her clothing definitely looked rumpled. There was even a run in her stockings, if one could believe that. He scrambled to fasten his pants for real now. Suddenly, having an extra layer of protection sounded like a good idea.

"I'm sorry about that. I was…" He nodded toward the bathroom. "I was a little preoccupied."

She refused to understand. Instead, she sat staring at him like an angry mongoose. Her beady eyes bored into him, intent on reading lies. It occurred to Sacha that there was very little human in those eyes. He gestured toward the bathroom, but it did no good.

"I was…in the *bathroom*."

"Oh my God!" Heather said, finally getting it. "That's disgusting, Sacha! I don't want to know about you doing *that*."

"Well, you *asked*," he said quietly. "Are you okay?" Then, because he knew she would hate it, Sacha leaned over to hug her. Heather's shoulders stiffened and she pushed him away.

"*Gross*, Sacha! Did you even wash your hands?" She stood rigid. The look on her face spoke volumes on the topic of how vulgar Sacha was. He did not miss the opportunity.

"Oops! Excuse me…" he said and ducked into the bathroom.

While he washed, Heather stormed into the living room. Sacha gave her enough time to look around for Jake, but not enough time to check out the bedroom. He made an awful racket by dropping Deli's soap dish in the sink, to warn her that he was done.

When he entered the living room, Heather sat primly at the dining table with her purse in her lap. She stared at him without blinking, which was unnerving. He kept himself civil because he still didn't know if she had a gun or not.

"What happened out there? You look a little freaked out."

"Nothing happened," she said far too quickly, then changed her tone. "I dented my car."

"Oh, gosh! Are you okay?" Sacha sounded truly concerned. He crossed to the kitchen and looked around for a glass. He found something suitable next to the sink.

"No, I am *not* okay. I was pulling out of the parking lot and a landscaping truck hit the front end of my car. The bastard was going too fast and he never even stopped! And now my car is *ruined!*"

She pushed out her lower lip. Then she looked directly at Sacha, filled her eyes with tears that would never spill, and gave him the full force of her pout.

"I'm so sorry…" He said, managing to stop himself before he added *honey*. The idea of this woman being anyone's *honey* was as terrible as it was fascinating. Instead, he handed her a jam jar filled with tap water. She took it with bad grace.

"Why don't I call the police? They'll get this straightened out."

"*No!*" Her arms jerked around, making the water in the jar slosh into her lap. She slammed the jar down on the table and stood up to brush it off before it seeped into her skirt.

"Don't! Uh, don't call the police. The guy is long gone. I didn't get his license plate number or anything. I don't want to waste my time filing a police report."

"Don't be silly! Your insurance company will need to see a police report if you want to make a claim."

He turned to Heather as he picked up his phone. She crossed the room in short choppy steps, adjusting her purse strap so that it pulled her blouse tight across her breasts. She stopped right in front of him, sliding her foot between his legs, then stepping closer. Sacha's mind went blank and he stopped dialing. She put her fingers to her lips to shush him, took the phone from his unresisting hand.

"I said I don't want you to call the cops, Sacha." She drew a sexy line down the side of Sacha's neck and along his chest.

"I don't understand. You love that car."

"I do! It's my baby. But right now, I have a bigger problem." Her fingers found their way to his belt and began to investigate.

Over the past two months, Sacha had learned to be wary when she initiated sex. It usually meant she wanted something. He could not imagine what she wanted now.

"I need a little help, baby." She whispered into his ear. "I just need one *teeny, tiny* favor." She licked his earlobe, and his brain scrambled for a moment. When he came back to his senses, he found himself nodding.

"What do you need?"

She grabbed his belt and pulled him closer. "I need the password to Sector Nine."

Sacha relaxed. For once, he didn't have to feel awkward about her requests. He couldn't give her the password even if he wanted to.

"Sorry, I don't have it. Carl changed it before he left and didn't tell me the update."

Heather snaked her hand into his front pocket, sliding it up and down in a rhythmic motion designed to keep his eyes rolled up in his head. It worked. Sacha stopped breathing, scared of what she was going to do next and terrified she might not do anything.

She pulled his cell phone from his pocket and studied it. Then she stepped back and tossed it at him like a bucket of cold water.

"Then I'm gonna need you to call my *lovely* ex and have a little chat."

Sacha tried to catch the phone, but his hands were shaking too much. He ended up knocking it to the floor instead.

"Wh-what for?"

"I *really* need that password, Sacha."

"But you *know* he won't give it to me. He'd never give out a password over an unsecure phone line."

"Just *try*," she said. Her smile stayed encouraging but lost some of its enthusiasm. "I'm sure you can get him to talk."

Sacha sighed. When Carl wanted something safe, it stayed safe. There was no way he was going to give him that password over the phone.

"What do you need it for, anyway?"

Heather stepped back another foot. She dropped her purse from her shoulder and caught it with one hand.

"Never mind what I *need* it for, Sacha, just get it. I don't care how you do it. But if you don't want things to go bad here, you damn well better do as I say."

She gave him a smile that started out sexy and ended with a shiny black gun pointed at the tuft of hair between his eyebrows.

* * *

If he had any energy after all of this is over, Jake was going to monkey-punch that traitorous jackass in the nuts. His strength was returning but more slowly than he'd anticipated. Although the feeling in his arms had come back and his mind was clearer, Jake still couldn't breathe very well. It was a strange sensation. The Elevator *was* working, though. He could feel his brain firing off ideas faster. It was incredible.

He listened intently to the conversation in the other room. Leave it to Sacha to fall for the oldest psycho-bitch trick in the book. Never once in the history of hot ex-girlfriends had one come back to sleep with the dorky roommate because she'd secretly been attracted to him all along. How had that dumbass not seen through that?

Out in the living room, he heard Heather asking Sacha for the password to Sector Nine.

That son of a bitch better keep his yap shut.

If only Jake could get through to him, Carl was going to go ape-shit.

CABIN OF THE *DORIS DAY*, HONG KONG 3:00 A.M.

DELI TRIED BLOTTING THE BLOOD from Carl's shirtfront but gave up after a few feeble swabs. There was just too much of it. She took his face in her hands and concentrated on his nose.

"It's not too bad," she said finally. "It might heal weird if you don't have it reset, though."

"Dat's okay. I can lib wid a crooked node."

"Don't be an idiot, Carl. I can reset it for you. But it's probably gonna hurt." She looked at him sideways. "A *lot*."

Carl blushed, which made his nose bleed more. So far on this trip, Deli had beaten three people into submission while escaping arrest and kidnapping. *Four* people, if the captain counted. Considering he was bound and gagged when she was through, Carl figured he probably did.

Carl, on the other hand, had stolen a boat and punched a wall. And stealing the boat didn't really count because in the end, Jin had taken pity on him. So he stuck his chin defiantly close to Deli and welcomed the chance to prove he wasn't a wimp.

"Dat would be grade!"

Deli raised her eyebrows but gave him no more warnings. Instead she walked over to the galley, checked the refrigerator and a few cupboards for supplies, and returned to Carl in his chair.

"Okay," she said. "First, you should look up."

Carl looked up.

"Stay there for a second."

Carl stayed there for a second. Deli poked at his face a little.

"Okay, now look at me."

Carl looked at her. In the same instant, Deli grabbed the bottom of her shirt and yanked it up, flashing the tiny bow at him again. Carl's eyes glazed over. Deli used the momentary distraction to reach over and crack his nose back into shape.

Carl did not yell, even though it sounded all squelchy and started bleeding again. He blinked back the water in his eyes, took a deep breath, and reached up to feel his realigned nose. When he was satisfied that all was well, he looked back at Deli.

"That's a very interesting diversionary tactic," he said. The blush had almost faded from his cheeks.

"Well, there wasn't any ice, so it was that or nothing,"

"It worked. Thank you."

"You're welcome."

She took his face in her hands again and examined his nose some more. Carl found it easier to shut his eyes when she was so close.

"It'll bleed for a while, but if you shove some tissues up there, it should quit sooner than later." To Carl's relief, she let go of him before he did anything stupid.

She disappeared into the bathroom to wash her hands. Carl became aware of a buzzing noise. It took him a few seconds to recognize that it was his phone. He stood up to get it, but his knee refused to bend properly so he limp-hopped across the cabin.

Carl hadn't had the heart to look at any of the stuff in his bag since he sat on it. Now he fished around inside and found his phone. The screen was cracked badly, but the display behind it still kind of worked. It was currently announcing a call from Sacha. Unfortunately, the screen was no longer touch sensitive, and Carl spent a frustrating five seconds trying to figure out how to connect the call.

"Carl!"

"Hey," Carl said. He held the phone carefully so it wouldn't fall apart. "What can I do for you?"

Deli emerged from the bathroom and questioned him with a look. Carl mouthed, "*Sacha.*" Deli nodded.

"Is everything okay?" said Sacha.

"How do you mean?" In all the running around, Carl had completely forgotten about his previous phone call.

Across the cabin, Deli busied herself in the kitchenette, finding something to drink. Carl watched her in the tantric way the phone has of putting your mind on hold. She had cleaned the blood from her lip, but the part of her chin where Lenny had punched her was turning a deep purple. Her t-shirt had some sort of rust-colored smudge down the front, and he wondered what it was, until it occurred to him that it was probably his blood. Somehow, that didn't seem fair.

"I *said*, did you find what you needed?" Sacha was yelling across the connection. Carl snapped back to the conversation.

"Oh, sorry, Sash, I'm exhausted. Yeah, I got her. Er, *it*. Did you check on Jake?"

"I can't [*beep*]. Did you change it?"

"I'm sorry, Sacha." Carl said, shaking the noise out of his ear. He looked at the shattered screen. Sure enough, his battery was almost dead.

"My phone is dying. I didn't catch that?"

"I said, did you change the password for Sector Nine before you left?"

"Yes, why do you need in there?"

"I don't. Jake [*beep*]."

"So you *did* find Jake?" Carl was happy to hear that. Maybe everything would be okay.

"He needs the password," was all Sacha said.

Carl breathed easier. Last night seemed so far away now. He had really been worried that Jake was in trouble.

"Give me an hour. I'll change it back to [*beep*]."

Sacha did not come back on the line. Carl looked at his phone and shrugged. It was completely dead.

Carl's eyebrows scrunched together as he stared at his phone.

"Everything okay back home?"

"I guess so. Jake needs me to change a password. I need to get connected so I can log in."

"Why don't we look at your loot from the *Marty-Lu* first," Deli said. "Maybe we can figure out what the hell we're doing."

Carl thought this was a good idea, so he dumped the contents of his bag onto the table. Cables and papers spilled out everywhere. Shards of glass from another cracked screen tinkled over them. He disgorged several more tiny gadgets and at least two computers, revealing something that Deli hadn't known until that very moment: Carl had been lugging close to forty pounds of crap around with him this whole time.

"I hope you found something good back there. I would hate to think Johnny shot at us for no reason." Deli's natural flair for sarcasm kicked into high gear.

"I got these." He gathered up the papers and gave them to Deli as though he were handing in homework.

Deli studied the papers and lowered her head slightly. "Carl, I don't want to alarm you but...*these are in Chinese.*"

"I think that's because they're a Chinese company." He nodded slightly but his face remained impassive. Deli was no longer sure if they were joking with each other.

"Yes, but you can't read Chinese...*can* you?"

"No." Carl smiled wide. "But Jin can."

AROUND THE TABLE

AS IT TURNED OUT, Captain Jin Chiu was more than a hopeless romantic. He was also slightly crazy, in an emergency-preparedness type of way. After they lost Johnny and his friends, Jin tucked the *Doris Day* into a bank of early morning mist and radioed someone. Whatever Jin said to them must have caused quite a stir because the answering voice shouted excited commands at them until they pulled into a secluded marina.

Deli's doubts regarding the sanity of their benefactor were confirmed as she watched the complicated handshake he performed with a guard at the dock. There were at least three different finger movements and an elbow bump. It was phenomenal. Then he smiled and gave everybody a thumbs-up. Jin was definitely in control of the situation.

She could see the buildings of Hong Kong shining in the distance, but other than kinda-far-outside-of-town, she had no idea where they were. Deli relaxed at the thought, reasoning that if *she* couldn't find them on a map, then maybe Johnny couldn't, either.

Jin sat cross-legged on the Not-Carl side of the table. Somewhere he'd found a pair of Aviators and insisted on wearing them, even in the dimness of the cabin. He still hadn't put on any pants.

"For buy," he said and pointed to the papers.

"For buy what?" Carl understood more of what Jin was saying, so Deli let him do all the talking. She did a lot of listening.

"Metal parts *bing*."

Carl shook his head. Jin drew a square in the air with his hands. Then he pretended to shiver.

"Bing," he said.

Carl thought about that for a moment before turning back to Jin. "Do you mean ice?" Carl shivered back. Jin gave him a thumbs-up and smiled.

"Yes! Ice, metal parts." He rotating motion with his hands.

"Refrigerator parts?"

"Yes, *refrigerator* parts." Jin gave him another thumbs-up. Deli wondered if his thumb was getting sore.

"Captain Jin," she said, turning to their pantless leader. He grinned wide, enjoying every moment.

"This address." Deli pointed to what she hoped was a street number. "Do you know it?"

Jin turned to Carl for the translation. Carl did the best he could.

"Yes!" Jin said. "Bad place. No good."

He shook his head against the idea and took off on a rant in Chinese. Carl almost stopped him to ask another question when Jin said something familiar.

"I'm sorry," Carl interrupted. "Did you just say *Hang Choy?*"

Jin's glasses looked up at him. "Yes, Hang Choy."

Carl turned to Deli. "I know that name. Where do I know that name?"

Deli shook her head and shrugged.

"Jin, is Hang Choy a food company?" Carl held his bruised hand up to his mouth in the universal sign of *I am eating a sandwich* and pretended to chew. Behind the Aviators, Jin's eyebrows shot up.

"Yes, food company!" he said, giving Carl yet another thumbs-up. This time, Carl returned it. He looked at Deli.

"Your brother spent thirty dollars at Hang Choy Dining the day before he disappeared."

"I thought he went to the Silver Hammer," Deli said.

"It might be the parent company."

"Oh, yeah," Deli said. "That makes more sense. So what do we do about it?"

"Well, we have an address," Carl said. He was sore and hungry and dead tired, but they might be finally getting somewhere.

"You want to go there and check it out?" Deli said.

"No," Jin replied. Both Carl and Deli looked at him. He smiled and shook his head.

"No," he said again. "No go."

"But we haven't got any more leads," he said. "Where else…"

"No go *now*. Sleep! Rest! We go *after*." Jin smiled broadly beneath the sunglasses and shot them a double thumbs-up.

He had a point.

* * *

Jin went topside to talk with the marina attendants, probably about the best ways to barnstorm a warehouse during a full moon.

"It's not like I think those are shorts, dude," Deli called after him as he walked up the stairs. "I know what boxers look like!"

Jin merely looked back and gave her another of his ubiquitous thumbs-up. Deli looked at Carl in disbelief.

"He knows he hasn't got any pants on, right?"

Carl barked out a laugh and winced when the pain hit him.

"I'm pretty sure he doesn't care," he said. He turned to the field of gadgetry in front of him on the table and picked up a cable.

"Jin was right. I need to take a nap. I am *exhausted*." She stretched her arms over her head. Carl kept his eyes on his computer.

"Don't you think you should take a break?"

"I can't," he said. "I told Sacha I'd get this password changed for Jake."

"Carl," she said louder. "When was the last time you slept?"

"I will when I'm done here."

"That's not the question I asked. You're hurt and you haven't slept in *how* long? I was unconscious for at least two hours and I'm *beat*. You have got to be tired."

"Really, I'm not."

Deli yawned at him.

He stared back.

Deli yawned at him again.

He did not yawn back. How was he resisting that? Deli yawned twice more just thinking about it.

"Fine," Deli said. "Have it your way. But just for that, you get the chair."

* * *

The side of the boat opposite the table consisted of a built-in couch that spanned the entire length of the cabin. It was large enough to fit two Delis end to end. Carl pretended not to watch as she shuffled around for blankets and pillows. When she had enough, she made a small nest in the middle.

He booted up his laptop as she took her shoes and socks off, focusing on jotting down notes to give her some privacy. But when she finished her socks and started unbuttoning her pants, Carl's fingers stopped making any sense. They just typed the same eight letters over and over mindlessly, as he glued his eyes to the screen. He did not want to be caught searching in case any tiny bows made an appearance.

She snuggled down into a nest of blankets, fidgeting now and again to get comfortable. After a while, she stopped moving, and Carl risked a glance in her direction. She had cocooned herself inside a moss-colored blanket and all he could see was the soft fringe of her eyelashes, her button nose, and the mesmerizing pucker of her lips.

"Good night, Carl," she said, not opening her eyes. He jumped at the sound of her voice.

"Oh, um… Good night," he said. But that didn't really seem like enough so he added, "Sleep well."

"I will, now that I'm all snuggly. It's too bad you're missing out on all these snugglies," she said with a contented giggle. Then she pulled the blanket up to her nose and didn't talk again.

Carl watched her sleep for a few minutes before forcing himself back to the computer problem. He usually used his phone to link in a satellite connection, but it was beyond dead. Without it, he would have to use the tablet or see if Jin had a connection. Both things were easy enough to do, but his brain kept wandering off toward fluffy pillow clouds and blanket nests. His concentration was shot. The computer problem was over six thousand miles away and as much as he'd like to pretend he wasn't, he was dog-tired.

He grabbed a light blanket and tried to make himself comfortable in the recliner, but after five claustrophobic minutes, he gave up. The only place large enough was the floor. He stripped down to his undershirt and shorts as quickly as possible before wrapping himself in the blanket. Then he stretched out alongside the couch. It felt wonderful to be lying down.

Staring at the wood paneling on the ceiling, Carl began to contemplate what *snugglies* might be. Were they blanket- or pillow-related? How many people were required?

It was some time before he fell asleep.

DELI'S APARTMENT, SEATTLE
11:30 A.M.

"HE SAID HE WOULD CHANGE IT BACK to something. Probably an old password."

"Which one?"

"I don't know. Give me a minute to think about it."

"Think hard," she said and stepped forward. The gun was within inches of his face.

"I can't," Sacha said. "You have a gun in my face."

Heather gave him a sour look that said she didn't think he was trying hard enough and lowered the muzzle several inches.

"Better?"

Sacha didn't think having a gun trained on his testicles was any better than having one aimed at his head, but he was wise enough to keep his mouth shut.

"I can only try two passwords every thirty minutes, or I'll be locked out for four hours."

Heather glared at him. "You aren't going anywhere until I get that password, Sacha, so you better get to work."

IN FRONT OF DELI'S APARTMENT

TOESY FELT QUEER ABOUT THE GREAT MAN. Sock Pants was up there right now, but he couldn't decide if that was good or not. Sock Pants wasn't really like any of the other human females he knew. Granted, he only knew Deli in depth, but she was a lot of person to know. Still, something niggled at the back of Toesy's mind.

When Deli got angry, she liked to punch things. Toesy understood that. For a human, she was very small, and she had so many emotions that her tiny body probably couldn't hold them all in.

When Sock Pants got angry, she had punched things too. But then she stopped being angry and started being something Toesy didn't know how to describe—sort of calm and horrible at the same time. At first, he dismissed the familiarity as simple déjà vu but that was before he remembered the raccoon.

It had wandered into the back parking lot, slavering and crazy. From the kitchen window, Toesy watched as it snapped at everything and shook its head. The neighbor cat, Snuffles, had been sunbathing on the porch. When the raccoon saw her, the same type of terrifying calm came over it. What happened after that, Toesy didn't like to remember.

It was a relief when the men in blue uniforms came with their shotguns.

Toesy thought about Snuffles and began to doubt the wisdom of letting Sock Pants near the Great Man. He willed the voice to hurry up with whatever it was doing, and set about trying to find a way into the building.

KINDA FAR OUTSIDE OF HONG KONG
7:00 A.M.

HIS DREAMS WERE A TUMBLED MESS of rocking and pitching and, at one point, a loud boom that shook the ground. But after the boom, the dreams quieted down and turned quite pleasant, nice even. There were lots of bows everywhere.

Carl woke on his side, cradling a fluffy green blanket in his arms. An abandoned pillow lay next to his head, rumpled and wrinkled where it had been slept on. The sound of laughter floated down from above, and he realized that he was alone.

Outside, the sun was mustering its forces, promising them a beautiful morning. His thoughts ran through the previous evening, and he found himself feeling optimistic about the day. Then he tried to move his head and changed his mind.

His nose, and all the face around it, was stiff and swollen. Carl had never had a broken nose before. It was an unusual feeling, painful and tight and somewhat badass. If his face was going to hurt *this* much, he hoped he at least had a black eye. That would be kind of cool.

He propped himself up on his elbows and took stock of the room. The computer setup had slid forward, but the lip around the table kept it from falling to the floor. His pants were still where he stashed them in his hurry to get under a blanket. Deli had thankfully been asleep for that part. He saw her tiny shoes lined up next to his huge ones near the couch. She must have gone upstairs barefoot.

Carl dug his dirty clothes out and stared at them. The button-down was crusty with blood. He could probably get away with wearing just his undershirt as long as no one noticed his lack of ripped pecs, delts, gammas, omegas, or whatever else the muscle-bound gorillas at Deli's gym had. It's not that he was out of shape. He was actually in rather good shape. It's just that his shape was more vertical than horizontal.

He toyed with the idea of ditching the pants too, but that was a little too risqué for him. Besides, there was no way Carl could pull off the pantsless look with as much style and grace as their fearless captain.

After the encounter with Military Mary and her incredibly sharp-toed shoes, Carl's knee thought bending was a stupid idea. It took a few tries, but eventually he persuaded the resisting joint to bend and he shimmied into his pants before his knee protested too much.

Once his pants were on, Carl noticed that the pocket stuck out at an odd angle. He tried sticking his hand in it to smooth it out but his fingers met with a lump of chewing gum. All the gymnastics during his rescue attempt caused the gum to work itself deep into his pocket lining. As he dug the Elevator out, Carl had to bite down on his tongue to keep from gagging. Chewed-up bubble gum grossed him out.

He finally got the nanobot free. Carl tried picking the gum from the lining, but it was no use. The pants were ruined. That was unfortunate because he really liked this suit. It was the only thing Heather ever gave him that he genuinely liked. On the other hand, Heather had given it to him so he wasn't exactly sad to see it go.

Carl held up the sticky nanobot and studied it the way one might study a ring. It was shaped like a kidney bean, each end slightly bulbous to accommodate the electromagnets. The sides were smooth with a faint line running down the middle where the casing snapped together. Even through the gum, Carl could see that Jake had put a lot of work into the design. He turned it around to read the letters on the back, but there was a blob of gum covering the etch marks, and all he could make out was the letter *R*. He grimaced as far as his poor face would let him.

Carl didn't want to be ungracious about Paul leaving them a clue, but would it have killed him to hide it somewhere less nauseating?

More laughing trickled down from above, and Carl decided he would deal with the Elevator later. A quick search of the galley produced a tiny spice jar full of red powder. He opened the stopper and dumped the powder in the sink. Then his lungs caught fire, and he coughed until he gagged.

When the air cleared, Carl dropped the Elevator in the bottle and stoppered it quickly. The bright green bits of leftover gum were immediately covered in spicy red dust, giving the nanobot a vaguely Christmassy feel. He tried not to imagine how it would taste; probably like spearmint-flavored napalm.

He stashed the bottle in his bag and turned his attention to the nest on floor. It seemed to Carl that there were twice as many blankets than there should be.

*   *   *

Deli sat on a plastic deck chair with her legs tucked underneath her. She was having an animated conversation with Jin, who sat nearby eating potato chips, unrepentant in his boxer shorts. Deli seemed to have gotten over it.

A man Carl had never met leaned against the railing, laughing and guessing at Deli's hand movements in Chinese. Between the three sat an empty chair and a plastic cooler used as a makeshift table. Maps and papers plastered the top. Jin kept them weighted down with his feet.

Carl walked up the stairs quietly so he wouldn't interrupt Deli. But he misjudged the door frame by a few inches and hit his head with a loud crack. All three turned to stare at him, as he held his head in pain.

"Wow, that's one way to wake up." Deli looked at him, smiling. "Good morning, sleepyhead."

Carl rubbed his forehead, feeling stupid. "Ouch," he said. It was an understatement.

Deli cleared the cooler off, opened it, and extracted two green bottles. They dripped ice water all over the deck.

"Here," she said, handing him one of the bottles. The other, she set down beside her chair. Then she grabbed a large chunk of ice and sloshed it onto the deck. She closed the cooler and helped Jin arrange their paperwork in much the same order it had been before Carl's head hit the door frame.

He looked at the bottle. The label was in Chinese, but Carl knew a cheap beer when he saw one. He put it on his forehead.

"No," Deli said. "That's your breakfast. Sit."

She pointed him to the empty chair. Carl sat. Deli grabbed the chunk of ice from the deck and the now-empty potato chip bag from Jin's lap. She dumped the crumbs overboard and dropped the ice in the bag.

"This is for your head."

She handed it to Carl, then stood over him to study the wreckage of his face. "That's a nice shiner you got there. Do you mind if I take a look?"

Carl didn't mind. Deli touched his nose lightly and he didn't wince, even though he thought strongly about doing so.

"Does that hurt?" she said.

"It doesn't feel great but it's not going to kill me."

"That's a good sign. It must have been a nice clean break. Keep the ice on it for a while, and hopefully the swelling will go down."

Carl watched her slide into the chair next to him. He *had* been feeling like a complete idiot for running into the door frame, but that was before he saw Deli's t-shirt. It was hot pink with the gigantic silk-screened head of a cartoon cat staring out at the world through two hypnotic dots. The bow on her ear was a field of red sequins.

"Nice shirt," he said from underneath the ice pack. "Did you mug a nine-year-old?"

She gave him the stink eye and stuck her tongue out. He would have laughed, but the stiffness from his nose prevented him from smiling too much.

"*Someone* bled all over my other shirt. Xing-Tiu here," she gestured politely to the unknown man, "kindly lent me some of his daughter's clothes."

The man looked at them when he heard his name, wiggling his eyebrows and giving them a thumbs-up. Carl set his ice pack down and cracked open the beer. He gave up trying to fight the pain and grinned broadly.

"Thank you, sir," Carl said, raising his bottle to Xing-Tiu. "I applaud your daughter's fashion sense. Deli loves Hello Kitty. I bet you didn't know that."

The man nodded, giving Carl a gigantic smile full of golden teeth and leftover breakfast.

"Hello Kitty!" he shouted and thrust his bottle in the air to join Carl's.

By the smell of his breath, Carl surmised that Hello Kitty wasn't the only cartoon celebrity he'd toasted that day. But Xing-Tiu's enthusiasm was infectious, and Carl hadn't felt this good in a long time, even counting the broken nose.

"Oh, I almost forgot to tell you," he said, turning to Deli. She looked up at him with interest.

"Third grade called. They're having a boy/girl party and wanted to invite you."

Deli flashed her plastic smile at him then kicked out her bare foot, meaning to hit him in the shin. But when her foot connected with Carl's leg, he grabbed it and held on, then he flipped it sideways and ran his icy beer along the inside of her arch. Deli gave a startled gasp and shook her foot loose. Carl smiled to himself and took a swig from his bottle.

"Thanks for the beer," he said and toasted her.

"Ha *ha*." She stuck out her tongue again. Carl laughed.

Deli waited until he picked up his ice pack again. When it was almost to his forehead, she reached over and shoved it, ice and all, into his face. This time, Carl winced.

"Now, shut up and drink your beer. You're going to need it when you hear Jin's idea."

AROUND THE COOLER

THE ADDRESS TURNED OUT TO BE a small packing plant on Kowloon Bay. Apparently, the plant was well known for being owned and operated by the Tridents, a local gang with ties to the Triads. Before that, it had been known for its pickled radishes. Jin and Xing-Tiu argued for ten minutes about which had been the better kind (spicy or spicy with garlic), unfazed by the whole mafia aspect of the venture. Deli watched the argument with fascination. Clearly, the men were passionate about their pickles.

From the shadow of his ice pack, Carl watched Deli. The bruise on her lip mesmerized him. He followed the way it moved when she laughed at the drunken Xing-Tiu and his spicy garlic pickle jihad.

Another five minutes were spent reminiscing about pickles before the men agreed that whichever flavor was best, it was a shame they no longer made them. Then the conversation turned serious.

The plan was simple: Jin would take them back to the harbor, where Xing-Tiu's cousin owned a small shipping business. They would dock at the shipyard. Xing-Tiu would stay and visit with his cousin while Carl, Jin, and Deli walked the short distance to the packing plant.

Xing-Tiu's cousin's girlfriend (or possibly niece) had access to the building next door to the defunct pickle-packing plant. The roofs were separated by a low wall, which Carl and Deli could easily climb. Once inside, they would look around for anything suspicious, like Paul tied to a chair or something. Xing-Tiu assured them that most days the place was deserted until evening, save for a few guards.

"How many guards?"

Carl made gun-like motions with his hands then pretended to count on his fingers. Xing-Tiu nodded and held up all his fingers. Ten guards.

At that point, Carl called a stop to the proceedings to get another beer. Everyone agreed this was a good idea.

As they put the makeshift table back together and sat back down, Deli's chair had somehow turned so that she could prop her bare feet up on Carl's armrest—which she promptly did. When he teased her about the stink, she picked them up and dropped both feet in his lap. They continued planning while Carl pretended not to notice ten tiny pink toes wiggling in his lap. His motivation for finding Paul began to wane.

"Jin," said Deli, "when are we leaving?" She made two little legs walking away with her fingers.

"Yes, leaving. One hour!" His thumb was in the air before she could blink.

Deli returned the thumbs-up and faced Carl. He sat with his head resting on the back of the lawn chair, swaying back and forth with the boat. She poked him in the thigh with her big toe. He grabbed at her foot and held it with both hands and didn't let go until she slapped his arm with the bottom of her other foot.

"Come on," she said. "I need to get moving or I'll never get out of here."

"Where are we going?"

He'd only asked the question to be polite. He didn't care at all. Frankly, if they never moved again, he would be okay with that. Deli put her beer bottle down and stood up.

"I'm not walking into a gangster-filled, spicy-pickle warehouse completely unarmed. I need to get some stuff. Plus, I don't know about you, but I need to eat something more substantial than beer and potato chips."

"That's a good idea. I'll get our stuff." He ducked down below while Deli got directions from Jin to the nearest market.

In the cabin, Carl found his bag. He checked the cash he had stashed in the zippy pocket. It was all still there. He counted out a few bills and stuffed them into the gum-free pocket of his trousers. Then he shoved his feet into his shoes, too quick to care about socks. Even though the morning was sultry with heat, Carl was shaking slightly.

In a few hours, they were going to break into a warehouse most likely owned and operated by the Chinese mafia. However, that did not concern him as much as breakfast did. Of course, it wasn't a date. Everybody has to eat.

Still, he worried that Deli would insist on going Dutch. Carl didn't see how she could, since she had no money with her, but she was proving to be a very resourceful woman. What if she'd borrowed money from Jin or something? He hoped she hadn't thought of that. It would make everything needlessly confusing.

He grabbed her shoes and scanned the cabin for anything else he might have forgotten. Over on the table, the computer setup reminded him of his promise to change the Sector Nine password for Jake. There was no time now.

Jake will be all right until later, he thought. *He always is.*

Carl shrugged his shoulders at no one in particular and bounded up the stairs, making sure to duck on the last stair to avoid any more concussions. He was eager to continue whatever he and Deli had been doing, even though he wasn't entirely sure what *it* was.

He joined Deli topside and held her hand as they climbed off the boat although he gave it back soon after. Together, they walked down the dock in search of pork noodles and zip ties.

BACK PARKING LOT OF
DELI'S APARTMENT BUILDING

TOESY'S FUR WAS NOW QUITE STIFF. The dried blood turned his naturally grey and white stripes into darkened plates of armor. The shards of glass crunched along his legs and back, making a sneak attack ill-advised. With one possible exception, no living creature within three city blocks of Toesy had enough nerve to try.

Sock Pants might be a different story.

He sat on the lid of the Dumpster, the heat from the sun toasting his bloody fur to a deep maroon. The voice in his head requested "deep sound resonance," which Toesy eventually figured out was a fancy way of asking him to purr. He purred, though he did not feel particularly content. He was still thinking about Snuffles.

After a minute or so, the voice asked if he could please try flexing his claws. Toesy did as requested.

He extended the claws of each paw one at a time: pointer, scratcher, scraper, then pinky. They worked just as well as they had two hours ago.

Then the voice asked him to try his thumbs.

Toesy was immediately skeptical. Those claws were useless. They never obeyed. All they were good for was getting him stuck in the damn couch. He refused.

The voice asked again. It took nothing to try, so why not? Toesy thought it was useless but acquiesced anyway.

Gingerly, he willed his dewclaws to stretch out. To his confounded delight, they obeyed his commands. He wiggled his thumb claws and they wiggled back at him happily. He pinched the thumb and pointer claw of each forepaw together and nearly drew his own blood in excitement.

Now, the voice told him, *we need a specific type of fuel.*

Toesy jumped into the Dumpster. He shifted garbage around in search of the things that the voice wanted him to eat. As he did so, the voice filled Toesy in on the powers of his new, highly capable thumbs.

Toesy was so pleased that he promoted the voice to Executive Wingman and named it Steve. Together, Toesy and Executive Wingman Steve formed a plan.

DELI'S CLOSET

HE SHOULD HAVE CALLED THE POLICE immediately, but when Jake heard the footsteps in the hall, he thought it was Heather coming back to finish him off. Now he'd been stuck in Deli's closet for *hours.* The not-moving part he was okay with, especially since every time he *did* move, it took him a few minutes to get his breath back. His throat was wicked dry, and he needed to pee so badly that his eyes were turning yellow—but worse than that, Jake was utterly, mind-numbingly, *devastatingly* bored.

And it was all Heather's fault.

Jake didn't hate many people unless they were Heather. That was okay though because it was one hundred percent mutual. The minute she'd met Jake, her bitch-powers had taken over and she'd dedicated her life to driving a wedge between him and Carl.

Carl and Heather met at the fourth annual PAX convention. Carl wasn't a huge celebrity outside a limited cohort of computer security geeks. To most, he was another tall dude in an ill-fitting suit. But to anyone interested in computer security, he was the guy who designed the double blind firewall, a nonstandard security measure that was almost impossible to hack.

Heather's boyfriend at the time was into *TerrorCity,* but thirty seconds after she found out who Carl was, that guy disappeared, and no one ever saw him again.

Four weeks after their first date, Jake had come home late and found Heather in their sys admin account, monkeying around with permissions. At the time, Jake hadn't really understood the law of girlfriends. He did what came naturally and proceeded to tell her off. Carl woke up when Heather started crying.

It all went downhill from there.

They dated for two dreadful years. In that time, she did everything she could to take the mickey out of Carl. She cut his hair and changed his clothes. She got him a real job at the investment firm of Stokem and Boyle, working for serious cash. Then she gave away all his mint edition collectibles—even the Christmas-themed Batman one, which was going on eBay for over three hundred dollars.

But worse than that, Heather made Carl move out of the Dungeon. She claimed it was unsuitable for a professional man to live in such squalor. Jake remembered the satisfaction on her face when Carl told him. She was radiant. Jake had been heartbroken.

Somehow, through the tightening grip of Heather, they remained friends. They even went so far as starting up the Elevator project again—long distance, of course.

For the last part of his Heather period, Carl and Jake communicated mostly by email and text. Carl had to wipe his phone clean every day after work so she wouldn't know. It was pathetic.

Then the blowup happened. When she found out about him and Carl working on the Elevators she was livid. She cornered Jake and threatened him. If he didn't leave Carl alone she would ruin him "fiscally and otherwise."

She had the skills to do it, too. Jake spent three days guarding the *TerrorCity* server from a cyber-attack when he realized that she hadn't been talking about the website. She never believed that *TerrorCity* made any money. Oh, she would have worked her way to it eventually, but her threat hadn't been about his business, it had been about his *inheritance*. Jake had a substantial one, invested heavily through the same brokerage that employed Carl as the head of their computer security team. When he put these two things together, he did a little bit of poking around and found out that Heather had been a very naughty girl indeed.

Carl didn't believe him at first, but Jake had the login tables. For months, Heather had free reign over the brokerage's customer accounts, moving things around and paving her way into something more fraudulent than just snooping. By the looks of it, she'd set Carl up as the fall guy.

Carl moved out immediately. Jake had offered to help him move all his stuff, but after eighteen months of living with Heather, he didn't have much left. So Jake did what he could and offered to buy him a beer when he was finished.

Heather came home at seven, but by then, Carl and Jake were halfway through their second pitcher of Mac & Jack's. Some time after eight, they decided to drink every time his cell phone rang. By eleven, they were so sloppy that the bartender called them a taxi. Jake remembered that hangover. It was totally worth it.

Jake always suspected she would come back and mess with Carl. He had the brains to outwit her and the common sense to kick her ass to the curb. But Heather was a classic Bunny Boiler, a grade-A psychopath. She wouldn't take that shit easily.

Jake sighed again.

Sacha had to be the dumbest asshole in the history of dumb assholes. He would stick his dick into anything. But *Heather*? That was like screwing a face hugger. You may be getting laid now, but you were also going to *die* soon. You had to be pretty fucking stupid to get involved with that amount of crazy.

And now they were camped out in the other room. He could hear the smile on Heather's face every time she mocked Sacha for being an idiot. She was ruthless. Sacha tried two new passwords every thirty minutes. With each failed attempt, Heather became more and more irrational. Jake had to do something soon. The idea of Heather shooting him *again* made his fists clench—well, sort of clench. His strength was definitely returning, but very slowly. Still, no one should have to be shot by that bitch *twice*.

He thought about calling the police, but Heather would certainly hear him talking. With his luck, she would recognize his voice. She had a way with voices. It was creepy.

He thought about texting the police, but he knew for a fact they had no texting capabilities yet because Darryl down at Computer Wizard worked part-time on their communication systems, and they still had major bugs in their location software.

He thought about texting someone *else* to call the police. But the only other person he trusted was Carl and he'd been trying to get in touch with Carl, since Sacha gave him his phone back. He'd sent him seventeen texts so far, and gotten nothing in return. Jake sincerely hoped that reason had everything to do with crazy sex and nothing whatsoever to do with being dead.

He thought about *TerrorCity*. Those guys would totally help him out if they could. But most of them were complete unknowns except for their avatars. Did he really want them to know that Il Serpiente de los Muertos, the Dark Mage Warrior, was really a fat guy named Jake who lived in his parents' basement apartment? It didn't matter that his parents only owned the house and didn't actually *live* there, it was just too stereotypical. He had a reputation to uphold. *TerrorCity* was out.

Jake grew maudlin. He was going to die in Deli's closet because he didn't have anyone else. All he had was a list of things that he had yet to do with his life, and on the top of it was Pizza Girl. And he didn't even mean that as a double entendre.

If he'd known Pizza Girl well enough, he had no doubt she would help. But he didn't know her—not personally, anyway. He knew her name, of course. And where she lived. And her roommate's name and where she went to college and that she once had a dog named BeeBoo and that she was allergic to horses—all that sort of stuff, but he didn't actually *know* her because they only ever talked when he ordered pizza. He didn't even like Pizza Joe's that much, but he still ordered it three nights a week. He wished he could order one now, just so he could hear her voice one last time. Also, because he was starving.

That's when Jake had a brilliant idea. It was a long shot and potentially embarrassing, but if it worked, he might get rid of the psycho *and* improve his chances with Pizza Girl. He just hoped his phone had enough battery left.

HANG CHOY FOODS WAREHOUSE, HONG KONG 10:00 A.M.

"OH DEAR LORD, HE'S SUMO-SIZED," said Deli.

She stood flat against the fire door, risking glances through the small window every seven seconds. Carl was counting.

Even though the pickle factory did not make pickles anymore, they seemed to be making *something*. They could hear the sounds of machines, clanking and hissing, down on the factory floor. The stairwell, however, was relatively quiet, so they whispered.

"What do we do?" said Carl. He shifted his weight from his left foot to his right and back again as Deli peeked through the window.

"Okay, I've got the big bastard on the left," Deli said. "You take the skinny guy on the right."

Deli pointed to the right, to give Carl a visual. He snuck a quick peek through the window to see what the guards looked like. The guard on the left was indeed Sumo-sized. The guard on the right was barely larger than Deli. Carl stepped back.

"Don't you think I ought to go for the bigger guy? I mean, he's at least four and a half times your size."

Deli looked Carl up. Then she looked him back down.

"No offense, Carl, but I watched you punch a wall yesterday. Do you think you could render *that* guy"—she motioned toward the massive guard to the left—"unconscious within ten seconds, *without* making a lot of noise?"

"Probably not."

"Then when we get out there, you run over," she pointed toward the shrimpy guard again. "And punch the little guy in the face as hard as you can."

"But what if I..." Carl started to say, but Deli held up a quieting hand.

"It's easy. Just look him in the eye." Deli looked Carl in the eye.

"Then make a fist." She held her hand out and showed him how to make a proper fist.

"Then you reach out." She reached out.

"And touch where you're looking *really hard*." She did not punch Carl. He knew enough by now to get out of the way.

"I know you can do this." She chucked him on the shoulder and waited five and a half more seconds until the guards had their backs turned.

"Now, go!"

Deli opened the fire door and pushed Carl out in front. The Sumo-sized guard turned toward them, a look of surprise growing on his face. Deli did not let it get very far. Once Carl was out of the way, she launched herself at his neck.

Carl did what Deli told him to do. He hurried along the wobbly catwalk, as quietly as he could, although the clanking machinery down below made this unnecessary. A Viking could have stormed the catwalk and not been heard. But Carl didn't want to make a mistake, so he tried emulating the funny little rolling step he saw Deli use when she was sneaking.

It must have worked because as he reached the end of the catwalk, the shrimpy guard turned from staring out at the open warehouse floor and jumped in surprise.

Carl didn't waste time. He looked the guy directly in the eye, then punched where he was looking. There was a crunching sound as his fist connected with the guard's nose. Then the guard clutched at his face and sunk to his knees. Carl was flabbergasted.

I actually punched a guy in the face! And by the looks of the fetal position he'd crawled into, broken his nose in the process.

"I'm sorry about that. I know how much it hurts."

The guard rocked back and forth with his face in his hands. At the sound of Carl's voice, he peered around his fingers. Carl smiled and pointed to his own black and blue face and nodded in an enthusiastic way before reaching down and grabbing one of the man's arms. He zipped a plastic tie around it.

"Same thing happened to me yesterday." He zipped the man's other arm.

"Carl!"

Deli stood at the end of the catwalk, one foot on the unconscious guard's back, signaling for Carl to hurry up. He finished tying the man's arms and shoved the rag Deli had given him for this very purpose into the guy's mouth. The man started heaving. He couldn't breathe through the torrent of blood from his nose. Carl didn't want him to suffocate, so he pulled the rag back out again. Deli had warned him to keep the guy quiet, but Carl didn't think anyone would hear him over the noise down below.

"Don't shout, okay?" he said. "I have to go." He turned to leave but spun back around immediately. The guard flinched.

"You might want to have someone look at that," he said. Then he ran, not quietly at all, back down to Deli.

Deli stood next to a small mountain of unconscious guard as Carl bounded down the catwalk at her. She half expected his tongue to loll out the side of his mouth. When it did not, she was mildly disappointed.

"I did what you said. I looked at him, then I punched where I looked, and it worked! I punched him right in the frickin' nose!"

He made a fist with his right hand and gave her a broad smile, which quickly turned into a frown.

"I'm really sorry, but I think might have broken it." Carl pointed to his own face. "He was doing that face-clutching thing."

He stared anxiously at Deli. She almost laughed.

"You don't have to apologize for hitting that guy, Carl. Getting your nose broken is standard in a job like this."

Carl paused for a breath. He was still holding his fist in the air.

"It was way more painful than that guy made it look," he said. He was hopping gently from foot to foot.

"Carl," said Deli.

"Yes?" said Carl.

Hop. Hop.

"Would you like to go punch someone else now?"

Hop. Hop.

"Yes, thank you. I think I would."

"I thought maybe you might," she said. "We need to get to the office." Deli pointed to their left. Thirty yards down the catwalk was another hallway. "I think it's over there."

Carl nodded. "We came in the southeast corner of the building, so that would be the northeast side. Yes, I believe you are correct."

Deli scowled at him, but in his excitement, Carl didn't see it. "Let's try and sneak up on the guards if we can. I think you'll find it's easier to punch them if they don't know what's coming."

Carl nodded enthusiastically. The cowlicks on his head mimicked his fervor, agreeing wholeheartedly to her plan.

"Let me see your fist," she said. Carl held out his hand and Deli took it. She shaped his fingers into a fist. "Don't forget to keep your thumb free, like this." She contorted his thumb outward.

"Thumb free, you bet!" Carl said. He was looking down at her with crazy eyes and a triumphant smile on his face.

"Be careful, Carl," Deli said. "You might be having fun, but these guys aren't playing a game. They will kill you if they get the chance. *Remember that* when you go charging in." She squeezed his hand lightly.

The wild light in Carl's eyes dimmed and his face grew serious.

"I remember everything you tell me," he said. He didn't say anything else. He just focused on her.

Deli broke his stare by looking down at her feet, horribly tongue-tied for the moment. She stayed like that until her fighting instincts came back. Then she put her game face on and looked up at Carl.

"Then let's go get 'em, tiger!"

Her hand shot out and spanked Carl square on the backside. He jumped. She smiled. They turned down the catwalk together, keeping close to the wall.

"Carl," Deli said as they stalked. Carl perked up his attention.

"Some of the things I've said…well…some of them may not be true anymore."

She focused on the hallway ahead instead of looking at Carl. It was easier.

"You were lying?" It was a simple question, not an accusation. Carl never made accusations unless he had tangible proof, but Deli didn't know that.

"No."

She wanted to explain, but they were close to the hallway and needed to be quiet. Deli tiptoed up to the corner and peeked around to study the situation.

There was a door halfway down the hall. On either side of the door sat two men, each holding a gun and looking bored.

Deli ducked back to Carl and motioned for him to come closer. Carl crouched down next to her, and she leaned up to his ear.

"There's a door about twenty feet down. Two guards, one on each side of the door."

Carl nodded.

"I'll take the first guy. You go for the guy farther down."

Carl nodded again and showed her a fist with his thumb free. Deli smiled in approval. He tried to stand up all the way, but Deli pulled him down again.

"I didn't lie to you, Carl. It's just that I've changed my mind about some things."

Carl stood up straight and stared at Deli. After a few seconds of scrutiny from an unblinking Carl, Deli felt uncomfortably bare. She grabbed his arm and tugged to break his trance. He shook his head and started hopping again. Deli relaxed.

Let's go, she mouthed.

They went.

WAREHOUSE HALLWAY

CARL STEPPED INTO THE HALLWAY FIRST. His size commanded the beefy guard's attention immediately. He swung his gun around to face Carl, but Deli was already on him.

Like a little backpack of doom, Carl thought.

He smiled through his adrenaline rush and crossed to the far side of the door in three steps. The guard there was trying to see past Deli, aim his gun at Carl, and figure out what was happening with his partner all at the same time. It was not going so well.

Carl walked up to the confused guard and looked him in the eye.

"I'm sorry about this," he said, and punched where he was looking.

The guard dropped, his gun clattering to the floor. This, paired with the shouting, was enough to bring two more guards to attention. They came out of the office, weapons at the ready. Deli was faster. As the first one emerged, she kicked him with ninety-eight pounds of fury right in the nuts. Carl momentarily felt bad for the guy.

The next guard tried to run out the door but found himself climbing over his comrade. Carl looked him in the eye and punched, *super* hard. He went down the same way the other two had. Carl felt victorious.

He dragged them one at a time to a broom closet at the end of the hall, where Deli awaited them with a pocket full of zip ties. She worked fast, tying their arms and legs in a crazy mess, the right arm of one guard to the left leg of another, and so on. The resulting chaos looked like one of those endless knots the Celts are so fond of, only instead of dragons, this one was full of incapacitated thugs.

Deli nodded back toward the office. Carl went immediately.

It was a large room, its notice-covered walls jaundiced from nicotine. A bank of computers lined the far wall. Carl headed straight for it. The system was ancient, some of it dating back to the late nineties. That was good. Then he saw the monitor and rolled his eyes. Someone had logged in and walked away from the screen.

Carl shook his head. It took him less than twenty seconds to find the root directory and another ten seconds to figure out how to connect his portable hard drive. After that, getting access to their shipping and lading records was simple.

As the computer divested its secrets, Carl searched through the clutter of papers around the desk. Most were shipping documents for Hang Choy Foods, exactly like the ones he stole from the *Marty-Lu*. Because they were in Chinese, they were not much help.

He checked on the file download and found it halfway done. The computer continued to churn through the last sixty days' worth of transactions, and Carl went back to rifling through the desk. Underneath the stack of shipping documents, he found odds and ends: memos, advertisements, and a letter on university stationery.

The first thing Carl noticed was that it was in English. Sent from a Professor Konjin, the letter detailed a robotics project that claimed to increase the speed and ease of packing radishes into glass jars using a sorting method referred to as numerical substitution. Carl couldn't see what numerical substitution had to do with radish sizes. He set the letter on the pile of papers he'd already gone through, scanning it one last time for anything out of the ordinary. That's when he saw the numbers.

Down below the signature sat the usual paragraph of contact information. The work and fax numbers meant nothing to him, but the cell phone number he knew by heart.

He had called that number three times a day for almost two years.

"Carl!"

Carl stuffed all the papers into his bag and ran to the doorway. Deli stood just outside the hallway on the catwalk. Her mouth was a tight line. She held her arms halfway in the air and away from her body.

"What's wrong?"

"We have a slight problem." Deli took a step forward. The metallic shine of a gun muzzle followed her. She took another step forward and the smiling face of Johnny appeared around the corner.

* * *

He stood with his legs apart, a half-dead cigarette hanging from his mouth. He wore grey suit pants and a dress shirt that was valiantly trying to contain the bulge of his belly. Somehow, he appeared to have more pinky rings than pinkies.

"Johnny," said Carl. He gave a short nod in his direction, but his eyes never left Deli.

"What are you doing *here*, Agent Sanderson?" Johnny said in a friendly voice. "When you should be on a plane back to your beloved American justice system?"

"My prisoner has decided to cooperate in the investigation," he said.

"You see now, *that* is very interesting," Johnny said. "Because I thought you said you were investigating a spider woman named Bunny. But *this* woman..." He shoved Deli forward with his free hand. Carl winced. "...Is *not* the Bunny Spider."

Deli tripped and stumbled, throwing her arms out in front of her to catch herself. Watching her fall, Carl made a promise to himself that somehow he would find the opportunity to look Johnny in the face and punch really, *really* hard.

"It's Bunny *the* Spider. And what makes you think that, Johnny?"

"Oh, I hear things. For instance, I hear that this woman here has a brother named Paul."

At the mention of Paul's name, Deli jerked her head around to look at Johnny. "You know Paul?"

"Of course I know him. He is a very helpful man. He helped me find *you*." He pointed the gun at Deli. "And *you* helped me find him!" Johnny pointed all his pinkies at Carl and laughed heartily.

"That's it," Deli yelled, staring at Carl. "I officially hate that guy now. Don't call me his sister anymore. I have no love *left* for that asshole."

As she said the word *left*, her eyes widened slightly. Carl squinted in acknowledgment. Johnny was too busy gloating to notice.

"I make you a deal, Miss Pell-ham," he said. "Between Agent Sanderson and Brother Paul, I let you choose which one I shoot first."

Deli didn't even pause for breath. "I choose Paul. You can shoot him right now if you let me smack him first."

Johnny laughed long and hard at that. "You Yanks are a very surprising people! I offer you the chance to redeem your family honor, Miss Pelham, and all you want is vengeance." He shook his head slightly. "*Smack him*! I like that. You are a very funny lady. Now, if you please."

Using the gun muzzle as a pointer, Johnny motioned toward the door where Carl stood. When Deli didn't move right away, he reached out and shoved her again. She fell forward in a controlled manner that Carl thought might have been on purpose.

As she stood again, Carl watched her feet do a small shuffling step. She curled her left hand into a fist, thumb out, and waggled it surreptitiously at him.

Get ready, it said.

Johnny, busy with his anemic cigarette, saw neither the foot shuffle nor the fist waggle. He did see the defiant stance Deli took as soon as she was back on her feet, though.

"You push me one more time, and I'm going to take that gun away from you. Then I'm going to beat you with it."

His eyebrows arched in surprise. He brought his gun up and aimed it at her, then thought better of it, and used it to push her in the shoulder. Every ounce of diplomacy left Deli's face. Carl tensed for whatever came next, but no smackdowns were delivered. Before Deli had the chance to throw a punch, a shadow appeared behind Carl.

Johnny concentrated on Deli's defiance, ignoring Carl until the shadow was almost in full view. By then, the man already had a bead on him.

"Johnny, my good friend," said the shadow man. "It is a fancy meeting you here."

Johnny's eyes shifted, then widened.

"Zarubin."

Neither lowered their weapons. Carl turned his head enough to see the man from the corner of his eye. In the flickering fluorescent light of the hallway, Carl couldn't see much of him. The only thing that stood out was the circular scar around his eye.

Dammit.

Carl had *completely* forgotten about that guy.

PIZZA JOE'S KITCHEN, SEATTLE

KIX PRINTED THE ORDER off the computer, smiling when she read the name. She liked Jake Denny. He was a super nice guy and he usually tipped well. Then she read the rest of the order form and stopped smiling.

"Hey, Marco," she called across the kitchen. "What do you make of this?"

Marco looked up from the ball of dough he was working. His mustache had a light dusting of flour. Kix shook the pizza order at him.

"I am too busy, Miss Kix! Get Frank, he will help you. Now, go away. I must make enough damn dough for rush tomorrow. Ask Frank." He made dusty shooing motions with his hands.

"Just read it," she said.

On the order form, under the "special instructions" heading was typed:

> *Please bring the police with you when you deliver. I have been shot and a friend is being held captive. Also, I am not a vampire. Can you go lighter on the garlic?*

Marco read it. When he finished, he made a disgusted sound in the back of his throat.

"Light garlic? This is for sissy boys. Never get involved with sissy boys. Big mistake."

"Well, I'm calling the police anyway," she said, but Marco had already gone back to his dough.

HANG CHOY FOODS WAREHOUSE

"HELLO JOHNNY." The man spoke in a thick Russian accent filled with good intentions and brotherly love. "It is good to see you again."

Carl risked a look at the Johnny-filled doorway. The man had not moved a muscle since the Russian appeared. It dawned on him that he and Deli were now caught between two longtime enemies.

He focused on Deli. They needed to get out of here before these guys went to war. Deli stared back at him and raised one eyebrow slowly. *We can use this,* it said.

Carl didn't know how to move just one of his eyebrows, so he blinked to show he understood. Deli blinked back at him. Carl wasn't sure if that had anything to do with anything.

"Zarubin, *comrade*. What is it I can do for you?" Johnny sounded as friendly as Zarubin, but did not lower his gun.

"Odessa has a problem Johnny. They are looking for a woman much like the one you now have in your hands. In fact, I am positive it is the same one."

Johnny grunted but did not say anything.

"She has something important, they say. You must follow her and find out what it is, they say. And when I come here I find you making fuss over this same woman. I find this interesting. Do you not think this is interesting?"

"It is," said Johnny not sounding convinced at all.

"Yes, it *is*. In fact, it is *so* interesting that Odessa has asked to have a word with you about it." He flashed an expansive smile that stopped just shy of his eyes and kept his gun trained on Johnny's head.

Deli looked at the floor, then back up. *You, get down.*

Carl agreed with another quick blink. Deli flared her nostrils wide for half a second.

Nostrils? What was *that* about?

Then she did it again, and Carl understood. On her third nostril flare, Carl leaned to the left and fell to the floor. Deli bent double, into a forward roll.

Johnny was in the middle of asking what it is that Odessa wanted to talk about when his human shield toppled over. The Russian's trigger hand reacted instantly. Johnny's courageous shirtfront blossomed with two red flowers, and he fell.

Before his body even touched the ground, Deli was up. Carl had seen her move fast when she fought the guy at the ferry terminal. The brawl on the ship had been more impressive still, but this wasn't really moving so much as going from one state of being to another, like a Deli-flavored quantum jump. She appeared to have so much energy that her body didn't need to do the intervening steps of moving her arm up and aiming it at Zarubin's throat. First she was standing, then he was bent over double, gagging.

She followed with a direct kick to the groin. The Russian's gun sailed through the air and landed exactly where Carl had been standing before Deli's warning.

"That way!"

Carl ran where she pointed.

They reached the catwalk while the Russian spluttered around trying to get his breath. Their feet pound out a hollow rhythm on the plywood floor, and they ran toward the stairwell that led to the roof.

As they neared the fire door, it cracked open an inch. Deli aimed herself at it and jumped. She twisted her legs around in the air to kick the door closed again. Carl, running close behind Deli, saw a greasy-looking man collide with the wire mesh window and fall backward. The roof was a no-go.

Ahead of them lay a staircase leading down to the open factory floor. Deli headed for it. Because he was watching the man knock himself out on the fire door, Carl missed the turn. Deli ran down the stairs two at a time and Carl raced past her, still up on the catwalk.

It didn't take long for them to figure out what happened, but by then, the guard from the fire door had regained his footing, and somewhere, he'd found a friend. Carl could not go back.

He ran alongside the railing, looking down at Deli for help.

"There!" She pointed in front of him.

The catwalk circled, or rather *rectangled*, the factory. Two sides of the rectangle had stairs leading down to the floor. Carl aimed for the south side stairs.

He almost made it.

Just before he turned the corner to the south side of the catwalk, a small door opened wide and disgorged another armed thug. Carl was beginning to *really* dislike those guys.

"Nope!" he shouted and punched the guy, right in the nose. The thug fell, clutching his face. Carl was so keyed-up and angry that he only felt sort of bad about it.

"Carl!" Deli shouted from down below again. He ran back to peer over the railing. She pointed to the south stairs. Two men scrambled up them like rats. Both of his exits were now covered in guards.

Deli waved and pointed to the railing of the catwalk. "Can you jump it?" she said and pantomimed a little hop so Carl would get the idea.

Carl got the idea. He nodded and backed up. He ran to the railing, throwing the weight of his bag behind him. As he hit the rail, he launched himself forward, grabbing on with both hands and twisting in midair, just like his stunt on the *Marty-Lu*.

* * *

Deli scanned the floor until she found a likely exit on the other side of the building. She practiced running there in her mind. Up above she heard a loud pop and the railing sounded out a deep gong. Someone was shooting.

She saw Carl jump to the outside of the catwalk. His bag swayed back and forth, knocking him off balance and he wobbled for a second to keep from falling. It made Deli nervous to see him standing still like that. He needed to get moving. You were harder to shoot if you were moving.

Carl saw her staring up at him and smiled. He opened his mouth to say something when his face suddenly contorted into a grimace and he swayed dangerously off the railing. Deli watched in horror as his right arm went limp and he slipped a few inches. A trickle of red oozed down his fingers and for the first time that she could remember, Deli screamed in fear.

DELI'S LIVING ROOM

"SHE DID *WHAT?*" Heather shouted into the phone. Sacha, ticking away at the keyboard next to her, ducked his head just in case.

"Get rid of that bitch! Shoot her if you have to!" She scowled angrily, then her eyes widened.

"No, wait! Don't shoot her. Let me talk with Zarubin." She tossed her hair back like a snotty teenager and sighed impatiently. Sacha kept his eyes glued to the screen in front of him.

"I don't give a fuck what he's got aimed at your head, put him on."

From the corner of his eye, Sacha could see her glaring at him. He did not look up. He wanted her to think she had complete privacy, even though he was listening to every word she said. She took her conversation to the kitchen, and Sacha started banging away on the keyboard, so she could hear how fixated he was on hacking into Sector Nine.

He was trying to work his way around the password shutout, but they both knew he had little chance of getting past it. Carl built this system. Sacha probably had a better shot at hijacking Air Force One for a joy ride through North Korean airspace.

Heather knew he wouldn't be able to get through Carl's security. He suspected that's why she made him try. She enjoyed watching people fail.

Sacha kept one ear on her conversation and continued with the seismic typing.

"I'm glad we could work things out to our mutual benefit, Mr. Zarubin. If you'll just call me when you've done it, please. I'll need the phone number."

She disconnected the call and walked back to the living room.

"Everything okay?" Sacha asked.

If he had taken the offensive approach and made her angry, she would have shot him hours ago. But his mindless banter seemed to work. At least it kept her temper down to a mere berating every ten minutes or so.

"No," she said. "Everything is *not* okay. Carl's little booty-call is fucking things up."

Sacha felt it was unwise to point out that Heather was standing in the booty-call's apartment, so he kept silent and let her vent.

"I don't know what he sees in her. I bet she's all manly and horrible in bed. Oh, poor Carl." Sacha looked back to the computer screen, suddenly hoping she would go back to yelling at him.

"He was always so generous, too." She stared out the window and sighed.

Sacha tried willing his ears not to hear any more. He did *not* want to hear anything else about Carl's generosity, so he hid behind a wall of black curls and redoubled his efforts to find a way into Sector Nine.

"When Carl realizes his mistake, he's going to be pretty embarrassed." She gave him a self-satisfied smirk.

Sacha didn't ask why. He crossed his toes and hoped she wouldn't tell him. He would have crossed his fingers, but she might notice that. The timer on his computer screen said he had three minutes until his next password attempt. Sacha wasn't a religious man, but he prayed like hell that the March password from three years ago would work.

HANG CHOY FOODS WAREHOUSE

HE FELL.

It was horrible.

A short drop for such a tall guy, the sound he made as his backside hit the cement floor was gruesome. At least his bag managed to break his fall again.

"Carl?" Deli shouted. "Carl, are you okay?"

She was at his side immediately. Carl didn't say anything. He couldn't. It was too painful. His head throbbed, and his tailbone was definitely broken. Or maybe that was his spine. He couldn't tell.

"Carl?" Deli said, less forceful this time. "Carl, please say something." Up above, three sets of footsteps ran for the stairs.

He didn't hear her words. He was too busy taking stock of all the parts, willing each arm and leg to bend. They did, but none were happy about it.

"I'm still in one piece," he said. "But I'm pretty sure my computer is dead."

Deli, who had been crouching down next to him, searching for a heartbeat, snapped her head up. Tears ran down her face, and she laughed.

"We need to get out of here," she said.

"I agree," Carl said. He coughed once and fell back on the floor with his legs splayed out in front of him. "We have about thirty-three seconds before they shoot us for real." He sat up on his elbows.

"Can you stand?"

He could not. She asked him something else, but Carl didn't really follow it. He wasn't following much of anything at the moment. Her hands were on him, moving his arms up and out. He focused on her hands. As tiny as they felt, they were now hauling him across the floor.

Wow, he thought, gaining a little more reality with the movement. *She is really strong.*

Deli dumped him, a bit unceremoniously, in the space between a gigantic mixer and the south wall. Then she left.

Carl sat with his back against the wall, legs scrunched up against the mixer. Sunlight fought through the high, dusty windows, making shadows along the factory floor. From his hidey-hole, Carl couldn't see much. He listened as intently as possible to the confusing orchestra of pickle-making machinery, creaking floorboards, and physical violence.

Clink, oof, cling, creak, hiss.

He risked a peek around the mixer. An endless row of empty glass jars clinked their way down a small conveyor belt toward the belly of a machine. Every ten jars or so, the machine belched out a great plume of steam.

A loud pop and a zing broke his trance. Carl thought it sounded like a gun, mainly because that was exactly what it sounded like earlier when someone shot him in the shoulder.

His shoulder! He looked at the blood oozing down his arm. He should probably do something about that. Carl didn't know much first aid, but he was pretty sure that raising a bleeding wound above your heart was the right thing to do, so he used his left hand to pull his right hand over his head. Once it was there, he propped his elbow against the wall to keep it elevated. Now all he had to do was wait for Deli to come back to him. He hoped she would come back soon.

"Well, the guards are neutralized, but I can't find Zarubin."

Her voice came from out of nowhere, making Carl jump in surprise. This caused his right arm to flop down to his lap with a painful *whump.*

"Oh God, Carl," Deli said. "You're bleeding everywhere."

He turned around to see that Deli had weaseled her way behind the mixer from the other side.

"I think that's because I got shot." He tried to hold up his arm for Deli to see, but the effort winded him. Black spots burst into his vision. He exhaled with a groan. Deli squished herself down next to him.

"Don't," she said and took his hand into her hers. "Let me do that."

Carl nodded. His eyelids drooped, and his breathing slowed. Deli slipped one leg across his lap and held his arm gingerly. Carl's breath picked up again.

"This might hurt," she said

"No problem," said Carl.

She grabbed his t-shirt by the neck and tried ripping it with her bare hands. When she couldn't get the ribbing to tear, she bent over and used her teeth. The thin cotton shirt tore away cleanly. Carl, bleeding and groggy, looked away in embarrassment. Deli didn't notice. She manhandled the sleeve from his right shoulder and Carl continued thinking about how nice her hands were.

His left shoulder was goopy with blood. Deli used as much care as she could to remove his shirt entirely. Her fingers were cold as they ran up and down his arm. Carl was grateful for that. It was easier to focus on her hands touching his skin than the pain in his shoulder.

Using his t-shirt as a bandage, she wrapped his arm as best she could. When she finished, she looked at him gravely.

"It's not great," she said. "It could be worse, though." Then, in a quieter voice, she added, "I thought you were..."

"Dead?"

Deli nodded. She was still sitting in his lap. Even though Carl was bruised and bleeding, he managed to smile.

"Sorry, but you still owe me some soggy French fries," he said. Then he passed out.

*   *   *

Deli managed to prop Carl's arm back up over his head. He was hurt pretty bad, but if she could keep the bleeding stanched, he should be okay. She checked his pulse, then felt his temperature. She had no idea what was normal for Carl. She'd never really done first aid on anyone so tall.

She tested his response to stimuli by sweeping her hand along his cheek and down his neck. He woke enough to follow her touch with his head. That would have to do for now. Deli didn't want to leave him, but she needed to scout an escape route.

She peeked around the mixer. No one was there. She scooted to the front of the mixer. Still no one was there. She scooted out farther. Then she heard the click.

"Hello, Miss Booty-Call." Zarubin stood behind her, a sleek pistol aimed at her heart. "I would like for you to come with me."

"Thank you," said Deli. "But I have other plans for the evening."

"Let me rephrase myself," he said, adjusting his aim to her left. "I would like for you to come with me, or I will shoot your boyfriend in the head."

DELI'S BEDROOM WINDOW

FROM THE FIRE ESCAPE, Toesy pointed himself toward the outside window ledge and jumped. It wasn't his most graceful jump, but he did stick the landing. Executive Wingman Steve gave him an eight-point-one, which Toesy accepted without argument.

He clung to the sill, hind claws biting into the brick, front paws struggling against the wooden sash. Using his head, Toesy pushed the window open until he had enough space to squeeze in and drop to the floor. He landed in a drift of dirty clothes. They smelled of Deli and...*cheese?*

He looked up.

The Great Man was alive! Toesy broke into a hearty purr, full of goodwill and dynamic sound activation. Executive Wingman Steve adjusted adenosine triphosphate levels accordingly.

* * *

The kitchen was filled with shouting for the moment, so Jake hazarded a whisper. "Hey, buddy, I'm glad you're here! I was worried she got you, too."

Toesy trotted over to him, intent on a joyous head-butt. Luckily, Jake's reflexes were still strong and he grabbed a pair of Deli's jeans to fend off any lacerating nuzzles. Deli soon had a new pair of cutoffs.

"What happened to you, man?"

He tried picking the glass from Toesy's fur, but it was no use. The shards stuck fast in their mortar of dried blood.

Jake gave up de-spiking the cat and found a small spot, less dangerously serrated, just inside Toesy's ear. He gave it a happy scratch. The cat purred louder, and Jake's stomach did a funny little backflip.

He looked down to the hole in his shirt and back to the gory cat. His brow wrinkled and his gaze bounced between Toesy's chest and his own.

"Is that my blood or yours?"

Jake didn't believe that animals understood more than a few key words: *bath, food, treats, outside*—stuff like that. But as soon as he'd asked the question, Toesy looked down at his grisly coat for a second, then brought his nose up and pointed it at the bloodiest part of Jake's shirt. He twitched his left ear in a way that said *both*. Jake nodded gravely.

"What a bitch," he said.

Toesy's eyes squinted into a question.

Who?

"Heather," Jake said. Out in the kitchen, the shouting had quieted down to angry mumbling. Jake dropped his voice even lower.

"Carl's ex-girlfriend."

Toesy stared at Jake, the breadth of his intentions vibrating his long whiskers in angry twitches. Jake knew exactly what the cat was thinking because he'd thought it many, *many* times before.

"We're gonna need a plan," he said.

Fortunately, Executive Wingman Steve already had one.

HANG CHOY FOODS WAREHOUSE

HE WOKE UP TO A CHEAP PLASTIC FLIP-PHONE sitting on his chest, singing an electronic rendition of "Yankee Doodle Dandy." He knew without looking that it wasn't his phone because Carl did not believe in ringtones.

Where was Deli?

The phone rang on. He looked around and, seeing no one in the immediate area, assumed the call was for him. Carl reached out and unflipped the phone.

"Hello?" he said, and immediately wished he hadn't. His head almost split open at the sound.

"Hi, honey! How's your head?" The voice was bright and chipper, and it made Carl's blood run cold.

"Heather."

A sharp spike of fear shot through his stomach. He looked around but couldn't see Deli. Scenes from the past seventy-two hours ran through his mind: Zarubin walking up the steps to the apartment, Deli in customs, finding her shoes on the floor of the ladies room.

"What have you done with her?"

"Oh, sweetheart," said Heather in a sexy growl. "Don't be like that. You can drop the charade now. I've got everything figured out."

"What are you talking about?"

"Our plan, sweetie. Don't tell me you forgot?" She *tsk*ed at him. "You silly boy! I knew you would. Good thing *I* remembered." The mania in her voice was impossible to disguise. Carl knew better than to challenge her.

"I must have forgotten it. Why don't you remind me?"

As he spoke, he flexed his arm. The muscles were stiff and crusty with blood, but the t-shirt bandage was tight and it held the wound closed enough that the bleeding had stopped. Carl sat up.

"Oh, I don't know. I think that would be cheating, don't you?"

"Am I supposed to guess, then?"

Carl tried interjecting some friendliness or at least interest into his voice. It wasn't easy. He flexed his knees a few times. That wasn't easy either.

"I'm sure it will come to you soon. Until then, I'd like to have the password to Sector Nine."

"What do you need with Sector Nine?" Carl disguised the anxiety in his voice by using that moment to hoist himself to his feet. He walked up and down the floor a few times to get his muscles moving.

"It's not important. Just give me the password."

"Ungh," he said. "I'm lightheaded. I'm trying to remember." This was not entirely a lie.

Carl walked cautiously around the factory floor, poking his head around corners and in darkened alcoves, breathing heavily every time he put weight on his right leg.

"Are you hurt? I told those nasty men not to hurt you. *Oh, sweetie pie.*"

"No, I'm just a little tired is all." He said this with all the remembered intimacy he could muster. It made him feel traitorous and weak and he wondered if she engineered it that way. She loved making people feel weak.

"Oh, baby! If they hurt one hair on your head, I will personally make sure they pay for it. Now, what's the password?"

Carl doubted that highly and continued searching the factory floor. He made his way toward the west wall.

"Let me think. I changed it a few months ago."

"*I'm not stupid, Carl.* I happen to know you changed it yesterday, *sweetie.* Now, you just think really hard, and I'm sure you'll come up with it."

"And *how* do you know that?" Carl said. Despite his best efforts, his voice gave away the irritation he felt.

"Ooopsie! Sorry, honey, I forgot to tell you about that part. I've been on the Dungeon server for a few months now."

"You *have*?" Carl was somewhat confused but mostly horrified.

"Yeah, Mr. Big-Shot Pauley boy was a terrific help there. Between you and me, hon, I think he might have been a virgin."

Carl almost choked. "You slept with Paul?"

"It was only so I could make our plan work, honey," she said. "Are you mad?"

"Uh..." Carl didn't know what to say. He wasn't mad. He was nauseated and astounded at the thought, but not mad. "No?"

The far wall was dark as pitch under the catwalk, so he felt around until he found a light switch. A fluorescent bulb bucked to life down a narrow hallway on the right.

"What do you mean *no*? I fucked your roommate in your unmade bed while you were at work, and you don't *care*?"

Carl held the phone away from his ear and shook his head violently. Oh God, *yuck*. He did not need that mental picture right now.

Down the short hallway was an imposing metal door. The door handle was probably locked, but he had to try.

"You're not saying anything, Carl. I think you're mad."

He could hear the excitement in her voice. She was getting off on this.

"Okaaay, I *am* mad. What do you want me to do, Heather?"

She laughed. "That's what I thought. You poor thing. I did it for us, you understand? Now, you need to give me the password to Sector Nine."

"What are you going to do?" Carl grabbed the door handle and turned slowly. Surprisingly, it wasn't locked.

"Never you mind."

"What happens if I don't give it to you?"

"I think we both know the answer to that. Did you find her yet?"

"Find who?"

The steel door opened up to an antechamber of iron bars, like a three-sided dog pen stretching from floor to ceiling. Carl had seen something like it in an old Gothic-style bank before. It was a vault room, designed to keep the money in and the people out. You could see in, but unless you had the key, you stayed out.

Inside the vault, tied to a rickety cane chair, sat Deli. Her mouth was gagged with a dirty blue rag. Underneath the chair was a metal box surrounded by a mess of wires.

"Your little booty-call. What's her name again — *Polly*?"

Carl did not move. He could barely breathe. "Delilah."

"Why are you doing this, Heather?"

"I can't believe you even need to ask," she said. "You've had your fun, Carl. Now it's time we got serious. Give me the password."

"This...this isn't about the Elevators, is it?"

Heather laughed. "Those things? Good Lord, no. That was just convenient. I needed you gone so I could access your Euro-Stock security system backup. I can't believe how well your silly little project worked out for me, though."

"I don't have a backup," Carl said into the phone. His eyes were locked on Deli's, ten feet away and completely inaccessible.

"Don't be stupid, Carl. I know you keep a personal backup of the security protocols. You keep a personal backup of *everything*. It's one of the things I love most about you." She giggled. Carl swallowed the bile in his throat.

"Now, why don't you give me the password, and when the upgrade goes live tomorrow, you and I will be home free. Then we can finally be together, Carl. We won't ever have to work again." Her voice was soft, almost loving.

"I can't, Heather. You know I can't."

"Yes, you can, baby. This line is totally secure. I made sure." When Carl didn't answer immediately, she got snippy.

"This is all your fault, you know. I almost had it, but you changed the damn password before you left. I just needed to make a few little modifications in your code. You wouldn't even have known until later. You weren't supposed to change that password."

"What was I *supposed* to do?" Carl wanted to keep Heather talking, stall her into making a mistake. He didn't know how yet, but he was going to get Deli out of there. She looked so small.

"Oh, you did everything else right, *eventually*. But that was my mistake, baby. I misjudged how much you still loved me. I know you've been kinda lonely since I left. I just assumed you'd tag along with her from the start, no matter what she looked like. I should have gone for a blonde, shouldn't I? Oh well, what's done is done. Did she like the upgrade?"

"Heather, what are you talking about?"

For the first time, Carl broke eye contact with Deli. He looked at the phone.

"The kidnapping was a nice touch. Of course, I didn't think they'd take me literally about the whorehouse, but it worked better than expected. Did you get to see her naked?"

Heather was laughing now. For Deli's sake, Carl tried not to look horrified.

"I think the detective was the weakest link, don't you? I didn't think he'd cave so quickly. You must have been quite forceful. I bet she fell for you as soon as you stepped through the door. Did you wear the grey Armani? You look so sexy in that suit."

"Would you believe Johnny just wanted to kill her outright? Honestly, he's such a brute. Oh wait, I guess he *was* a brute. I understand there's been a hostile takeover on your end."

"*Heather? What are you saying?*" Carl shouted.

"I'm saying, my dear, that if you don't give me the fucking password, you can kiss that little bitch goodbye." Carl jerked his attention back to Deli.

"Yankee Doodle Dandy" began to play again. This time, it came from the nest of wires below Deli's chair. Both of them jumped at the sound. Underneath Deli, the digital timer flashed on. It read 5:00 then flashed off. When it flashed back on, it read 4:59. Carl's eyes bugged out. Deli began to struggle against her bonds.

"I'm trying to set us up for success, Carl," Heather said. "Why are you not helping me?"

"Stop it, Heather. I'll give you anything. Just stop it."

"I want the password to Sector Nine," she said.

"*Omenstep13* — sub out the number three for the E's," he shouted into the phone. Then he spelled it out, in case she heard it wrong.

"*Finally*," Heather said. "That wasn't so difficult now, was it? Thank you, sweetheart."

Carl held his breath as he looked at the counter. It blinked 4:57, then blinked off. He smiled and exhaled.

The counter blinked back on.

It flashed 4:56.

"Turn it off, Heather," Carl shouted into the phone. "You said you'd turn it off!"

"Yes, well, about that. It's just that I don't really think this a healthy relationship for you, Carl. I think you might be getting too attached.

I can't have that little slut taking you away from me now, can I? You should have left her on the boat where she belonged, babe, but if you leave now, you'll have plenty of time to get out of there. I'll meet you at the hotel tomorrow, okay? The Garden Suite, right? You always did know how to treat a girl nice."

He heard a click and the phone went dead.

DELI'S LIVING ROOM

"LET'S TALK ABOUT JAKE," she said.

The conversation with Carl had left her giddy, and she twirled the gun around her finger playfully. Then she grabbed it and pointed it very close to at Sacha's head. He continued to focus on the computer screen. It took all of his willpower to pretend she wasn't there.

"Where is he?" she yelled.

"Who?"

"Don't fuck with me, Sacha. Where is he?"

"I haven't seen him since yesterday." Sacha said it convincingly but just a fraction of a second too fast and Heather was unusually skilled at picking up lies. She drew herself in toward him, still aiming the gun.

"Where *is* he, Sacha? I know he was here last night. I shot him through the fucking cat."

"You shot her *cat*?" Even for Heather that was low. She wasn't just insane, she was depraved.

"What? It had mange. It looked like it was on its last legs, anyway. God, you make it sound like I shot a baby or something." She gave him half a smirk and shrugged. Regrettably, she still had the gun in her hand when she did so. Sacha did a fine bit of bobbing and weaving until Heather stopped giggling and exploded with rage.

"*Where the fuck is he, Sacha?*"

Sacha froze. His heart stopped beating and the color drained from his cheeks. She was going to shoot him, right here. Then he was totally going to die until he was all the way dead.

"You know, I don't think you properly appreciate the dynamic here. *You*" —she rested the gun on the fuzzy spot between his eyes—

"have a gun pointed at your head. Which means that *I* get to call the shots." She paused. "Okay, that's funny. Get it? I call the *shots.*" Heather laughed a semi-lucid giggle. Then she pointed the gun at Sacha's leg and pulled the trigger. He was so surprised that he didn't feel the pain right away. When it hit him two seconds later, he leaned over the carpet and threw up.

"Now, tell me where the fuck he is or the next time it won't be your fucking leg." She cocked the gun and used his shoulder to steady her aim.

Maybe she just wanted to talk with Jake. Maybe they could work this out.

No, that wasn't going to happen. Heather was nuts. She was going to shoot him. Then she would find Jake and shoot him, too. No matter what Sacha did, they weren't going to survive this woman. All of this was his fault. The only way to redeem himself now was to keep his mouth shut. He looked Heather in the eye and refused to speak.

"Have it your way," she said, but before she could pull the trigger, her phone started playing "Tennessee Waltz."

"That *damn well* better be Zarubin." She rolled her eyes and made a ridiculous show of checking her text messages. However, when she skimmed the screen, her eyes contorted into angry slits, and her face flushed red with fury. She threw the phone on the table and stalked past Sacha toward the kitchen.

With the hand not currently acting as a tourniquet, Sacha reached out and picked up her phone. The text was still open. It was from Jake.

COME AT ME, BITCH.

DELI'S BEDROOM

"HE'S IN HERE, ISN'T HE?"

She kicked the bedroom door with such force that it bounced off the closet wall and came back at her. She kicked it three more times in succession before the doorknob punched through the plaster and the door stuck open.

"Get out here, Jake. Where I can see you, you *bastard.*"

She spoke in a deadly growl, like a panther right before it eats the face off a baby squirrel. At least that's how Jake imagined it. He always thought of Heather as a face-eater. It was in the way she stared at you, like she was trying to decide what kind of sauce to serve with your cheeks. *God, he was hungry.*

"No."

He spoke so quietly that Heather was forced to step forward to hear him. The light from the kitchen cast her shadow into the room.

"You chickenshit coward. Come out and fight like the pathetic girl you are."

Heather's shadow scratched the back of its neck. She refused to step any farther into the room. Jake suspected that Toesy's growling had a lot to do with her hesitation. Even Jake was a little scared of Toesy at the moment, and he was pretty sure the cat had started worshipping him like some sort of canned-food-bearing god.

Her shadow stretched out an arm and the foot of Deli's bed exploded in a fit of feathers and stuffing. The boom made everyone jump. Heather jerked backward with the recoil. The growling stopped.

"What the fuck? Are you crazy?"

"I *hate* you, Jake. You took everything from me. My boyfriend, my home, my job—*everything*! Now, I'm going to take everything from you."

"I didn't take your damn boyfriend, Heather, you did that all by your crazy self."

"Shut up!"

Bullets hit the wall beneath the window and dust erupted from the fresh craters. Bits of plaster pattered to the floor like rain. The growling started again.

"I always knew you'd be back. You just can't let him be happy, can you? You soul-sucking harpy."

Deli's dressing mirror exploded in glittering shards, then a pane of glass in the window shattered. The growling deepened.

"What are you going to do, Heather—kill me? What the hell is so important on the Sector Nine drive that you'd go to prison for it?"

"Money, you idiot. *Lots and lots* of money. And if you think I'm going to prison for this, you're sadly mistaken. As soon as I've got the security patch installed, I'm out, you're dead, and Carl's little booty-call's fingerprints are all over the gun."

"Security patch?"

"For the stock exchange. My God, Jake, do I have to spell it out for you?" She laughed. "Never mind. I already know the answer to that."

She slowed her speech and talked louder. "Carl has been working on their security upgrade for two years. I just made one tiny tweak. It won't send up any flags. It just changes some numbers, that's all."

"Changes what numbers?"

"The number two...into anything I want, actually. Instead of twenty-five, I can make the screen read seventy-five or fifteen. That's all."

Jake could hear the smile in her voice. Toesy stood right next to him, sounding like a diesel-powered hellhound. He followed her reasoning backward for only a second before he saw what she intended to do. It was brilliantly simple.

"You're going to destroy the stock market," he said.

Heather groaned.

"You've never been very good at subtlety, have you, Jake? I have no intention of ruining the stock market, I want to *own* it. Think of it as extreme guerilla marketing, encouraging people to spend their money in certain ways. For a small fee, I can provide that kind of encouragement. A two turning into a three can be a problem, but not an *unfixable* problem."

"Jesus, Heather, that's sneaky," said Jake. "But you'll never get it to work."

"It already works, you idiot—or have you forgotten the South China Sea?"

"That was you!" Jake said. He *knew* that signal had been hinky somehow.

"You *finally* figured it out."

"So you're going to plunder the stock market and frame Carl. That will really make him want you back."

"*No!*" she yelled. Jake saw the shadow of her arm raise up and point the gun again. He tensed.

"I didn't frame Carl last time. He was supposed to meet me in Cabo for our anniversary. But *you* had to go sniffing around and ruin all of it." Her voice spiked in anger and her shadow crept forward.

"So I changed it up this time. He's already out of the country. All I have to do is make sure his sidekick plugs in the security patch and then I'll meet him in Hong Kong. He even booked a room for us at the Maxwell. The Garden Suite, isn't that just like him?"

Jake didn't know what to say. Heather was talking ten thousand percent loony-bird.

"Are you sure he's expecting you?" Her shadow grew larger as she stepped farther into the room.

"*Of course he is.* As soon as he gets rid of that little whore, he'll figure it out. So you see," she said, stepping in front of the closet. "I have no more use for *you.*"

She pointed the gun at Jake and fired.

HANG CHOY FOODS WAREHOUSE
4 MINUTES AND 55 SECONDS UNTIL
LIFE CHANGES DRASTICALLY

4:55

"Deli!"

Carl ran at the steel bars and kicked them as hard as he could, but the only thing that did was make his foot hurt. Deli stared at him through her hair, shaking her head slowly from side to side.

4:50

"Okay, we can do this. I can do this. You can do this. How do we do this?" he said. But of course Deli couldn't answer.

Carl hadn't thought about Heather in months. Why was she doing this? How dare she do this? After everything he'd gone through for that woman, she was still torturing him. Carl made a half turn toward the doorway and kicked the open door. It hurt his foot much less than the steel bars.

4:45

"Mmmph MmmmMMMmmmph" said Deli. Carl looked at her.

"Mmmph MmMMMPH" she said again, this time with more emphasis on the MMMPH part. Then she nodded toward something. Carl followed the vector of her nod toward the wall. He saw what she meant.

"That might work!" he said.

The steel bars, though formidable and likely impossible to breach, had been bolted into the aging plaster wall. They were *not* bolted to the ceiling or the floor. When Carl kicked the bars, one of the bolts popped loose. He set about kicking more of them. Most of them budged, some of them did not.

3:28

"There's one left," he said. "I can't get it to move!" His panic began to grow in volume. Carl ran at the wall, smashing his good shoulder against the bars over and over. Deli tried to spit out the rag out of her mouth but had to stop when she started to gag. He could see her working her hands up and down, trying to loosen the rope. He ran at the bars again, smashing himself into them with all his strength. Fresh blood began to seep through the bandage on his arm.

3:02

Deli's eyes sparkled in the light from the low bulb overhead. Even through her hair, he could see the tears forming.

"No, no, no, no, no, Deli," he said. "Please, I've almost got it. We're going to get you out of there."

The last time he hit the bars, he could swear that something moved. He kicked at them three times from every angle he could, then reared back to smash himself into them again.

"Listen to me," Carl said in a breathless voice. "I'm not going to let this happen. Can you hear me?" Deli nodded a sliver, but Carl could work with a sliver.

"Remember the time you punched Augie Terkle?" He ran at the bars again. Deli's eyebrows raised up half an inch.

"At Paul's Christmas party. You knocked him out. Remember?" Deli nodded slowly.

"Get angry like you did that night," he said. "Stay angry like that. We'll get out. I know we will. There is a"—he ran at the bars again—"ninety percent chance that this bolt will come loose within five seconds."

2:56

"Eighty-seven percent chance," he said as he gulped in air.

2:53

"Eighty three percent chance," said Carl, but he only whispered it.

2:31

Numb from the stomach up, Carl ran at the wall again. He couldn't continue to kid himself much longer. He had absolutely no strength left. He opened his mouth to say so, but at that moment the bolt, which had held so tightly to the wall, finally gave out. Like a revolving door, the steel bars pivoted forward with his momentum, and Carl found himself sprawled out on the floor. Deli gave an exaggerated grunt of victory. Carl couldn't have said it better himself.

2:12

The first thing he did was take the gag from her mouth.

"You saw me punch Terkle?" Deli said.

Carl didn't answer. He was very busy untying knots.

1:52

He pushed and pulled the stiff rope. It was no use. He couldn't get the knots undone. Deli turned her wrists sideways to give him some slack, but it wasn't working.

"Can we cut them?" Deli said.

"Good idea!" Carl shouted. Then looked around the room. "What with?"

"I dunno, do you have some glass or something?"

Carl almost said that he did not have any glass, but that wasn't true. He had at least three computer screens in his bag. Without thinking, he grabbed one, opened it and stepped on it, shattering the screen. He drew a shard out and tested it. It was too blunt to cut anything.

The second screen he tried came from his fancy cell phone. Since it was already cracked. he plucked a piece from the frame and tried it. To his surprise, it worked.

1:09

Deli's hands fell free. She reached down and untied the knots around her legs in less time than Carl could have imagined.

0:25

They ran.

0:00

Life became very interesting.

DELI'S BEDROOM

THE BULLET GRAZED JAKE'S HEAD, leaving a slash along his cheekbone. Later it would turn into a scar and an awesome story, but for now, Jake was petrified into inaction. Toesy, however, stuck to the plan.

An inhuman scream ripped through the air. From the corner of his eye, Jake saw pinpoints of light fly past. He watched as every razor-sharp part of Toesy (nearly all of him, by now) clamped down on Heather's hand and endeavored to separate it from the gun, or her wrist, whichever came loose first. Toesy didn't seem to care. Heather snarled and hissed, oblivious to the pain.

Out in the hall, a great walloping thump crashed into the front door. Jake felt the floor jerk. As improbable as it seemed, he could swear he smelled garlic.

* * *

Sock Pants dropped the gun. It bounced off a small hillock of t-shirts into the corner. To keep her from recovering it, Toesy bit down on her ankle. His fangs sunk so deeply into her leg that they hit something hard. Executive Wingman Steve suggested he bite down some more, just to see what would happen, but Toesy vetoed that. Humans tended to be sensitive about these things, he reasoned, even if it was for a good cause. Steve stored that directive for later.

The room rocked with another booming thud from the front door and still the woman did not stop. She kicked at Toesy with her cat-free foot and roared a feral growl. Blood splattered from her hands. She paid it no mind. The light of madness shone brilliantly in her eyes.

She dragged herself, cat and all, across the floor. Toesy saw what she intended and disengaged his jaw. They both made a mad dash for the gun, but Toesy, having twice as many feet, got there first. He grabbed it with his paw. Using his fabulous new thumbs, he dragged it away from the furious woman. She lunged at him. Toesy decided she was definitely Siamese, probably purebred. He held the gun to his chest and hoped the men in blue uniforms would come soon.

Snippets of voices carried through from the hall.

"Mr. Denny?"

"…This is the Seattle Police."

But the shouting and thumping at the front door had no effect on the scene unfolding in Deli's room. Neither Toesy nor Sock Pants blinked. The rest of the room ceased to exist as they stared each other down. She had turned an ashy grey color. Blood flowed from the tooth-shaped holes in her hand and leg. Her tight skirt and sock pants were slick with it.

She walked, calmly and deliberately, to the massive cat. Toesy backed up. He could take this woman down in a fight *if* she was normal, but she was no longer normal. She had gone rabid. Not even a bird dog was stupid enough to tangle with the rabid.

He tightened his grip on the gun and hauled it backward toward the Great Man. The room was so quiet that he could hear her heart beat. He stared into her angry, lifeless eyes and wondered for the first time what it would be like to lose a fight.

It will probably hurt.

Another boom on the front door and the tension in the room snapped.

Sock Pants grabbed for the gun at the same time Toesy lunged. He was fast, but the rabid animal in her had an incredible blocking reflex. She jabbed her arm sideways and smashed Toesy in the face, knocking him off his balance and shredding the skin of her forearm. She didn't even flinch.

With her left hand, she grabbed the gun from the floor and aimed it at the cat. Toesy rolled through the impact and was getting back to his feet when she pulled the trigger.

*   *   *

The bullet hit Toesy in the side, throwing him halfway across the room. Jake had never heard a cat scream like that before. A normal person would have soiled their pants upon hearing it. Heather just laughed.

"Fuck you," she said and kicked at the bleeding cat. "I've killed you twice now. *Stay dead this time.*"

The pop of gunfire electrified the sounds coming from outside the door. Someone was screaming something but Jake couldn't make out the words. He hoped they would break the door before Heather shot him.

"Heather," said a weak voice. Jake looked up from his laundry-covered foxhole to see Sacha standing in the doorway. Blood pooled below him on the carpet. His face had turned a ghastly shade of white.

"Heather, don't do this," Sacha said with the little energy he had left.

"I don't need you any more, Sacha," She drew the gun up. True to her word, Heather didn't shoot Sacha in the leg this time.

HANG CHOY FOODS WAREHOUSE

THEY MADE IT TO THE FAR SIDE of the factory floor before the explosion threw reality a few inches to the south. Wave after wave of empty jars lapped at the floor in a sea of broken glass. One of the machines buzzed and flashed red while jets of steam poured from its side. Through it all, Deli ran. Carl kept pace with her as best he could, but the energy it took to get her free had tapped him out. Deli was getting away.

The building rocked as smaller explosions sent spasms through the walls. Deli looked ahead to see the fire door twenty feet away. She looked behind. Carl wasn't there.

"Carl!" Deli screamed. "Carl! Where are you?" She turned on her heels and ran back searching the ground for anything remotely Carl-shaped. The air burned her nose, and billows of thick, black smoke made it difficult for her to see.

Instinctively, she ran toward the one thing she *could* see—the buzzing, flashing machine. She found him on the floor ten feet from it.

"Come on, Carl!" Deli shouted to hide the panic in her voice.

Carl didn't respond.

"Carl, wake up! For chrissake, don't die on me. We're in a pickle warehouse." Deli shook his arm. Carl still didn't respond but she could see his chest move with shallow breath. She rolled him over to his back, threw his beloved messenger bag on his stomach, stuck one hand under each armpit and started hauling him across the floor. It was slow going.

"I need you alive, Carl! Wake up!"

Deli found it increasingly difficult to catch her breath. Carl became dead weight. She could not pull him much longer in this haze.

She stopped to adjust the hold she had on his arms. When she let go of his left arm, his bag fell to the ground, spewing his hoard of electronics across the floor. She gathered up what she could reach without letting go of Carl: two phones, a small computer and a little glass jar.

A glass jar? What the hell was that for?

She studied the jar, bringing it close to her face to see it through the smoky haze. Inside it was a silver bean mottled with blobs of green and red powdery stuff.

This must be one of the Elevators!

She opened the jar and dumped the Elevator into her hand. What was all the green sticky stuff? Maybe it was some sort of biofilm? She couldn't even guess what the red powder was.

Carl said he didn't think it could make you invincible but he wasn't totally sure. Deli had nothing to lose.

She knelt down next to him, propped his head up in her lap and opened his mouth. The smoke was thinner down near the ground but it was still very hard to see. Deli wasn't exactly sure how it worked, so she jammed the bean as far down his throat as she could and hoped he wouldn't choke on it.

Carl's eyes blinked opened. Then he clutched at his throat and started coughing. Deli helped him sit up and hit him hard on the back. Beads of perspiration stood out on his forehead and he swallowed several times in a row before pulling in a great gulp of smoky air. This caused the Elevator to down shoot straight down his esophagus. He shook his head and cleared his throat a few times.

"That was...spicy," he said at last. His voice sounded shaky and painful. Carl looked at Deli. Her cheeks shimmered with tears.

"I think we should probably leave," he said.

"You *think*?"

It was difficult to laugh, cry, and talk at the same time. Deli choked a little. Carl lifted his arm up to her. She took his hand in both of hers, ducked under his arm, and hoisted him three-quarters of the way up to standing. Carl blinked and looked down.

"You are"—he said, wincing at the pain in his throat—"*really* short."

"Yeah, I know," she said.

As they shuffled along the floor to the emergency door, the heat in the air intensified. Flickering orange light cast shadows on the wall in front of them. Carl walked faster with each step. His strength was returning. They reached the door as a gigantic crash ripped through the ceiling, and the west side of the catwalk leaned toward the factory floor.

"I'm sorry for this," Carl said.

"Yeah, I know," said Deli.

They tumbled through the security door into a back alley filled with old furniture and rats.

Lots of rats.

Lots and *lots* of rats.

Deli was a sensible woman. There were way too many things to worry about at the moment to let seven million rats bother her, so she didn't. She pushed Carl out of the door, and pulled him to the middle of the alley.

The rats, preoccupied with escape, skittered around but paid them no heed. She hitched Carl's arm up around her neck and followed the river of beady eyes and whiskers toward the fresh air. Later, she promised herself a nice little freakout, but only after she had a stiff shot of whiskey.

DELI'S BEDROOM

ANOTHER BOOM SHOOK THE APARTMENT, followed by a splintering sound, but Jake knew they were too late. Heather turned to him. There was no life in her eyes that he could see, only malice and greed.

"I don't need you anymore, either, Jake." She laughed and pulled the trigger.

The gun made no noise.

Heather gave him a confused look. She walked closer to him, aimed the gun directly at his head and pulled the trigger again.

This time the blast was enough to pierce his eardrums. He looked down to see where he'd been shot but he still wore his black t-shirt so he couldn't see any blood right away. He looked back to Heather. She smiled wide with victory.

Jake's dying thought was that Heather had lipstick all over her teeth.

He second dying thought was the he didn't really feel much pain. He'd heard the gun go off, so he knew he'd been shot, but he couldn't feel where he'd been hit. He took a short inventory of himself and found that he wasn't in any more pain than he had been ten minutes ago. His head hurt like a son of a bitch. He was slightly damp and he no longer had to pee, but other than that, everything seemed okay. He looked again at Heather and realized that wasn't lipstick pouring out of her mouth.

"We need an ambulance now!" someone shouted.

"Mr. Denny!" someone else shouted. "Mr. Denny! Damn it, *Jake*, are you okay?"

He couldn't tell if he was okay or not. The voice kept asking, and after a moment, it occurred to him that he ought to say something so he nodded.

"Oh my God, Jake, I totally thought you were dead!"

Worn out from too many near-death experiences and not enough blood, Jake assumed he was hallucinating because the voice sounded remarkably like Pizza Girl.

"Nah," he whispered. "It's just a flesh wound."

The silky voice giggled, then burst into a full, throaty laugh. It was a wonderful laugh, all fluid and savory. He found sanctuary in such a laugh.

Jake tried to join in, but it hurt too much. So he settled for smiling until he passed out.

SHIPYARD ON THE
KOWLOON PENINSULA
1:00 P.M.

HE STOOD SHIVERING AND NAKED from the waist up, save for the grubby bandage of blackened t-shirt Deli had tied around his arm. His right side was crusty with blood. Jin procured a towel from somewhere and wrapped it around Carl's shoulders. Carl refused to go to the hospital on the grounds that Johnny's detective friends might still be looking for them. At least the towel covered the blood.

"Why not?" said Carl.

She didn't know why not. Going back to the hotel minutes after they escaped fiery death-by-homicidal-ex-girlfriend just didn't feel right. It would make the past thirty-six hours feel somewhat trivial, like they had been on an adventure cruise or something. But his arm needed tending, and housekeeping would definitely have a sewing kit. It had been a while since she'd had to sew anyone back together. Maybe they should stop and get some iodine.

Jin was reluctant to let them go, insisting that they come to the boat instead. Xing-Tiu had stayed with his cousin's family and would not return until tomorrow morning. He had plenty of room for them. He could patch Carl up and they would be ready to run in case the Russian came after them. Carl put up a woozy, semi-conscious argument that Zarubin thought they were dead and would therefore not come looking for them. Jin was not convinced.

Finally, Deli stepped in with a shrewd suggestion. "Captain Jin," she said.

"*Shi*! Jin." He pointed to himself.

"Would you come with us to the hotel? I can take care of Carl's arm, but I will need a few things and I cannot speak Chinese. Of course you can stay on the *Doris Day*, but it would be much easier if you came to the hotel with us. I'm sure we can get you your own room."

Carl opened his eyes wider. He translated her words as well as he could, making sure to explain that he would pay for Jin's hotel room. The offer delighted Jin, though he declined to let Carl pay for the room. They left immediately.

* * *

They walked through the front doors of the hotel, an unlikely trio of dirty, bleeding ruffians that surely had no legitimate business at the Maxwell. Patrons gawked. The ruffians paid no attention to them.

As they walked through the lobby, the doorman nodded surreptitiously at a security guard hiding behind a potted fern. The security guard gave him a knowing nod back. Jin saw the nod exchange and gave them both a thumbs-up. The security guard didn't know what to do with that, so he returned the gesture. Then he felt silly and went back to hiding behind his potted fern.

The concierge on duty that afternoon was an older gentleman with a shiny head of empty real estate and crooked yellow teeth that Deli appreciated. He had been practicing his "You might be more comfortable at…" speech as Carl approached.

"Has anyone come in and asked for room 742? Have there been any messages?" he said in a raspy, tired voice and held up the room key.

All five hairs in the concierge's eyebrows jumped in surprise. Room 742 was the Garden Suite. *These* people were staying in the Garden Suite?

"Sir," the concierge said, bowing his head slightly. Then, because he was good at his job, he checked the mail slots. Room 742 had one message. He handed it over to Carl with the air of someone trying to figure if an apology was necessary. Carl took it without smiling. He was too tired to smile.

Deli had learned a lot of sneaky tricks in a childhood full of Paul Pelham. One thing she learned was reading backward and in reverse.

The hotel stationery was nice thick paper, but a lamp on the counter lit it from behind and Deli couldn't help but read it through the other side.

Some "Bunny" missed you! I'm glad you're back!

—H

As Carl read the note, his eyes grew angry. When he finished, he ripped it in half. Then he crumpled it up. Then he threw it in a garbage can.

"Who was that from?" Deli asked.

"No one important," he said.

THE GARDEN SUITE

"IT'S ABOUT TIME. Where the fuck have you been?"

"Paul?" Deli said.

Paul sat in the living room of the Garden Suite, looking like a high roller and smelling like a fresh penny. His shoes were so glossy, she could see up his pant leg in the reflection.

"In the flesh!" he said, smiling and chipper. He had on a new suit, tailored to make him look taller. "What the hell have you guys been doing? Why are you all dirty? Wait, don't answer that. I'm sure I don't want to know. Are you enjoying your vacation?"

"What do you mean, *vacation*?" Deli said stiffly.

"Well, maybe not vacation. I don't know. I told Heather I didn't think it was a good idea. But she said Carl needed it." Paul didn't notice Deli glaring at him. "Tell her, Carl."

Carl was too dumbfounded to speak. He stared at Paul in disbelief.

"Come on, Carl! Tell her what Heather said." Carl did not say a word. Deli turned her glare on him.

"Yeah, Carl," she said in a small voice. "What did Heather say about your *vacation*?"

Carl shook his head and looked confused. Deli turned to Paul for an answer. Paul laughed.

"Oh, Heather was only trying to help, sis." Paul pointed at Carl. "She knew Carl wanted to impress you. So she thought if you two could take a break—you know, relax and all that crap, it would be good for you both. You know? Make sparks fly. Whatever." He made jazz hands and flew imaginary sparks around.

Deli's expression went from angry to furious. She turned to Carl. *"Did you know about this?"*

"No," said Carl. He put his hands up to show how much he didn't know. "That is not what happened."

Deli wasn't supposed to be mad at him. She was supposed to be happy they were alive and possibly willing to celebrate. Instead she stood in front of him, all spiky and murderous. Why wouldn't Paul shut up?

"How did you do it?" Her eyebrow arched high.

"Do what?" said Paul.

"*Was the bomb a plant, too?*"

"What bomb?" said Paul.

"No." Carl's eyes were wide with fear. The blood had drained from his face, making his bruises stand out. "I had n-no idea! Please, you have to believe me. I had no idea all this was going to happen."

"What bomb, guys?" Paul said in his whiny kid voice.

"*Shut up!*" they yelled in unison.

Carl stared intently at Deli, trying to make her see that he was telling the truth.

"You know what's funny?" she asked, implying there was nothing funny left in the universe.

"Um…" said Carl.

"That's exactly what Terkle said."

"Deli…" Carl said.

"Leave it," she snapped. "You can have the couch. I will leave you *fifty percent* of the pillows." Then she went into the bathroom and slammed the door behind her. Carl stared at the locked door.

"Jeez, what a bitch," Paul said. He scowled for a few seconds then brightened up. "What did you think about all the Beatles stuff?"

Carl didn't say anything.

"I mean, I thought it was kinda stupid but she said it would be perfect."

The sound of bathwater filling the tub brought Carl back to reality. He rounded on Paul.

"How did you get in here?"

"I paid the stupid old concierge twenty bucks to let me on the floor. Told him it was for a surprise party in a room down the hall. Then I found a housekeeping lady and told her I left my key in the room. She let me in. Can you believe that? For twenty bucks, I can get into your hotel room. What did you pay for it? Five hundred? Ha!"

"*Why* are you here, Paul?" Even though his voice had gained deadly levels of fury, Paul still paid it no attention. He strolled through the living room to look at himself in the reflection of the windows.

"Heather was supposed to call tonight with some business details, but I haven't heard from her. She told me not to bother you guys, but I can't stall any longer. I don't know anything about the product delivery date and this is a big-time deal. You don't walk away from a buyer like this. I need to know when she can deliver."

"This product," Carl said. "Is it an actual product or more of a service?"

"Funny you should ask. It's a service. She said she'd have a pricing structure and a definite drop date by tonight around—"

"Six Eastern time, right?"

"Yes," Paul said. He looked a little amazed. "Were you in on this, too? How did you know?"

"Because that's when the Euro-Stock upgrade goes live." He crossed the room in three long strides and grabbed the phone off the desk, intent on calling into work immediately. But after he fat-fingered the phone buttons three times in a row, he slammed the phone down and turned on Paul.

"What happened with Terkle?" he said.

"What? Augie Terkle? That was ages ago, man. Weren't you and Heather at that party? You saw what happened."

"*What the hell happened?*"

"Wow, okay! Calm the fuck down, man."

Carl stood up straight and stared down at Paul. "*Tell me.*"

"Terkle bet me a hundred dollars that he could get Deli to sleep with him."

Carl's left eye twitched. "That's the worst thing I've ever heard. Why would you do that to your sister?"

"Dude, *I bet against him.*"

Carl's left eye twitched again. He swallowed hard and looked Paul straight in the eyes as he walked calmly across the floor. His fist made such a satisfying smack against Paul's nose that Carl thought about pulling his arm back and doing it again. Instead, he picked Paul up by the shoulders and hauled him out of the room. Normally, Paul would have resisted such treatment, but after the initial shock had worn off, he was too busy clutching his face to protest much.

Carl *definitely* did not feel bad about it.

"I think you will find"—Carl said as he schlepped Paul to the door—"that your actions constitute a breach of contract. I found one of the Elevators stuck into a wad of gum in a restaurant. I'll take money from the escrow account to pay for damages." He dropped Paul to the floor as he hauled the front door open.

"That leaves one nanobot unaccounted for. The rest of your money will be held for an additional thirty days." He dragged the stunned and bleeding Paul into the hallway. "If you have not returned the outstanding hardware by then, the escrow account will become property of Sanderson & Denny, Inc., as per the rules of early contract dissolution," Carl said as he dumped Paul next to an alcove containing a gigantic silk flower arrangement.

"We will, of course, pay you for your time." He kicked Paul's leg away from the door. "But if I don't get my fucking robot back in thirty days, I will make your life miserable."

Then he slammed the door in Paul's face.

HALLWAY OUTSIDE
THE GARDEN SUITE

FUCKING *CARL.* He had always been such a pushover. Why did he have to pick this week to grow a pair? Paul was just doing what Heather told him to do—he'd never considered that he might get called out on breach of contract. Fuck.

Paul sat against the wall, legs stretched out, head back. Jesus, his nose hurt. He had already destroyed his handkerchief trying to stop the bleeding. His cornflower silk shirt was totally ruined, as well as the double-stitched, satin-lined pants. Fuck. Carl was going to pay for those. Paul grumbled about his ruined clothes as he tried to figure out what to do.

The truth was…well…the truth was that he hadn't looked up Carl and Deli just because Heather had gone MIA. Paul was worried about the buyer: He wasn't the most patient person alive, and he had an interesting way with guns—namely, he liked pointing them at people, then pulling the trigger.

He *had* hoped Carl would help him out. Sure, there was some bad blood between him and Heather, but that'll happen when a hot chick dumps you. You have to get over it. Deli was *totally* Carl's type, what with the books and all the thinking and stuff. Paul figured they would have some Chinese food, get drunk, and take it back to a swanky hotel. Then when they got back home, *wham!* Carl is over Heather, Deli has a boyfriend, and he wouldn't have to hide the fact that he and Heather were humping like rabbits every Thursday afternoon.

But Deli had to blow everything out of proportion *again*. She never appreciated any of his efforts. Ugh, his sister was impossible.

A polite ding announced the elevator. Paul, preoccupied with bloodstains and self-pity, did not pay attention. That was his first mistake.

"Hello, Mr. Pelham, Miss Spider told me I might find you here."

Paul looked up in surprise.

The man's eyes were hard. In the soft, recessed lighting of the hallway, his circular scar looked pink and fresh. The skin under his close-cropped hair shone with a greasy flicker as he walked toward Paul.

"Who the hell are you?"

"I am your new business partner."

"Fuck off, man," said Paul. "I got enough problems."

That was his second mistake.

THE GARDEN SUITE BATHROOM

SHE HEARD THEM ARGUE. She heard someone get hit. She heard the door slam. She heard Carl calling someone from the living room. She didn't know what to make of it all. She spent an hour and a half in the bathtub trying to come to a decision. Part of her wanted to tell Carl to leave. She would make her way home by herself, thank you very much. Part of her wanted to punch him. Another part of her wanted him to be telling the truth: that he had nothing to do with any of this.

She had more parts, and they all had their own opinions. It took a long time for her to come to a decision, but eventually she made up her mind.

She was round and pink and warm to the touch by the time she got out of the tub. Swaddling herself in the Godzilla-sized bathrobe, Deli waded out into the living room on a gust of almond- and honey-scented steam. Lights were on all over the room, but she didn't see Carl anywhere. Her heart sank.

She shuffled over to the TV area and picked up the phone. As she sat down to dial Jin's room, she stumbled and landed tailbone first on something very solid. She turned to find herself sitting on the steel bar of the hide-a-bed. The couch cushions were gone.

Rubbing her sore tailbone, Deli looked around. Not only were the couch cushions gone, but the cushions from both wingback chairs were gone as well. A quick survey of the room yielded no additional cushions or throw pillows of any kind. They were all missing.

Deli walked to the doorway of the bedroom. The king bed, so fluffy and inviting before, was now a towering arrangement of bolsters and throw pillows with a roof of peacock-blue cushions. There were two feet, clean but bare, sticking out the end of it. The legs wore plain flannel pajama pants.

"Carl?"

Immediately the overstuffed architecture crumbled as an earthquake of Carl proportions sat bolt upright. He must have gone to Jin's room and showered because his hair was still damp. He'd changed into pajama pants. The short sleeve of his cotton undershirt stopped short of the bandage he had wrapped around his arm. It was polka-dotted with red spots where the blood seeped through.

"Hey."

He moved slowly, as if he had been sleeping, but his eyes were alert. She did not walk into the room. There were too many pillows.

"Carl, what the hell are you doing?" Deli asked.

"Nothing," he said too quickly. Then he stood up and started picking up the pillows off the floor and arranging them on the bed. He concentrated on the pillows as he spoke.

"Are you making a pillow fort?"

"No," he said. "Maybe."

Deli stopped herself from smiling.

"I called Jake," he said.

"How's everything going back home?" She tried to sound noncommittal.

"He, uh…he didn't answer," Carl said. Then he stood straight up and focused on nothing at all. When he spoke again, it all came out in a jumble.

"He was staying with your cat. Sacha hadn't cleaned the bathroom, and I guess you did. Whatever. I knew he was there, so I kept calling. But then you went missing, so I called Sacha, only he was sleeping with Heather, too. I'm not really sure how that happened. I thought he knew better than that. But I guess…whatever. She had him over a barrel, and then your cat got involved, and I finally got smart enough to just call your home phone." He turned to her, wringing a gold brocade throw pillow nervously in his hands.

"Carl, what are you trying to tell me?"

"They've been shot," he said.

"Who?"

"Jake and Sacha. She shot them both."

Deli gasped. She walked over to the bed and sat down.

"Jesus, are they okay?" she said. Carl continued pummeling the poor pillow. He walked absently to the bed and sat next to Deli—not too close, though. He was careful about these things.

"Somehow Jake got the pizza delivery girl involved. She called the police. They were at your place. It was her I talked to at the hospital. She told me that Jake was conscious but Sacha was still in surgery. Apparently, he's pretty bad."

"Heather is dead. The police broke your door in and shot her before she could do any more damage."

Deli had no idea what to say. She stared, open-mouthed, at Carl.

"I didn't do this." He waved the pillow around to indicate everything that had happened. "I can't lie to you; the past two days have been incredible in lots of ways." He stopped waving the pillow and looked at Deli. "But I promise you, this wasn't my idea. I did not start any of this." He hung his head.

"For what it's worth, I think you're telling the truth." Deli reached over and hesitantly put a hand on Carl's knee. "I'm so sorry about Jake and Sacha."

"Thanks," said Carl.

"Not so much about Heather, though," she said.

"Yeah," Carl said. "That's okay." He gave Deli a halfhearted smile.

She moved closer to Carl. "When will you know about Sacha?"

"I talked to Kix about thirty minutes ago. She said she would call me back when she had news. She had no idea when that would be, though."

Deli cocked her head to the side. "Kix *Welty*?"

"Sure, I guess. I don't know her last name."

"Carl, I know Kix. If she's at the hospital with Jake, she'll make sure he's okay. You can trust her." Carl looked surprised at that.

"You *know* her?"

"Sure I do. She's been training with me for the last year and a half. She's very sweet. She's also pretty deadly." Deli gave him half a smile.

Carl smiled back at her, then hung his head again. They stayed like that for some time.

A SUITABLE AMOUNT
OF TIME LATER

"CAN I ASK YOU SOMETHING?"

"Sure." Carl said this into his lap.

"What were you *really* doing before I came in?"

Carl looked at Deli. His eyes were blank for a second. Then he turned a brilliant shade of red.

"Nothing," he said, and stood up. He walked across the room and started picking up pillows again. "I was just thinking through something."

"Did you come up with anything good?"

"No, I still couldn't figure it out."

"Figure what out?"

Deli hopped off the bed and walked over to where Carl was sorting pillows. She picked up the missing couch cushion and tossed it out to the living room.

Carl looked down. He blushed again. He looked up. He gave Deli an embarrassed smile and fidgeted with his bare feet.

"It's just that, well, on the boat with Jin, when you were falling asleep, you told me I was missing out on all the, uh"—Carl cleared his throat—"*snugglies.*"

Carl looked at the floor, avoiding eye contact for the moment. His mouth had dried up, and he was having a difficult time getting the words out.

"I was, uh…just trying to…um…figure out what you meant by that."

Although his throat was still very sore, Carl swallowed back his unease with an animated gulp. He could not look at Deli.

"You want me to tell you?"

Carl, still flushed from embarrassment, brought his head up with a snap.

"Oh, no, that's okay." He said this reflexively, to avoid the feeling of dread boiling over in his stomach. He hadn't been prepared for such impulsive honesty.

Deli's eyes dulled and her face fell slightly. It was not the reaction Carl had been anticipating. Since Paul had opened his mouth and ruined everything, he'd been sick to his stomach imagining all the ways she would turn him down, *had already* turned him down. But she just stood there, looking dejected.

Then he realized what he said.

"Oh, *God*! That's not…"

He stepped closer, holding his hands up to mediate the words coming out of his mouth.

"I didn't mean… It's just that…"

He looked up, willing himself to stop being an idiot. His heart pounded in his ears and all the words he knew were meaningless because his mouth had stopped working.

Deli stared at him without blinking. The air between them buzzed with indecision. Carl took two more steps toward her—slowly, in case she was still mad.

"I'm sorry. That isn't what I meant."

His stupid stomach chose that instant to practice tying knots. Breaking Paul's nose wasn't punishment enough for what he and Terkle did. But Deli stood close to him, making it impossible for him to ignore how he felt. She was more than beautiful. She was fascinating and exotic and strong, and if she thought all this was a setup, then so be it. He hoped she wouldn't punch him too hard, but he didn't want to take *no* for an answer anymore.

He reached out and brushed his fingers along the line of Deli's chin, sweeping her hair back. He bent over and let the delicate scent of her skin consume his thoughts. The green and purple bruise from Lenny stood out. He was careful not to touch it.

Deli went rigid. Carl's mutinous heart beat violently, embarrassing him. He tried to etch the smell of her into his brain so he could remember it after she smacked him. But she didn't smack him. Instead, she did the most amazing thing. She closed her eyes and stepped into him, closing the minute gap between their bodies. Carl exhaled.

He felt her body tremble underneath the layers of bathrobe and breathed deeply. He needed everything about her—the captivating lines of neck, the perfect bow of her lips, the plump little lobe of her ear, so round he wanted to taste it. Everything about her that he'd kept himself from thinking, all the desires he'd held in check came crashing back to him. He remembered so many things.

Deli opened her eyes and looked at him with an intoxicating candor, undecided and unashamed. The words came back.

"What I meant to say is that I have a working hypothesis, but I need a little help testing it out."

Deli's laugh came easy.

"That was the nerdiest pickup line I've ever heard," she said (but nicely, because she also thought it was cute).

"It wasn't a pickup line," he said. Then he kissed her on the soft spot behind her ear, and Deli stopped laughing.

AFTERWARD

THEY MADE THEIR WAY BACK TO SEATTLE three days later. Jin was sorry to see them go, but delighted when they made him promise to visit the next time he was in Seattle. For now, he had the formidable Mrs. Jin to manage, so he waved goodbye, snapped his Aviators in place, and strolled away. He looked back one time. Carl gave him a thumbs-up.

They arrived at Deli's apartment to find it sealed with crime scene tape. She broke through the tape, armed with nothing but her teeth and some very sharp words.

Everything was in shambles. There was glass everywhere. Several of the windows were broken, and the living room was literally a bloody mess. Deli would have been devastated—or at the very least put out—but Carl pointed to the kitchen where a shredded bag of kibble-crumbs sat uselessly on the floor.

"You don't want to stay here tonight anyway," he said, wiggling his eyebrows. "I understand there is an eighty percent chance of toxic fumes."

Carl helped her pack. Then he took her to Horsey House, where he tucked her into the upstairs studio apartment. It hadn't been rented out all summer, and Carl still had an old key.

Jake didn't mind. He was still trying to find a way to explain the cat.

* * *

For everything that had happened to him, Jake spent a surprisingly short time in the hospital. The ER doctors were amazed to find him in such good shape, considering he'd been shot in the chest. Judging by the size of the hole, a small-caliber bullet had entered his chest through the third and fourth ribs near the sternum on his right side. For some reason, the bullet had been travelling at an exceptionally low rate of speed. When it hit Jake's sternum, it bounced sideways and exited the body through the fourth and fifth ribs to his side. It missed every major artery and most of the smaller ones, too. The end result was a collapsed lung, a lot of initial blood loss, and not much else. They put him under observation for two days, but by the second day, the doctors couldn't find anything wrong with him, so they sent him home with a round of antibiotics, some ointment for the wound on his face, and strict instructions to avoid sick people. He would definitely have a scar, but Jake said he could live with that.

No one said anything about a small bean-shaped object stuck in Jake's stomach, probably because the radiologist only took x-rays of his lungs.

Jake wasn't sure if the Elevator was still there or not, but when he got back to the Dungeon, Toesy greeted him with thirty minutes of raucous purring, and he felt kind of invincible.

THE DUNGEON

"I'M SORRY I MADE YOUR CAT INDESTRUCTIBLE," Jake said, because there really was no other way to put it.

"Don't you mean *immortal*?" Deli said.

"Oh no! He's definitely not immortal," Jake said. "You could probably kill him if you chopped his head off or something. You'd have to sneak up on him first, though." He didn't add that sneaking up on Toesy was probably a bad idea.

Deli grimaced. "What the hell, Jake? You turned my cat into a *Highlander*? How am I supposed to feed him?"

"Yeah, you probably won't have to worry about that anymore." There was a note of nervousness in his voice that Deli caught immediately.

"*Why not?*"

"He's just, well… I'm not really sure he's a pet anymore."

"*What do you mean?*" Deli squinted and pulled her mouth into a disapproving line.

Jake didn't answer. How could he describe it? She just had to see it. He held one hand up to signal for patience and called the cat.

"Psst, hey, Toesy! You around here, man?"

Mmrrrooooaaawwwrrr, said Toesy, stalking into the room.

He'd been a large cat when she left for Hong Kong, but the cat in front of her could do some serious feline-related trauma to a Saint Bernard. Whiskers filled his cheeks in dense mutton chops of white. His shredded ears had knitted themselves back together, and he walked with a swagger that Deli knew for a *fact* Dr. Bartlett had surgically removed five years ago. He looked as if he'd eaten another cat and assimilated the parts.

"Look who's here, man!" said Jake and pointed to Deli. Toesy gazed at her with sleepy eyes and began to purr so enthusiastically that Deli felt it vibrate through the cement floor.

He stomped up to his favorite alpha female and head-butted her joyfully. Carl reached over and caught Deli as she fell.

"You get used to that after a while," said Jake.

* * *

The general opinion of Sacha's treason amounted to him being a complete dumbass, blinded by his own dick. But as stupid and dangerous as his behavior had been, everyone agreed that he did most of his penance in the ICU while a team of doctors worked for seven hours to keep his lungs and heart alive.

They still kicked him out of the Dungeon, though—just not as far as they would have otherwise. Jake moved him to the north-facing apartment on the second floor. The student living there had moved to France during the winter, and he had yet to find a new renter. Some type of furry animal had taken up residence in the kitchen cupboards, but Toesy dispatched it quickly, and Sacha did not complain.

Paul made it back to the States sooner than anyone would have guessed, sporting an interesting set of bruises and a light blue walking cast. No one believed it was a waterskiing accident.

He pleaded with Carl to stay on at the house, but after everything that happened, Carl couldn't stand to be in the same room with him. Neither could the partners at Stokem and Boyle. When word got out about his unprofessional behavior, he was asked to pack up his things and leave quietly. The last Deli heard, her twin brother was living in their mom's basement. She gave him three months before he went back to school just so he could move back to his former frat house.

Carl and Deli did *not* move in together. Carl moved back into his old room in the Dungeon while Deli stayed in the third-floor studio. She liked having her own apartment. Besides, she'd only really *known* Carl for a month. There was no way she was going to move in with someone she'd only really known for a month. What if he was a slob? What if he was a morning person? *What if he didn't know how to cook?* Deli liked him a lot, but she had standards. She never dated men who couldn't cook.

Carl didn't mind. He liked having his own space. He liked that Deli liked having her own space, too. He *really* liked that her space was only three floors up from his space, and that he could walk there in his bare feet.

* * *

Toesy wasn't sure how much he approved of the new situation. Most of it was profoundly gratifying. With the advent of thumbs, he no longer needed human intervention to gain access to closed doors. Now that they lived upstairs to the Great Man, Toesy spent a great deal of time in worship, especially late afternoons when the chance of spontaneous napping was greater.

But he also had the Tall Man problem.

He liked the Tall Man well enough. He had a very large lap, and that was something of which Toesy highly approved. He often allowed Toesy access to his expansive lap, even going so far as to scratch behind his ears. Toesy was particularly susceptible to ear scratches. They made him break into hearty fits of purring.

And therein lay his problem. Every time he achieved a position so comfortable that he could not contain himself, Deli allowed him five minutes of purring (maximum) before she grew agitated and tossed him, unceremoniously, out the front door. She would inevitably cite some feeble excuse like "I need to talk with him alone," or "Don't you have something to do *elsewhere*?" or (worse still), "Go away."

Then he would have to go downstairs to the Great Man for sympathy and pizza. Sometimes, if he got there early enough of an evening, he would call the Angel of Delivery and ask her to put those tiny little fish on Toesy's half.

This just went to prove how venerable the Great Man truly was. He knew the value of Seafood Flavor.

PREVIEW OF
WIZZY WIG
BOOK TWO OF THE THANATOS RISING SERIES

FALL 2014

This time, he's got thumbs.

SEATTLE
SATURDAY, OCTOBER 14TH

"WHAT THE HELL IS THAT?"

"A fedora. Why? Is it too much?"

"Not if your name is Elwood, no."

"Should I not wear it?"

"That depends," said Jake. His eyes lit up with good-natured devilment. "Are you on a mission from God?"

"No, Deli and I are going to that costume party, remember?"

"Oh, well, in that case, you should definitely wear it." Jake smiled, but his eyes dimmed, and he sat back down at his computer.

"We're meeting some of her friends at Shorty's first. You *really* don't want to go?"

Jake tilted his head slightly. "Who are you meeting?"

"Nicole and Jo," said Carl. Then he winced in apology and added, "Sorry, man, Deli tried to get her to come out with us but she's working a double."

Jake remained impassive.

"You should come anyway. Nicole thinks you're funny, and Deli would be happy to see you."

Carl and Deli had been dating since the summer. Jake liked Deli. She was smart and funny and she never complained about Thursday gaming nights. Most importantly, she was friends with Kix, the pizza delivery girl.

"That's okay. I'm good here."

"You sure?"

"I'm sure. I want to get started on this Christmas wash for the swamp zombies anyway. It's almost November, for God's sake."

"I thought you and Sacha were gonna start that tomorrow?"

"I don't trust him. He told me the other day that Santa Claus is a materialistic excuse for overindulgence. What the fuck is that about?"

Carl shrugged his shoulders. "He's *Jewish*, Jake. He's *allowed* not to believe in Santa Claus."

"Bullshit. *I'm* more Jewish than that clown, *and* I've got a Catholic-guilt hotline."

He pointed across the room to an old, hotel-style phone and answering machine combo sitting on its own table. Ostensibly, it was for tenants to call if they had problems with the plumbing or heating, but everyone knew the best way to reach Jake was just to go downstairs and knock on the door. They only person who actually called that number was his mom, Gloria. She thought it was his cell phone number.

Carl nodded, conceding the point.

"Besides," Jake went on. "Santa Claus hasn't got anything to do with religion, man. Everybody knows Christmas is all about little kids and presents and blowing shit up on your computer all afternoon."

"You sure you don't want to come out for a beer?"

Jake leaned back in his chair, stretching his arms over his head. "Thanks, but I'm good. There's nothing like drawing tiny Santa hats on homicidal monsters to put the shine on a Saturday night." He did not add that he also intended to order pizza for dinner. Carl had probably figured that part out on his own.

"Well, if you change your mind, text me." Carl straightened his tie and grabbed his coat.

"Wait a minute," Jake said. He swiveled his chair to face the desk behind him. There were four screens, all with various themes of red and green. He dug behind the lower left one and extracted a pair of sunglasses.

"You're gonna need these," he said and tossed the sunglasses across the room.

Carl's hand whipped up and snatched the glasses from the air. He put them on. "Later." he said.

ACKNOWLEDGMENTS

Several key people must be acknowledged before this book is properly finished.

First and foremost I would like to thank my motley crew: Catfish, Admiral, Candy Sunick, Bill Root, Nancy Mueller, Kathryn Minturn, Rachel Calhoun and (most especially) C. Bill Solo. Without you all, this book would still be goofy ideas and crazy talk.

Approximately four metric tons of praise must also be heaped upon the wonderful people at Booktrope. It has been a privilege to work with Stephanie Konat, Magdalen Powers, Melody Paris, Katherine Sears, Jesse James Freeman and the many other Booktropers involved with the production of this book. I thank you all for the incredible opportunity and continued support.

Let's do it again soon.

MORE GREAT READS
FROM BOOKTROPE

Touched by A.J. Aalto (Paranormal) The media has a nickname for Marnie Baranuik, though she'd rather they didn't; they call her the Great White Shark. A forensic psychic twice-touched by the Blue Sense, Marnie is too mean to die young, backed up by friends in cold places, and has a mouth as demure as a cannon's blast.

Fool's Game by **Heather Huffman** (Romantic Suspense) Targeted for assassination, government agent Caitlyn O'Rourke finds herself working alongside the man who broke her heart and betrayed her long ago.

A Tainted Mind by **Tamsen Schultz** (Romantic Suspense) Vivi DeMarco is a woman running from her demons, but now she's facing the worst demon of all: a twisted mind that leaves behind a string of corpses that look suspiciously like Vivi.

Joe Vampire by **Steven Luna** (Paranormal / Humor) Hey, folks. I'm Joe, and I'm a vampire – not by choice, mind you, but by accident…a fate-twisting, fang-creating, blood lust-inducing misunderstanding.

Mocha, Moonlight and Murder by **MaryAnn Kempher** (Romantic Suspense) Scott and Katherine face jealousy, misunderstandings, lust, and rivals, not to mention attempted murder—and all before their first real date.

Discover more books and learn about our
new approach to publishing at **booktrope.com**.

CPSIA information can be obtained at www.ICGtesting.com
Printed in the USA
LVOW10s2202160914

404434LV00001B/72/P